Out toward the rim of the galaxy hangs Alastor Cluster, a whorl of thirty thousand live stars in an irregular volume twenty to thirty light-years in diameter. The surrounding region is dark and unoccupied except for a few hermit stars; Alastor presents a flamboyant display of star-streams, luminous webs, sparkling nodes.

Scattered about the cluster are three thousand inhabited planets with a human population of approximately five trillion persons. The worlds are diverse, the populations equally so; nevertheless they share a common language and all submit to the authority of the Connatic at Lusz, on the world Numenes.

To the casual observer, Alastor Cluster is a system placid and peaceful. The Connatic knows differently. . . .

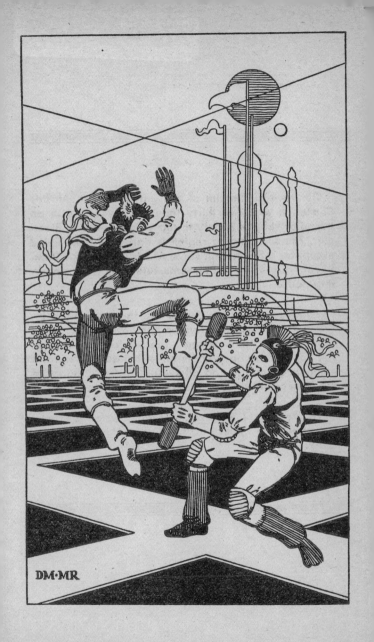

DM·MR

# TRULLION:

## Alastor 2262

## JACK VANCE

**DAW BOOKS, INC.**
DONALD A. WOLLHEIM, PUBLISHER
1633 Broadway, New York, N.Y. 10019

FIRST DAW PRINTING, JANUARY 1981

1 2 3 4 5 6 7 8 9

DAW TRADEMARK REGISTERED
U.S. PAT. OFF. MARCA
REGISTRADA. HECHO EN U.S.A.

PRINTED IN U.S.A.

# TRULLION:
## Alastor 2262

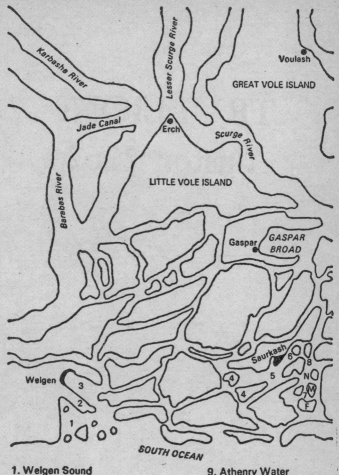

1. Welgen Sound
2. Welgen Spit
3. Blacklyn Broad
4. Lace Islands
5. Ripil Broad
6. Mellish Water
7. Near, Middle, Far Islands
8. Seaward Broad
9. Athenry Water
10. Rorquin's Tooth
11. Clinkhammer Broad
12. Sarpassante Island
13. Sarpent Channel
14. Tethryn Broad
15. Prefecture Commons
16. Zeur Water

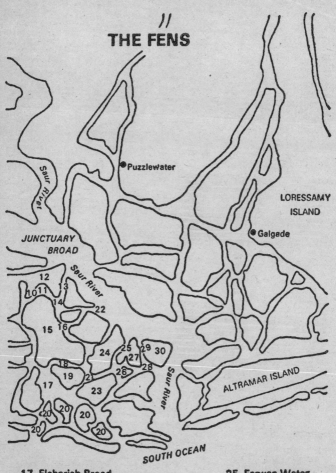

# THE FENS

Puzzlewater

LORESSAMY
ISLAND

Galgade

Saur River

JUNCTUARY
BROAD

Saur River

12
10 11
13
14
22
15 16
24 25 29 30
27
18 28 28
19 21
17 26
23
20
20 20
20
20 20

Saur River

ALTRAMAR ISLAND

SOUTH OCEAN

17. Fleharish Broad
18. Ilfish Water
19. Bellicent Island
20. Five Islands
21. Selma Water
22. Vernice Water
23. Fogle Island
24. Harkus Island

25. Farwan Water
26. Ambal Island
27. Rabendary Island
28. Ambal Broad
29. Gilweg Water
30. Gilweg Island

☆ ☆ ☆ ☆ ☆ ☆ ☆ ☆

Out toward the rim of the galaxy hangs Alastor Cluster, a whorl of thirty thousand live stars in an irregular volume twenty to thirty light-years in diameter. The surrounding region is dark and, except for a few hermit stars, unoccupied. To the exterior view, Alastor presents a flamboyant display of star-streams, luminous webs, sparkling nodes. Dust clouds hang across the brightness; the engulfed stars glow russet, rose, or smoky amber. Dark stars wander unseen among a million subplanetary oddments of iron, slag and ice: the so-called "starments."

Scattered about the cluster are three thousand inhabited planets with a human population of approximately five trillion persons. The worlds are diverse, the populations equally so; nevertheless they share a common language and all submit to the authority of the Connatic at Lusz, on the world Numenes.

The current Connatic is Oman Ursht, sixteenth in the Idite succession, a man of ordinary and undistinguished appearance. In portraits and on public occasions he wears a severe black uniform with a black casque, in order to project an image of inflexible authority, and this is how he is known to the folk of Alastor Cluster. In private Oman Ursht is a calm and reasonable man, who tends to under- rather than over-administrate. He ponders all aspects of his conduct, knowing well that his slightest act—a gesture, a word, a symbolic nuance—might start off an avalanche of unpredictable consequences. Hence his effort to create the image of a man rigid, terse and unemotional.

To the casual observer, Alastor Cluster is a system placid and peaceful. The Connatic knows differently. He recognizes that wherever human beings strive for advantage, disequilibrium exists; lacking easement, the social fabric becomes taut and sometimes rips asunder. The Connatic conceives his function to be the identification and relief of social stresses.

9

Sometimes he ameliorates, sometimes he employs techniques of distraction. When harshness becomes unavoidable he deploys his military agency, the Whelm. Oman Ursht winces to see an insect injured; the Connatic without compunction orders a million persons to their doom. In many cases, believing that each condition generates its own counter-condition, he stands aloof, fearing to introduce a confusing third factor. *When in doubt, do nothing:* this is one of the Connatic's favorite credos.

After an ancient tradition he roams anonymously about the cluster. Occasionally, in order to remedy an injustice, he represents himself as an important official; often he rewards kindness and self-sacrifice. He is fascinated by the ordinary life of his subjects and listens attentively to such dialogues as:

OLD MAN (*to a lazy youth*): If everybody had what they wanted, who would work? Nobody.

YOUTH: Not I, depend on it.

OLD MAN: And you'd be the first to cry out in anguish, for it's work what keeps the lights on. Get on with it now; put your shoulder into it. I can't bear sloth.

YOUTH (*grumbling*): If I were Connatic I'd arrange that everyone had their wishes. No toil! Free seats at the hussade game! A fine space-yacht! New clothes every day! Servants to lay forth delectable foods!

OLD MAN: The Connatic would have to be a genius to satisfy both you and the servants. They'd live only to box your ears. Now get on with your work.

Or again:

YOUNG MAN: Never go near Lusz, I beseech you! The Connatic would take you for his own!

GIRL (*mischievously*): Then what would you do?

YOUNG MAN: I'd rebel! I'd be the most magnificent starmenter* ever to terrify the skies! At last

---

* starmenters: pirates and marauders, whose occasional places of refuge are the so-called "starments."

I'd conquer the power of Alastor—Whelm, Connatic and all—and win you back for my very own.

GIRL: You're gallant, but never never never would the Connatic choose ordinary little me; already the most beautiful women of Alastor attend him at Lusz.

YOUNG MAN: What a merry life he must lead! To be Connatic: this is my dream!

GIRL: (*makes fretful sound and becomes cool.*)

YOUNG MAN *is puzzled. Oman Ursht moves away.*

Lusz, the Connatic's palace, is indeed a remarkable structure, rising ten thousand feet above the sea on five great pylons. Visitors roam the lower promenades; from every world of Alastor Cluster they come, and from places beyond—the Darkling Regions, the Primarchic, the Erdic Sector, the Rubrimar Cluster, and all the other parts of the galaxy which men have made their own.

Above the public promenades are governmental offices, ceremonial halls, a communications complex, and somewhat higher, the famous Ring of the Worlds, with an informational chamber for each inhabited planet of the cluster. The highest pinnacles contain the Connatic's personal quarters. They penetrate the clouds and sometimes pierce through to the upper sky. When sunlight glistens on its iridescent surfaces, Lusz, the palace of the Connatic, is a wonderful sight and is often reckoned the most inspiring artifact of the human race.

# Chapter 1

### ★ ★ ★

Chamber 2262 along the Ring of the Worlds pertains to Trullion, the lone planet of a small white star, one spark in a spray curling out toward the cluster's edge. Trullion is a small world, for the most part water, with a single narrow continent, Merlank,* at the equator. Great banks of cumulus drift in from the sea and break against the central mountains; hundreds of rivers return down broad valleys where fruit and cereals grow so plentifully as to command no value.

The original settlers upon Trullion brought with them those habits of thrift and zeal which had promoted survival in a previously harsh environment; the first era of Trill history produced a dozen wars, a thousand fortunes, a caste of hereditary aristocrats, and a waning of the initial dynamism. The Trill commonalty asked itself: Why toil, why carry weapons when a life of feasts, singing, revelry and ease is an equal option? In the space of three generations old Trullion became a memory. The ordinary Trill now worked as circumstances directed: to prepare for a feast, to indulge his taste for hussade, to earn a pulsor for his boat or a pot for his kitchen or a length of cloth for his *paray*, that easy shirtlike garment worn by man and woman alike. Occasionally he tilled his lush acres, fished the ocean, netted the river, harvested wild fruit, and when the mood was on him, dug emeralds and opals from the mountain slopes, or gathered *cauch*.** He worked perhaps an hour each day, or occasionally as much as two or three; he spent considerably more time musing on the verandah of his ramshackle house. He dis-

* Merlank: a variety of lizard. The continent clasps the equator like a lizard clinging to a blue glass orb.
** cauch: an aphrodisiac drug derived from the spore of a mountain mold and used by Trills to a greater or lesser extent. Some retreated so far into erotic fantasy as to become irresponsible, and thus the subject of mild ridicule. Irresponsibility, in the context of the Trill environment, could hardly be accounted a critical social problem.

13

trusted most technical devices, finding them unsympathetic, confusing and—more important—expensive, though he gingerly used a telephone the better to order his social activities, and took the pulsor of his boat for granted.

As in most bucolic societies, the Trill knew his precise place in the hierarchy of classes. At the summit, almost a race apart, was the aristocracy; at the bottom were the nomad Trevanyi, a group equally distinct. The Trill disdained unfamiliar or exotic ideas. Ordinarily calm and gentle, he nonetheless, under sufficient provocation, demonstrated ferocious rages, and certain of his customs—particularly the macabre ritual at the *prutanshyr*—were almost barbaric.

The government of Trullion was rudimentary and a matter in which the average Trill took little interest. Merlank was divided into twenty prefectures, each administered by a few bureaus and a small group of officials, who constituted a caste superior to the ordinary Trill but considerably inferior to the aristocrats. Trade with the rest of the cluster was unimportant; on all Trill only four space-ports existed; Port Gaw in the west of Merlank, Port Kerubian on the north coast, Port Maheul on the south coast, and Vayamenda in the east.

A hundred miles east of Port Maheul was the market town Welgen, famous for its fine hussade stadium. Beyond Welgen lay the Fens, a district of remarkable beauty. Thousands of waterways divided this area into a myriad islands, some tracts of good dimension, some so small as to support only a fisherman's cabin and a tree for the mooring of his boat.

Everywhere entrancing vistas merged one into another. Gray-green menas, silver-russet pomanders, black jerdine stood in stately rows along the waterways, giving each island its distinctive silhouette. Out upon their dilapidated verandahs sat the country folk, with jugs of homemade wine at hand. Sometimes they played music, using concertinas, small round-bellied guitars, mouth-calliopes that produced cheerful warbles and glissandes. The light of the Fens were pale and delicate, and shimmered with colors too transient and subtle for the eye to detect. In the morning a mist obscured the distances; the sunsets were subdued pageants of lime-green and lavender. Skiffs and runabouts slid along the water; occasionally an aristocrat's yacht glided past, or the ferry that connected Welgen with the Fen villages.

In the dead center of the Fens, a few miles from the village of Saurkash, was Rabendary Island, where lived Jut Hulden, his wife Marucha, and their three sons. Rabendary Island comprised about a hundred acres, including a thirty-acre forest of mena, blackwood, candlenut, semprissima. To the south spread the wide expanse of Ambal Broad. Farwan Water bounded Rabendary on the west, Gilweg Water on the east, and along the north shore flowed the placid Saur River. At the western tip of the island the ramshackle old home of the Huldens stood between a pair of huge mimosa trees. Rosalia vine grew up the posts of the verandah and overhung the edge of the roof, producing a fragrant shade for the pleasure of those taking their ease in the old string chairs. To the south was a view of Ambal Broad and Ambal Isle, a property of three acres supporting a number of beautiful pomanders, russet-silver against a background of solemn menas, and three enormous fanzaneels, holding their great shaggy pompoms high in the air. Through the foliage gleamed the white façade of the manse where Lord Ambal long ago had maintained his mistresses. The property was now owned by Jut Hulden, but he had no inclination to dwell in the manor; his friends would think him absurd.

In his youth Jut Hulden had played hussade for the Saurkash Serpents. Marucha had been *sheirl** for the Welgen Warlocks; so they had met, and married, and brought into being three sons, Shira and the twins Glinnes and Glay, and a daughter, Sharue, who had been stolen by the merlings.**

* sheirl: an untranslatable term from the special vocabulary of hussade—a glorious nymph, radiant with ecstatic vitality, who impels the players of her team to impossible feats of strength and agility. The sheirl is a virgin who must be protected from the shame of defeat.
** merlings: amphibious half-intelligent indigenes of Trullion, living in tunnels burrowed into the riverbanks. Merlings and men lived on the edge of a most delicate truce; each hated and hunted the other, but under mutually tolerable conditions. The merlings prowled the land at night for carrion, small animals, and children. If they molested boats or entered a habitation, men retaliated by dropping explosives into the water. Should a man fall into the water or attempt to swim, he had intruded into the domain of the merlings and risked being dragged under. Similarly, a merling discovered on land was shown no mercy.

# Chapter 2

## ★ ★ ★

Glinnes Hulden entered the world crying and kicking; Glay followed an hour later, in watchful silence. From the first day of their lives the two differed—in appearance, in temperament, in all the circumstances of their lives. Glinnes, like Jut and Shira, was amiable, trusting, and easy-natured; he grew into a handsome lad with a clear complexion, dusty-blond hair, a wide, smiling mouth. Glinnes entirely enjoyed the pleasures of the Fens: feasts, amorous adventures, star-watching and sailing, hussade, nocturnal merling hunts, simple idleness.

Glay at first lacked sturdy good health; for his first six years he was fretful, captious and melancholy. Then he mended, and quickly overtaking Glinnes was thenceforth the taller of the two. His hair was black, his features taut and keen, his eyes intent. Glinnes accepted events and ideas without skepticism; Glay stood aloof and saturnine. Glinnes was instinctively skillful at hussade; Glay refused to set foot on the field. Though Jut was a fair man, he found it hard to conceal his preference for Glinnes. Marucha, herself tall, dark-haired, and inclined to romantic meditation, fancied Glay, in whom she thought to detect poetic sensibilities. She tried to interest Glay in music, and explained how through music he could express his emotions and make them intelligible to others. Glay was cold to the idea and produced only a few lackadaisical discords on her guitar.

Glay was a mystery even to himself. Introspection availed nothing; he found himself as confusing as did the rest of his family. As a youth his austere appearance and rather haughty self-sufficiency earned him the soubriquet "Lord Glay"; perhaps coincidentally, Glay was the only member of the household who wanted to move into the manor house on Ambal Isle. Even Marucha had put the idea away as a foolish if amusing daydream.

Glay's single confidant was Akadie the mentor, who lived

in a remarkable house on Sarpassante Island, a few miles north of Rabendary. Akadie, a thin long-armed man with an ill-assorted set of features—a big nose, sparse curls of snuff-brown hair, glassy blue eyes, a mouth continually trembling at the verge of a smile—was, like Glay, something of a misfit. Unlike Glay, he had turned idiosyncrasy to advantage, and drew custom even from the aristocracy.

Akadie's profession included the offices of epigrammatist, poet, calligrapher, sage, arbiter of elegance, professional guest (hiring Akadie to grace a party was an act of conspicuous consumption), marriage broker, legal consultant, repository of local tradition, and source of scandalous gossip. Akadie's droll face, gentle voice, and subtle language rendered his gossip all the more mordant. Jut distrusted Akadie and had nothing to do with him, to the regret of Marucha, who had never relinquished her social ambitions, and who felt in her heart of hearts that she had married below herself. Hussade sheirls often married lords!

Akadie had traveled to other worlds. At night, during starwatchings,* he would mark the stars he had visited; then he would describe their splendor and the astounding habits of their peoples. Jut Hulden cared nothing for travel; his interest in the other worlds lay in the quality of their hussade teams and the location of the Cluster Champions.

When Glinnes was sixteen he saw a starmenter ship. It dropped from the sky above Ambal Broad and slid at reckless speed down toward Welgen. The radio provided a minute-by-minute report of the raid. The starmenters landed

---

* star-watching: at night the stars of Alastor Cluster blaze in profusion. The atmosphere refracts their light; the sky quivers with beams, glitters, and errant flashes. The Trills go out into their gardens with jugs of wine; they name the stars and discuss localities. For the Trills, for almost anyone of Alastor, the night sky was no abstract empyrean but rather, a view across prodigious distances to known places—a vast luminous map. There was always talk of pirates—the so-called "starmenters"—and their grisly deeds. When Numenes Star shone in the sky, the conversation turned to the Connatic and glorious Lusz, and someone would always say, "Best to steady our tongues! Perhaps he sits here now, drinking our wine and marking the dissidents!"—creating a nervous titter, for the Connatic's habit of wandering quietly about the worlds was well known. Then someone always uttered the brave remark: "Here we are—ten (or twelve or sixteen or twenty, as the case might be) among five trillion! The Connatic among us? I'll take that chance!"

At such a star-watch, Sharue Hulden had wandered off into the darkness. Before her absence was noticed the merlings had seized her and had taken her away underwater.

17

in the central square, and seething forth plundered the banks, the jewel factors, and the cauch warehouse, cauch being by far the most valuable commodity produced on Trullion. They also seized a number of important personages to be held for ransom. The raid was swift and well-executed; in ten minutes the starmenters had loaded their ship with loot and prisoners. Unluckily for them, a Whelm cruiser chanced to be putting into Port Maheul when the alarm was broadcast and merely altered course to arrive at Welgen instead. Glinnes ran out on the verandah to see the Whelm ship arrive—a beautiful stately craft enameled in beige, scarlet and black. The ship dropped like an eagle toward Welgen and passed beyond Glinnes' range of vision. The voice from the radio cried out in excitement: "—they rise into the air, but here comes the Whelm ship! By the Nine Glories, the Whelm ship is here! The starmenters can't go into whisk*; they'd burn up from the friction! They must fight!"

The announcer could no longer control his voice for excitement: "The Whelm ship strikes; the starmenter is disabled! Hurrah! it drops back into the square. No, no! Oh horror! What horror! It has fallen upon the market; a hundred persons are crushed! Attention! Bring in all ambulances, all medical men! Emergency at Welgen! I can hear the sad cries . . . The starmenter ship is broken; still it fights . . . a blue ray . . . Another . . . The Whelm ship answers. The starmenters are quiet. Their ship is broken." The announcer fell quiet a moment, then once more was prompted to excitement. "Now what a sight! The folk are crying with rage; they swarm in at the starmenters; they drag them forth . . ." He began to babble, then stopped short and spoke in a more subdued voice. "The constables have intervened. They have pushed back the crowds and the starmenters are now in custody, and this to their own rue, as well they know, for they desperately struggle. How they writhe and kick! It's the prutanshyr for them! They prefer the vengeance of the crowd! . . . What a dreadful deed they have done upon the hapless town Welgen . . ."

Jut and Shira worked in the far orchard grafting scions to the apple trees. Glinnes ran to tell them the news. " . . . and at last the starmenters were captured and taken away!"

"So much the worse for them," Jut said gruffly, and continued with his work. For a Trill, he was a man unusually self-

*whisk: star-drive.

contained and taciturn, traits that had become intensified since the death of Sharue by the merlings.

Shira said, "They'll be sweeping off the prutanshyr. Perhaps we'd better learn the news."

Jut grunted. "One torturing is much like another. The fire burns, the wheels wrench, the rope strains. Some folk thrive on it. For my excitement I'll watch hussade."

Shira winked at Glinnes. "One game is much like another. The forwards spring, the water splashes, the sheirl loses her clothes, and one pretty girl's belly is much like another's."

"There speaks the voice of experience," said Glinnes, and Shira, the most notorious philanderer of the district, guffawed.

Shira did in fact attend the executions with his mother Marucha, though Jut kept Glinnes and Glay at home.

Shira and Marucha returned by the late ferry. Marucha was tired and went to bed; Shira, however, joined Jut, Glinnes and Glay on the verandah and rendered an account of what he had seen. "Thirty-three they caught, and had them all in cages out in the square. All the preparations were put up before their very eyes. A hard lot of men, I must say—I couldn't place their race. Some might have been Echalites and some might have been Satagones, and one tall white-skinned fellow was said to be a Blaweg. Unfortunates all, in retrospect. They were naked and painted for shame: heads green, one leg blue, the other red. All gelded, of course. Oh, the prutanshyr's a wicked place! And to hear the music! Sweet as flowers, strange and hoarse! It strikes through you as if your own nerves were being plucked for tones . . . Ah well, at any rate, a great pot of boiling oil was prepared, and a traveling-crane stood by. The music began—eight Trevanyi and all their horns and fiddles. How can such stern folk make such sweet music? It chills the bones and churns the bowels and puts the taste of blood in your mouth! Chief Constable Filidice was there, but First Agent Gerence was the executioner. One by one the starmenters were grappled by hooks, then lifted and dipped into the oil, then hung up on a great high frame; and I don't know which was more awful, the howls or the beautiful sad music. The people fell down on their knees; some fell into fits and cried out—for terror or joy I can't tell you. I don't know what to make of it . . . After about two hours all were dead."

"Hmmf," said Jut Hulden. "They won't be back in a hurry. So much, at least, can be said."

19

Glinnes had listened in horrified fascination. "It's a fearful punishment, even for a starmenter."

"Indeed, that's what it is," said Jut. "Can you guess the reason?"

Glinnes swallowed hard and could not choose between several theories. Jut asked, "Would you now want to be a starmenter and risk such an end?"

"Never," Glinnes declared, from the depths of his soul.

Jut turned to the brooding Glay. "And you?"

"I never planned to rob and kill in the first place."

Jut gave a hoarse chuckle. "One of the two, at least, has been dissuaded from crime."

Glinnes said, "I wouldn't like to hear music played to pain."

"And why not?" Shira demanded. "At hussade, when the sheirl is smirched, the music is sweet and wild. Music gives savor to the event, like salt with food."

Glay offered a comment: "Akadie claims that everybody needs catharsis, if it's only a nightmare."

"It may be so," said Jut. "I myself need no nightmares; I've got one before my eyes every moment." Jut referred, as all knew, to the taking of Sharue. Since that time, his nocturnal hunts for merling had become almost an obsession.

"Well, if you two twits aren't to be starmenters, what will you be?" asked Shira. "Assuming you don't care to stay in the household."

"I'm for hussade," said Glinnes. "I don't care to fish, nor to scrape cauch." He recalled the brave beige, scarlet and black ship that had struck down the starmenters. "Or perhaps I'll join the Whelm and lead a life of adventure."

"I know nothing of the Whelm," said Jut ponderously, "but if it's hussade I can give you one or two useful hints. Run five miles every day to develop your stamina. Jump the practice pits until you can make sure landings blindfolded. Forbear with the girls, or there'll be no virgins left in the prefecture to be your sheirl."

"It's a chance I am willing to take," said Glinnes.

Jut squinted through his black eyebrows at Glay. "And what of you? Will you stay in the household?"

Glay gave a shrug. "If I could, I'd travel space and see the cluster."

Jut raised his bushy eyebrows. "How will you travel, lacking money?"

"There are methods, according to Akadie. He visited twenty-two worlds, working from port to port."

"Hmmf. That may be. But never use Akadie for your model. He has derived nothing from his travels but useless erudition."

Glay thought a moment. "If this is true," he said, "as it must be, since you so assert, then Akadie learned his sympathy and breadth of intellect here on Trullion which is all the more to his credit."

Jut, who never resented honest defeat, clapped Glay on the back. "In you he has a loyal friend."

"I am grateful to Akadie," said Glay. "He has explained many things to me."

Shira, who teemed with lewd ideas, gave Glay a sly nudge. "Follow Glinnes on his rounds, and you'll never need Akadie's explanations."

"I'm not talking about that sort of thing."

"Then what sort of thing are you talking about?"

"I don't care to explain. You'd only jeer at me, which is tiresome."

"No jeering!" declared Shira. "We'll give you a fair hearing! Say on."

"Very well. I don't really care whether you jeer or not. I've long felt a lack, or an emptiness. I want a weight to thrust my shoulder against; I want a challenge I can defy and conquer."

"Brave words," said Shira dubiously. "But—"

"But why should I so trouble myself? Because I have but one life, one existence. I want to make my mark, somewhere, somehow. When I think of it I grow almost frantic! My foe is the universe; it defies me to perform remarkable deeds so that ever after folk will remember me! Why should not the name 'Glay Hulden' ring as far and clear as 'Paro' and 'Slabar Velche'?* I will make it so; it is the least I owe myself!"

Jut said in a gloomy voice, "You had best become either a great hussade player or a great starmenter."

"I overspoke myself," said Glay. "In truth I want neither fame nor notoriety; I do not care whether I astonish a single person. I want only the chance to do my best."

There was silence on the verandah. From the reeds came

* Paro: a hussade player, the darling of the cluster, celebrated for his aggressive and daring play.
Slabar Velche: a notorious starmenter.

the croak of nocturnal insects, and water lapped softly against the dock; a merling perhaps had risen to the surface, to listen for interesting sounds.

Jut said in a heavy voice, "The ambition does you no discredit. Still I wonder how it would be if everyone strove with such urgency. Where would peace abide?"

"It is a difficult problem," said Glinnes. "Indeed, I had never considered it before. Glay, you amaze me! You are unique!"

Glay gave a deprecatory grunt. "I'm not so sure of this. There must be many, many folk desperate to fulfill themselves."

"Perhaps this is why people become starmenters," suggested Glinnes. "They are bored at home, at hussade they're inept, the girls turn away from them—so off they go in their black hulls, for sheer revenge!"

"The theory is as good as any," agreed Jut Hulden. "But revenge cuts both ways, as thirty-three folk discovered today."

"There is something here I can't understand," said Glinnes. "The Connatic knows of their crimes. Why does he not deploy the Whelm and root them out once and for all?"

Shira laughed indulgently. "Do you think the Whelm sits idle? The ships are constantly on the prowl. But for every living world you'll find a hundred dead ones, not to mention moons, asteroids, hulks and starments. The hiding places are beyond enumeration. The Whelm can only do its best."

Glinnes turned to Glay. "There you are: join the Whelm and see the cluster. Get paid while you travel!"

"It's a thought," said Glay.

# Chapter 3

★ ★ ★

In the end it was Glinnes who went to Port Maheul and there enlisted in the Whelm. He was seventeen at the time. Glay neither enlisted in the Whelm, played hussade, nor became a starmenter. Shortly after Glinnes joined the Whelm,

Glay also left home. He wandered the length and breadth of Merlank, from time to time working to gain a few ozols, as often living off of the land. On several occasions he attempted the ruses Akadie had recommended in order to travel to other worlds, but for one reason or another his efforts met no success, and he never accumulated sufficient funds to buy himself passage.

For a period he traveled with a band of Trevanyi,* finding their exactness and intensity an amusing contrast to the imprecision of the average Trill.

After eight years of wandering he returned to Rabendary Island, where everything went about as before, although Shira at last had given up hussade. Jut still waged his nocturnal war against the merlings; Marucha still hoped to win social acceptance among the local gentry, who had absolutely no intention of allowing her to succeed. Jut, at the behest of Marucha, now called himself Squire Hulden of Rabendary, but refused to move into Ambal Manse, which, despite its noble proportions, grand chambers and polished wainscoting, lacked a broad verandah overlooking the water.

The family regularly received news from Glinnes, who had done well in the Whelm. At bootcamp he had earned a recommendation to officer training school, after which he had been assigned to the Tactical Corps of the 191st Squadron and placed in command of Landing Craft No. 191-539 and its twenty-man complement.

Glinnes could now look forward to a rewarding career, with excellent retirement benefits. Still, he was not entirely happy. He had envisioned a life more romantically adventurous; he had seen himself prowling the cluster in a patrol boat, searching out starmenter nests, then putting into remote and picturesque settlements for a few days' shore-leave—a life far more dashing and haphazard than the perfectly organized routine in which he found himself. To relieve the monotony he played hussade; his team always placed high in fleet competition, and won two championships.

Glinnes at last requested transfer to a patrol craft, but his request was denied. He went before the squadron commander, who listened to Glinnes' protests and complaints

---

* Trevanyi: nomadic folk of a distinctive racial stock, prone to thievery, sorcery, and other petty chicaneries; an excitable, passionate, vengeful people. They consider cauch a poison and guard the chastity of their women with fanatic zeal.

23

with an attitude of easy unconcern. "The transfer was denied for a very good reason."

"What reason?" demanded Glinnes. "Certainly I am not considered indispensable to the survival of the squadron?"

"Not altogether. Still, we don't want to disrupt a smoothly functioning organization." He adjusted some papers on his desk, then leaned back in his chair. "In confidence, there's a rumor to the effect that we're going into action."

"Indeed? Against whom?"

"As to this, I can only guess. Have you ever heard of the Tamarchô?"

"Yes indeed. I read about them in a journal: a cult of fanatic warriors on a world whose name now escapes me. Apparently they destroy for the love of destruction, or something of the sort."

"Well then, you know as much as I," said the commander, "except that the world is Rhamnotis and the Tamarchô have laid waste an entire district. I would guess that we are going down on Rhamnotis."

"It's an explanation, at least," said Glinnes. "What about Rhamnotis? A gloomy desert of a place?"

"On the contrary." The commander swung about, fingered buttons; a screen burst into colors and a voice spoke: "Alastor 965, Rhamnotis. The physical characteristics are—" The annunciator read off a set of indices denoting mass, dimension, gravity, atmosphere, and climate, while the screen displayed a Mercator projection of the surface. The commander touched buttons to bypass historical and anthropological information, and brought in what was known as "informal briefing": "Rhamnotis is a world where every particular, every aspect, every institution, conduces to the health and pleasure of its inhabitants. The original settlers, arriving from the world Triskelion, resolved never to tolerate the ugliness which they had left behind them, and they pledged a covenant to this effect, which covenant is now the prime document of Rhamnotis, and the subject of great reverence.

"Today the usual detritus of civilization—discord, filth, waste, structural clutter—have been almost expelled from the consciousness of the population. Rhamnotis is now a world characterized by excellent management. Optimums have become the norms. Social evils are unknown; poverty is no more than a curious word. The work-week is ten hours, in which every member of the population participates; he then devotes his surplus energy to the carnivals and fantasies,

24

which attract tourists from far worlds. The cuisine is considered equal to the best of the cluster. Beaches, forests, lakes and mountains provide unsurpassed scope for outdoor recreation. Hussade is a spectator sport, although local teams have never placed high in Cluster rankings."

The commander touched another button; the annunciator said: "In recent years the cult known as Tamarchô has attracted attention. The principles of Tamarchô are unclear, and seem to vary from individual to individual. In general, the Tamarchists engage in wanton violence, destruction and defilement. They have burned thousands of acres of primeval forests; they pollute lakes, reservoirs and fountains with corpses, filth and crude oil; they are known to have poisoned waterholes in game preserves, and they set poison bait for birds and domestic animals. They fling excrement-bombs into the perfumed carnival crowds and urinate from high towers upon the throngs below. They worship ugliness and in fact call themselves the Ugly People."

The commander tapped a button to dull the screen. "So there you have it. The Tamarchô have seized a tract of land and won't disperse; apparently the Rhamnotes have called in the Whelm. Still, it's all speculation; we might be going down to Breakneck Island to disperse the prostitutes. Who knows?"

Standard strategy of the Whelm, validated across ten thousand campaigns, was to mass a tremendous force so extravagantly overpowering as to intimidate the enemy and impose upon him the certain conviction of defeat. In most cases the insurgence would evaporate and there would be no fighting whatever. To subdue Mad King Zag on Gray World, Alastor 1740, the Whelm poised a thousand Tyrant dreadnoughts over the Black capitol, almost blocking out the daylight. Squadrons of Vavarangi and Stingers drifted in concentric evolutions under the Tyrants, and at still lower levels combat-boats darted back and forth like wasps. On the fifth day twenty million heavy troops dropped down to confront King Zag's stupefied militia, who long before had given up all thought of resistance.

The same tactics were expected to prevail against the Tamarchists. Four fleets of Tyrants and Maulers converged from four directions to hover above the Silver Mountains, where the Ugly People had taken refuge. Intelligence from the surface reported no perceptible reaction from the Tamarchists.

25

The Tyrants descended lower, and all during the night netted the sky with ominous beams of crackling blue light. In the morning the Tamarchists had broken all their camps and were nowhere to be seen. Surface intelligence reported that they had taken cover in the forests.

Monitors flew to the area, and their voice-horns ordered the Ugly Folk to form orderly files and march down to a nearby resort town. The only response was a spatter of sniper fire.

With menacing deliberation the Tyrants began to descend. The Monitors issued a final ultimatum: surrender or face attack. The Tamarchists failed to respond.

Sixteen Armadillo sky-forts dropped upon a high meadow, intending to secure the area for a troop-landing. They encountered not only the fire of small arms, but spasms of energy from a set of antique blue radiants. Rather than destroy an unknown number of maniacs, the Armadillos returned into the sky.

The Operation Commander, outraged and perplexed, decided to ring the Silver Mountain with troops, hoping to starve the Ugly Folk into submission.

Twenty-two hundred landing craft, among them No. 191-539, commanded by Glinnes Hulden, descended to the surface and sealed the Tamarchists into their mountain lair. Where expedient, the troops cautiously moved up the valleys, after sending Stinger combat-boats ahead to flush out snipers. Casualties occurred, and since the Tamarchô represented neither threat nor emergency, the Commander withdrew his troops from zones of Tamarchist fire.

For a month the siege persisted. Intelligence reported that the Tamarchists lacked provisions, that they were eating bark, insects, leaves, whatever came to hand.

The Commander once again sent Monitors over the area, demanding an orderly surrender. For answer the Tamarchists launched a series of break-out attempts, but were repulsed with considerable harm to themselves.

The Commander once more sent over his Monitors, threatening the use of pain-gas unless surrender was affected within six hours. The deadline came and went; Vavarangi descended to bombard shleter areas with cannisters of pain-gas. Choking, rolling on the ground, writhing and jerking, the Tamarchists broke into the open. The Commander ordered down a "living rain" of a hundred thousand troops, and after a few brisk fire-fights the area was secure. The Tamarchist captives, numbered less than two thousand persons of both sexes. Glinnes was astounded to discover that some were little more than children, and very few older than himself. They lacked ammunition, energy, food and medical supplies. They grimaced and snarled at the Whelm troops—"Ugly Folk" they were indeed. Glinnes' astonishment increased. What had prompted these young people to battle so fanatically for a cause obviously lost? What, indeed, had impelled them to become Ugly Folk? Why had they defiled and defouled, destroyed and corrupted?

Glinnes attempted to question one of the prisoners who pretended not to understand his dialect. Shortly thereafter Glinnes was ordered back aloft with his ship.

Glinnes returned to base. Picking up his mail, he found a letter from Shira containing tragic news. Jut Hulden had gone out to hunt merling once too often; they had laid a cunning trap for him. Before Shira could come to his aid, Jut had been dragged into Farwan Water.

The news affected Glinnes with a rather irrational astonishment. He found it hard to imagine change in the timeless fens, especially change so profound.

Shira was now Squire of Rabendary. Glinnes wondered what other changes might be in store. Probably none—Shira had no taste for innovation. He would bring in a wife and breed a family; so much at least could be expected—if not sooner, then later. Glinnes speculated as to who might marry bulky balding Shira with the red cheeks and lumpy nose. Even as a hussade player, Shira had found difficulty enticing girls into the shadows, for while Shira considered himself bluff, friendly and affable, others thought him coarse, lewd and boisterous.

Glinnes began to muse about his boyhood. He recalled the hazy mornings, the festive evenings, the starwatchings. He recalled his good friends and their quaint habits; he remembered the look of Rabendary Forest—the menas looming over russet pomanders, silver-green birches, dark-green pricklenuts. He thought of the shimmer that hung above the water and softened the outline of far shores; he thought of the ramshackle old family home, and discovered himself to be profoundly homesick.

Two months later, at the end of ten years' service, he resigned his commission and returned to Trullion.

# Chapter 4

## ★ ★ ★

Glinnes had sent a letter announcing his arrival, but when he debarked at Port Maheul in Staveny Prefecture, none of his family was on hand to greet him, which he thought strange.

He loaded his baggage onto the ferry and took a seat on the top deck, to watch the scenery go by. How easy and gay were the country folk in their parays of dull scarlet, blue, ocher! Glinnes' semi-military garments—black jacket, beige breeches tucked into black ankleboots—felt stiff and constricted. He'd probably never wear them again!

The boat presently slid into the dock at Welgen. A delectable odor wafted past Glinnes' nose, which he traced to a nearby fried-fish booth. Glinnes went ashore and bought a packet of steamed reed-pods and a length of barbecued eel. He looked about for Shira or Glay or Marucha, though he hardly expected to find them here. A group of off-worlders attracted his attention: three young men, wearing what seemed to be a uniform—neat gray one-piece garments belted at the waist, highly polished tight black shoes—and three young women, in rather austere gowns of durable white duck. Both men and women wore their hair cropped short, in not-unbecoming style, and wore small medallions on their left shoulders. They passed close to Glinnes and he realized that they were not off-worlders after all, but Trills . . . Students at a doctrinaire academy? Members of a religious order? Either case was possible, for they carried books, calculators, and seemed to be engaged in earnest discussion. Glinnes gave the girls a second appraisal. There was, he thought, something unappealing about them, which at first he could not define. The ordinary Trill girl dressed herself in almost anything at hand, without over-anxiety that it might be rumpled or threadbare or soiled, and then made herself gay with flowers. These girls looked not only clean, but fastidious as well.

Too clean, too fastidious . . . Glinnes shrugged and returned to the ferry.

The ferry moved on into the heart of the fens, along waterways dank with the scent of still water, decaying reedstalks, and occasionally a hint of a rich fetor, suggesting the presence of merling. Ripil Broad appeared ahead, and a cluster of shacks that was Saurkash, the end of the line for Glinnes; here the ferry veered north for the villages along Great Vole Island. Glinnes unloaded his cases onto the dock, and for a moment stood looking around the village. The most prominent feature was the hussade field and its dilapidated old bleachers, once the home-field of the Saurkash Serpents. Almost adjacent was The Magic Tench, the most pleasant of Saurkash's three taverns. He walked down the dock to the office where ten years before Milo Harrad had rented boats and operated a water-taxi.

Harrad was nowhere to be seen. A young man whom Glinnes did not know sat dozing in the shade.

"Good day, friend," said Glinnes, and the young man, awaking, turned toward Glinnes a look of mild reproach. "Can you take me out to Rabendary Island?"

"Whenever you like." The young man looked Glinnes slowly up and down and lurched to his feet. "You'd be Glinnes Hulden, unless I'm mistaken."

"Quite right. But I don't remember you."

"You'd have no reason to do so. I'm old Harrad's nephew from Voulash. They call me Young Harrad, and I expect that's what I'll be the rest of my life. I mind when you played for the Serpents."

"That's some time ago. You've got an accurate memory."

"Not all that good. The Huldens have always been hussade types. Old Harrad talked much of Jut, the best rover Saurkash ever produced, or so said old Milo. Shira was a solid guard, right enough, but slow in the jumps. I doubt I ever saw him make a clean swing."

"That's a fair judgment." Glinnes looked along the waterway. "I expected him here to meet me, or my brother Glay. Evidently they had better things to do."

Young Harrad glanced at him sidewise, then shrugged and brought one of his neat green and white skiffs to the dock. Glinnes loaded his cases aboard and they set off eastward along Mellish Water.

Young Harrad cleared his throat. "You expected Shira to meet you?"

"I did indeed."

"You didn't hear about Shira then?"

"What happened to him?"

"He disappeared."

"Disappeared?" Glinnes looked around with a slack jaw. "Where?"

"No one knows. To the merling's dinner-table, likely enough. That's where most folk disappear."

"Unless they go off to visit friends."*

"For two months? Shira was a great horn, so I've been told, but two months on cauch would be quite extraordinary."

Glinnes gave a despondent grunt and turned away, no longer in the mood for conversation. Jut gone, Shira gone—his homecoming could only be a melancholy occasion. The scenery, ever more familiar, ever more rich with memories, now only served to increase his gloom. Islands he knew well slid by on each side: Jurzy Island, where the Jurzy Lightning-bolts, his first team, had practiced; Calceon Island, where lovely Loel Issam had resisted his most urgent blandishments. Later she became sheirl from the Gaspar Triptanes, and finally, after her shaming, had wed Lord Clois from Graven Table, north of the fens . . . Memories thronged his mind; he wondered why he had ever departed the fens. His ten years in the Whelm already seemed no more than a dream.

The boat moved out upon Seaward Broad. To the south, at the end of a mile's perspective, stood Near Island, and beyond, somewhat wider and higher, Middle Island, and yet beyond, still wider, still higher, Far Island: three silhouettes obscured by water-haze in three distinct degrees, Far Island showing only slightly more substance than the sky at the southern horizon.

The boat slid into narrow Athenry Water, with hushberry trees leaning together to form an arch over the still, dark water. Here the scent of merling was noticeable. Harrad and Glinnes both watched for water swirls. For reasons known best to themselves, merlings gathered in Athenry Water—perhaps for the hushberries, which were poisonous to men, perhaps for the shade, perhaps for the savor of hushberry roots in the water. The surface lay placid and cool; if merlings

---

* going off to visit friends: a euphemism for cauch-crazy lovers going off to camp in the wilds.

were nearby, they kept to their burrows. The boat passed out upon Fleharish Broad. On Five Islands, to the south, Thammas Lord Gensifer maintained his ancient manse. Not far away a sailboat rode high across the Broad on hydrofoils; at the tiller sat Lord Gensifer himself: a hearty round-faced man ten years older than Glinnes, burly of shoulder and chest if rather thin in the legs. He tacked smartly and came foaming up on a reach beside Harrad's boat, then luffed his sail. The boat dropped from its foils and rode flat in the water. "If I'm not mistaken it's young Glinnes Hulden, back from starfaring!" Lord Gensifer called out. "Welcome back to the fens!"

Glinnes and Harrad both rose to their feet and performed the salute due a lord of Gensifer's quality.

"Thank you," said Glinnes. "I'm glad to be back, no doubt about that."

"There's no place like the fens! And what are your plans for the old place?"

Glinnes was puzzled. "Plans? None in particular . . . Should I have plans?"

"I would presume so. After all, you're now Squire of Rabendary."

Glinnes squinted across the water, off toward Rabendary Island. "I suppose I am, for a fact, if Shira is truly dead. I'm older than Glay by an hour."

"And a good job too, if you want my opinion . . . Ha, hmm. You'll see for yourself, no doubt." Lord Gensifer drew in the sheet. "What about hussade? Are you for the new club? We'd certainly like a Hulden on the team."

"I don't know anything about it, Lord Gensifer. I'm so bewildered by the turn of affairs I can't give any sensible answer."

"In due course, in due course." Lord Gensifer sheeted home the sail; the hull, surging forward, rose on its foils and skimmed across Fleharish Broad at great speed.

"There's sport for you," said Young Harrad enviously. "He had that contraption brought out from Illucante by Interworld. Think of the ozols it cost him!"

"It looks dangerous," said Glinnes. "If it goes over, he and the merlings are out there alone."

"Lord Gensifer is a daredevil sort of chap," said Harrad. "Still, they say the craft is safe enough. It can't sink, first of all, even if it did go over. He could always ride the hull until someone picked him up."

31

They continued across Fleharish Broad and out into Ilfish Water, with the Prefecture Free Commons on their left—an island of five hundred acres reserved for the use of casual wanderers, Trevanyi, Wrye, lovers "visiting friends." The boat entered Ambal Broad, and there ahead—the dear outline of Rabendary Island: home. Glinnes blinked at the moisture that came to his eyes. A sad homecoming, in truth. Ambal Island looked its loveliest. Looking toward the old manor, Glinnes thought to perceive a wisp of smoke rising from the chimneys. A startling theory came to him, which would account for Lord Gensifer's sniff. Had Glay taken up residence in the manor? Lord Gensifer would consider such an action ridiculous and discreditable—a vulgarian trying to ape his betters.

The boat pulled up to Rabendary dock; Glinnes unloaded his luggage, paid off Young Harrad. He stared toward the house. Had it always lurched and sagged? Had the weeds always grown so rank? There was a condition of comfortable shabbiness which the Trills considered endearing, but the old house had gone far past this state. As he mounted the steps to the verandah, they groaned and sagged under his weight.

Flecks of color caught his eye, across the field near Rabendary Forest. Glinnes squinted and focused his gaze. Three tents: red, black, dull orange. Trevanyi tents. Glinnes shook his head in angry disparagement. He had not returned too soon. He called out, "Hallo the house! Who's here but me?"

In the doorway appeared the tall figure of his mother. She looked at him incredulously, then ran forward a few steps. "Glinnes! How strange to see you!"

Glinnes hugged and kissed her, ignoring the overtones of the remark. "Yes I'm back, and it feels strange to me too. Where is Glay?"

"He's off with one of his comrades. But how well you look! You've grown into a very fine man!"

"You haven't changed by so much as a twitch; you're still my beautiful mother."

"Oh, Glinnes, such flattery, I feel old as the hills and I look it too, I'm sure . . . I suppose you've heard the sad news?"

"About Shira? Yes. It grieves me terribly. Doesn't anyone know what happened?"

"Nothing is known," said Marucha rather primly. "But sit down, Glinnes; take off those fine boots and rest your feet. Would you care for apple wine?"

"I would indeed, and a bite of whatever is handy. I'm ravenous."

Marucha served wine, bread, a cold mince of meat, fruit, and sea-jelly. She sat watching him eat. "It's so very nice to see you. What are your plans?"

Glinnes thought her voice almost imperceptibly cool. Still, Marucha had never been demonstrative. He answered, "I don't have any plans whatever, I've only just heard about Shira from Young Harrad. He never took a wife then?"

Marucha's mouth pursed into a disapproving line. "He could never quite make up his mind . . . He had friends here and there, naturally."

Again Glinnes sensed unspoken words, knowledge which his mother did not care to communicate. He began to feel a few small inklings of resentment, and carefully put them aside. It would not do to start out his new life on such a footing. Marucha asked in a bright, rather brittle voice, "But where is your uniform? I so wanted to see you as a captain in the Whelm."

"I resigned my commission. I decided to come home."

"Oh." Marucha's voice was flat. "Of course we're glad to have you home, but are you sure it's wise giving up your career?"

"I've already given it up." In spite of his resolve, Glinnes' voice had taken on an edge. "I'm needed here more than in the Whelm. The old place is falling apart. Doesn't Glay do anything whatever?"

"He's been most busy with—well, his activities. In his own way, he's quite an important person now."

"That shouldn't prevent him from fixing the steps. They're literally rotting away . . . Or—I saw smoke from Ambal Isle. Is Glay living over there?"

"No. We've sold Ambal Isle, to one of Glay's friends."

Glinnes started, thunderstruck. "You've sold Ambal Isle? What possible reason . . ." He gathered his thoughts. "Shira sold Ambal Isle?"

"No," said Marucha in a cool voice. "Glay and I decided to let it go."

"But . . ." Glinnes halted and chose his words deliberately. "I certainly don't want to part with Ambal Isle, nor any other part of our land."

"I'm afraid that the sale has been effected. We assumed that you were making a career in the Whelm and wouldn't be home. Naturally we would have considered your feelings had we known."

Glinnes spoke politely. "I most definitely feel that we should void the contract.* We certainly don't want to give up Ambal."

"But my dear Glinnes, it's already given up."

"Not after we return the money. Where is it?"

"You'll have to ask Glay."

Glinnes reflected upon the sardonic Glay of ten years before, who always had stayed aloof from the affairs of Rabendary. That Glay should make large decisions seemed altogether inappropriate and more, insulting to the memory of his father Jut, who loved each square inch of his land.

Glinnes asked, "How much did you take for Ambal?"

"Twelve thousand ozols."

Glinnes' voice cracked with angry astonishment. "That's giving it away! For a beauty spot like Ambal Isle, with a manor house in good condition? Someone's insane!"

Marucha's black eyes sparkled. "Surely it's not your place to protest. You weren't there when we needed you, and it isn't proper for you to cavil now."

"I'm doing more than cavil; I'm going to void the contract. If Shira is dead, I'm Squire of Rabendary, and no one else has authority to sell."

"But we don't know that Shira is dead," Marucha pointed out, sweetly reasonable. "He may only have gone off to visit friends."

Glinnes asked politely, "Do you know of any such 'friends'?"

Marucha gave her shoulder a disdainful jerk. "Not really. But you remember Shira. He has never changed."

"After two months he'd surely be home from his visit."

"Naturally we hope that he is alive. In fact we can't presume him dead for four years, which is the law."

"But by then the contract will be firm! Why should we part with any of our wonderful land?"

"We needed the money. Isn't that reason enough?"

"You needed money for what?"

"You'll have to ask that question of Glay."

"I'll do so. Where is he?"

---

* By Trill law, a contract for land sale is considered provisional for a period of a year, for the protection of both parties.

34

"I really don't know. He'll probably be home before too long."

"Another matter: are those Trevanyi tents down by the forest?"

Marucha nodded. By now, neither was making any pretense of amiability. "Please don't criticize either me or Glay. Shira allowed them upon the property, and they have done no harm."

"Possibly not, but the year is young. You know our last experience with Trevanyi. They stole the kitchen cutlery."

"The Drossets are not that sort," said Marucha. "For Trevanyi, they seem quite responsible. No doubt they're as honest as they find necessary."

Glinnes threw up his hands. "It's pointless to wrangle. But one last word about Ambal. Certainly Shira would never have wanted the Isle sold. If he's alive, you acted without his authorization. If he's dead, you acted without mine, and I insist that the contract be voided."

Marucha gave a cold shrug of her slender white shoulders. "This is a matter you must take up with Glay. I am really quite bored with the subject."

"Who bought Ambal Isle?"

"A person named Lute Casagave, very quiet and distinguished. I believe that he's an off-worlder; he's much too genteel to be a Trill."

Glinnes finished his meal, then went to his baggage. "I've brought a few oddments back with me." He gave his mother a parcel, which she took without comment. "Open it," said Glinnes. "It's for you."

She pulled the tab and drew forth a length of purple fabric embroidered with fantastic birds in thread of green, silver and gold. "How utterly wonderful!" She gasped. "Why Glinnes—what a delightful gift!"

"That's not all," said Glinnes. He brought forth other parcels, which Marucha opened in a rapture. Unlike the ordinary Trill, she delighted in precious possessions.

"These are star-crystals," said Glinnes. "They haven't any other name, but they're found just like this, facets and all, in the dust of dead stars. Nothing can scratch them, not even diamond, and they have very peculiar optical properties."

"My, how heavy they are!"

"This is an antique vase, no one knows how old. The writing on the bottom is said to be Erdish."

"It's charming!"

"Now this isn't very distinguished, just something that caught my fancy—a nut-cracker in the shape of an Urtland crotchet. I picked it up in a junkshop, if the truth be known."

"But how cunning. It's for cracking nuts, you say?"

"Yes. You put the nuts between these mandibles and press down the tail . . . These were for Glay and Shira—knives forged from proteum. The cutting edges are single chains of interlocked molecules—absolutely indestructible. You can strike them into steel and they never dull."

"Glay will be delighted," said Marucha in a voice somewhat stiffer than before. "And Shira will also be pleased."

Glinnes gave a skeptical snort, which Marucha took pains to ignore. "Thank you very much for the gifts. I think they're all wonderful." She looked out the door down across the verandah to the dock. "Here is Glay now."

Glinnes went out to stand on the verandah. Glay, coming up the path from the dock, halted, though he showed no surprise. Then he came forward slowly. Glinnes descended the steps and the brothers clapped each other's shoulders.

Glay was wearing, Glinnes noted, not the usual Trill paray, but gray trousers and dark jacket.

"Welcome home," said Glay. "I met Young Harrad; he told me you were here."

"I'm glad to be home," said Glinnes. "With just you and Marucha, it must have been gloomy. But now that I'm here I hope we can make the house the place it used to be."

Glay gave a noncommittal nod. "Yes. Life has been somewhat quiet. And things change, certainly, I hope for the better."

Glinnes was not sure he knew what Glay was talking about. "There's a great deal to discuss. But first, I'm glad to see you. You're looking remarkably wise and mature, and—what would be the word?—self-possessed."

Glay laughed. "When I look back, I see that I always pondered too much and tried to resolve too many paradoxes. I've given all that up. I've cut the Gordian knot, so to speak."

"How so?"

Glay made a deprecatory gesture. "It's too complicated to go into right now . . . You look well too. The Whelm has been good for you. When must you go back?"

"Into the Whelm? Never. I'm through, since I now seem to be Squire of Rabendary."

"Yes," said Glay in a colorless voice. "You've got an hour's edge on me."

"Come inside," said Glinnes. "I've brought you a gift. Also something for Shira. Do you think he's dead?"

Glay nodded gloomily. "There's no other explanation."

"That's my feeling. Mother feels he's 'visiting friends.'"

"For two months? Not a chance."

The two entered the house, and Glinnes brought out the knife he had bought at the Technical Laboratories in Boreal City on Maranian. "Be careful of the edge. You can't touch it without slicing yourself. But you can hack through a steel rod without damage."

Glay picked up the knife gingerly and squinted along the invisible edge. "It frightens me."

"Yes, it's almost weird. Now that Shira's dead, I'll keep the other one for myself."

Marucha spoke from across the room. "We're not sure that Shira is dead."

Neither Glay nor Glinnes made response. Glay put his knife on the mantelpiece of smoke-darkened old kaban. Glinnes took a seat. "We'd better clear the air about Ambal Isle."

Glay leaned back against the wall and inspected Glinnes with somber eyes. "There's nothing to say. For better or worse, I sold it to Lute Casagave."

"The sale was not only unwise, it was illegal. I intend to void the contract."

"Indeed. How will you proceed?"

"We'll return the money and ask Casagave to leave. The process is very simple."

"If you have twelve thousand ozols."

"I don't—but you do."

Glay slowly shook his head. "No longer."

"Where is the money?"

"I gave it away."

"To whom?"

"To a man called Junius Farfan. I gave it; he took it; I can't get it back."

"I think that we should go to see Junius Farfan—at this very moment."

Glay shook his head. "Please don't begrudge me this money. You have your share—you are Squire of Rabendary. Let me have Ambal Isle as my share."

"There's no question of shares, or who owns what," said Glinnes. "You and I both own Rabendary. It's our home-place."

37

"That certainly is a valid point of view," said Glay. "But I choose to think differently. As I told you before, changes are coming over the land.

Glinnes sat back, unable to find words to convey his indignation.

"Let it rest there," said Glay wearily. "I took Ambal; you've got Rabendary. It's only fair, after all. I'll now move out and leave you in full enjoyment of your holding."

Glinnes tried to cry out a dissent, but the words clogged in his throat. He could only say, "The choice is yours. I hope you'll change your mind."

Glay's response was a cryptic smile, which Glinnes understood to mean no response at all. "Another matter," said Glinnes. "What of the Trevanyi yonder?"

"They are folk I traveled about with—the Drossets. Do you object to their presence?"

"They're your friends. If you insist upon changing your residence, why not take your friends with you?"

"I don't quite know where I'm going," said Glay. "If you want them gone, simply tell them so. You're Squire of Rabendary, not I."

Marucha spoke from her chair. "He's not squire until we know about Shira!"

"Shira is dead," said Glay.

"Still, Glinnes has no right to come home and instantly make difficulties. I vow, he's as obstinate as Shira and as hard as his father."

Glinnes said, "I've made no difficulties. You've made them. I've got to find twelve thousand ozols somewhere to save Ambal Isle, then evict a band of Trevanyi before they call in their whole clan. It's lucky I came home when I did, while we've still got a home."

Glay stonily poured himself a mug of apple wine. He seemed only bored . . . From across the field came a groaning, creaking sound, then a tremendous crash. Glinnes went to look from the end of the verandah. He turned back to Glay. "Your friends have just cut down one of our oldest barchnut trees."

"One of your trees," said Glay with a faint smile.

"You won't ask them to leave?"

"They wouldn't heed me. I owe them favors."

"Do they have names?"

"The het is Vang Drosset. His woman is Tingo. The sons

38

are Ashmor and Harving. The daughter is Duissane. The crone is Immifalda."

Going to his luggage, Glinnes brought forth his service hand-gun, which he dropped into his pocket. Glay watched with a sardonic droop to his lips, then muttered something to Marucha.

Glinnes marched off across the meadow. The pleasant pale light of afternoon seemed to clarify all the close colors and invest the distances with a luminous shimmer. Glinnes' heart swelled with many emotions: grief, longing for the old sweet times, anger with Glay which surged past his attempts to subdue it.

He approached the camp. Six pairs of eyes watched his every step, appraised his every aspect. The camp was none too clean, although, on the other hand, it was not too dirty; Glinnes had seen worse. Two fires were burning. At one of these a boy turned a spit stuck full with plump young woodhens. A caldron over the other fire emitted an acrid herbal stench: the Drossets were preparing a batch of Travanyi beer, which eventually colored their eyeballs a startling golden yellow. The woman stirring the mess was stern and keen-featured. Her hair had been dyed bright red and hung in two plaits down her back. Glinnes moved to avoid the reek.

A man approached from the fallen tree, where he had been gathering barchnuts. Two hulking young men ambled behind him. All three wore black breeches tucked into sagging black boots, loose shirts of beige silk, colored neckerchiefs—typical Treyanyi costume. Vang Drosset wore a flat black hat from which his taffy-colored hair burst forth in exuberant curls. His skin was an odd biscuit-brown; his eyes glowed yellow, as if illuminated from behind. Altogether an impressive man, and not a person to be trifled with, thought Glinnes. He said, "You are Vang Drosset? I am Glinnes Hulden, Squire of Rabendary Island. I must ask you to move your camp."

Vang Drosset motioned to his sons, who brought forward a pair of wicker chairs. "Sit and take refreshment," said Vang Drosset. "We will discuss our leaving."

Glinnes smiled and shook his head. "I must stand." If he sat and drank their tea he became beholden, and they then could ask for favors. He glanced past Vang Drosset to the boy turning the spit, and now he saw that it was not a boy but a slender, shapely girl of seventeen or eighteen. Vang Drosset spoke a syllable over his shoulder; the girl rose to her feet and went to the dull red tent. As she entered, she turned

39

a glance back over her shoulder. Glinnes glimpsed a pretty face, with eyes naturally golden, and golden-red curls that clung about her head and dangled past her ears to her neck.

Vang Drosset grinned, showing a set of gleaming white teeth. "As to moving camp, I beg that you give us leave to remain. We do no harm here."

"I'm not so sure. Trevanyi make uncomfortable neighbors. Beasts and fowl disappear, and other items as well."

"We have stolen neither beast nor fowl." Vang Drosset's voice was gentle.

"You have just destroyed a grand tree, and only to pick the nuts more easily."

"The forest is full of trees. We needed firewood. Surely it is no great matter."

"Not to you. Do you know I played in that tree when I was a boy? Look! See where I carved my mark! In that crotch I built an eyrie, where sometimes I slept at nights. That tree I loved!"

Vang Drosset gave a delicate grimace at the idea of a man loving a tree. His two sons laughed contemptuously, and turning away, began to throw knives at a target.

Glinnes continued. "Firewood? The forest is full of dead wood. You need only carry it here."

"A very long distance for folk with sore backs."

Glinnes pointed to the spit. "Those fowl—only half-grown; none have raised a brood. We hunt only the three-year birds, which no doubt you've already killed and eaten, and probably the two-year birds as well, and after you devour the yearlings none will be left. And there, on that platter—the ground fruit. You've pulled up entire clumps, roots and all; you've destroyed our future crop! You say you do no harm? You brutalize the land; it won't be the same for ten years. Strike your tents, load your wagons* and go."

Vang spoke in a subdued voice. "This is not gracious language, Squire Hulden."

"How does one graciously order a man off his property?" asked Glinnes. "It can't be done. You require too much."

Vang Drosset swung away with a hiss of exasperation and stared off across the meadow. Ashmor and Harving were now engaged in a startling Trevanyi exercise that Glinnes had never before witnessed. They stood about thirty feet apart

---

* Trevanyi wagons are ponderous boats with wheels, capable on either land or water.

and each in turn threw a knife at the other's head. He toward whom the knife was aimed flicked up his own knife to catch the hurled knife in some miraculous manner and send it spinning into the air.

"Trevanyi make good friends but bad enemies," said Vang Drosset in a soft voice.

Glinnes replied, "Perhaps you have heard the proverb: 'East of Zanzamar* live the friendly Trevanyi.'"

Vang Drosset spoke in a voice of spurious humility. "But we are not all that baneful! We add to the pleaures of Rabendary Island! We will play music at your feasts; we are adepts at the knife dances . . ." He twitched his fingers at his two sons, who hopped and jerked and swung their knives in shivering arcs.

By accident, by jocular or murderous design, a knife darted at Glinnes' head. Vang Drosset cawed, in either warning or exultation. Glinnes had been expecting some such demonstration. He ducked; the knife struck into a target behind him. Glinnes' gun jerked out and spat blue plasma. The end of the spit flared and the birds dropped into the coals.

From the tent darted the girl Duissane, her eyes projecting a dazzle as fierce as that of the gun. She snatched at the spit and burned her hand; she rolled the birds out on the ground with a stick, all the time crying out curses and invective: "Oh you wicked urush,** you've spoiled our meal! May your tongue grow a beard. And you with your vile paunch full of dog-guts, get away from the place before we name you a stiff-leg Fanscher. We know you, never fear! You're a worse spageen*** than your horn of a brother; there were few like him . . ."

Vang Drosset held up his clenched hand. The girl closed her mouth and grimly began to clean the birds. Vang Drosset turned back to Glinnes, a hard smile on his face. "That was not a kind act," he said. "Did you not enjoy the knife games?"

"Not particularly," said Glinnes. He brought out his own new knife, and pulling the Trevanyi knife from the target, sliced off a shaving as if he were paring a withe. The Drossets stared in fascination. Glinnes sheathed the knife.

---

* Zanzamar: a town at the far eastern tip of Cape Sunrise.
** urush: derogatory Trevanyish cant for a Trill.
*** spag: state of rut; hence *spageen*: individual in such a condition.

41

"The common land is only a mile down Ilfish Water," said Glinnes. "You can camp there to no one's detriment."

"We came here from the Common," cried Duissane. "The spageen Shira invited us; isn't that good enough for you?"

Glinnes could not comprehend the basis for Shira's generosity. "I thought it was Glay you traveled with."

Vang Drosset made another gesture. Duissane turned on her heel and took the birds to a serving table.

"Tomorrow we go our way," said Vang Drosset in a plangent, fateful voice. "*Forlostwenna** is on us, in any event: we are ready for departure."

Vang Drosset spat into the dirt. "It's Fanscherade which is on him. He's now too good for us."

"Too good for you as well," muttered Harving.

Fanscherade? The word meant nothing, but he would solicit no instruction from the Drossets. He spoke a word of farewell and turned away. As he crossed the field, six pairs of eyes stung his back. He was relieved to pass beyond the range of a thrown knife.

# Chapter 5

★ ★ ★

Avness was the name of that pale hour immediately before sunset: a sad quiet time when all color seemed to have drained from the world, and the landscape revealed no dimensions other than those suggested by receding planes of ever paler haze. Avness, like dawn, was a time unsympathetic to the Trill temperament; the Trills had no taste for melancholy reverie.

Glinnes found the house empty upon his return: both Glay and Marucha had departed. Glinnes was plunged into a state of gloom. He went out on the verandah and looked toward the Drosset tents, half of a mind to call them over for a fare-

---

* *Forlostwenna*: a word from the Trevanyi jargon—an urgent mood compelling departure; more immediate than the general term "wanderlust."

well feast—or more particularly Duissane, beyond dispute a fascinating creature, bad temper and all. Glinnes pictured her as she might look in a kindly mood . . . Duissane would enliven any occasion . . . An absurd idea. Vang Drosset would cut his heart out at the mere suspicion.

Glinnes went back into the house and poured himself a draught of wine. He opened the larder and considered the sparse contents. How different from the open-hearted bounty he remembered from the happy old times! . . . He heard the gurgle and hiss of a prow cutting water. Going out onto the verandah, Glinnes watched the approaching boat. It contained not Marucha, whom he expected, but a thin long-armed man with narrow shoulders and sharp elbows, in a suit of dark brown and blue velvet cut after that fashion favored by the aristocrats. Wispy brown hair hung almost to his shoulders; his face was mild and gentle, with a hint of impish mischief in the cast of his eyes and the quirk of his mouth. Glinnes recognized Janno Akadie the mentor, whom he remembered as voluble, facetious, at times mordant or even malicious, and never at a loss for an epigram, an allusion, a profundity, which impressed many but irked Jut Hulden.

Glinnes walked down to the dock and, catching the mooring line, made the boat fast to the bollard. Jumping nimbly ashore, Akadie gave Glinnes an effusive greeting. "I heard you were home and couldn't rest till I saw you. A pleasure having you back among us!"

Glinnes gave polite acknowledgment to the compliments, and Akadie nodded more cordially than ever. "I fear we've had changes since your departure—perhaps not all of them to your liking."

"I really haven't had time to make up my mind," said Glinnes cautiously, but Akadie paid no attention and looked up at the dim house. "Your dear mother is away from home?"

"I don't know where she is, but come drink a pot or two of wine."

Akadie made an acquiescent gesture. The two walked up the dock toward the house. Akadie glanced toward Rabendary Forest, where the Drosset's fire showed as a flickering orange spark. "The Trevanyi are still on hand, I notice."

"They leave tomorrow."

Akadie nodded sagely. "The girl is charming but fey—that is to say, burdened with a weight of destiny. I wonder for whom she carries her message."

Glinnes lofted his eyebrows; he had not thought of Duissane in so dire a connection, and Akadie's remark struck reverberations within him. "As you say, she seems an extraordinary person."

Akadie settled into one of the old string chairs on the verandah. Glinnes brought out wine, cheese and nuts, and they sat back to watch the wan colors of the Trullion sunset.

"I take it you are home on leave?"

"No. I've left the Whelm. I now seem to be Squire of Rabendary—unless Shira returns, which no one considers likely."

"Two months is indeed an ominous period," said Akadie, somewhat sententiously.

"What do you think became of him?"

Akadie sipped his wine. "I know no more than you, in spite of my reputation."

"Quite bluntly, I find the situation incomprehensible," said Glinnes. "Why did Glay sell Ambal? I can't understand it; he'll neither explain nor give back the money so that I can void the contract. I never expected to find so troublesome a situation. What is your opinion on all this?"

Akadie placed his mug delicately upon the table. "Are you consulting me professionally? It might well be money wasted, since, offhand, I see no remedy for your difficulties."

Glinnes heaved a patient sigh; here again: the Akadie with whom he never quite knew how to deal. He said, "If you can make yourself useful, I'll pay you." And he had the satisfaction of seeing Akadie purse his lips.

Akadie arranged his thoughts. "Hmmf. Naturally I can't charge you for casual gossip. I must make myself useful, as you put it. Sometimes the distinction between social grace and professional help is narrow. I suggest that we put this occasion on one basis or another."

"You can call it a consultation," said Glinnes, "since the matter has come to rest on these terms."

"Very well. What do you wish to consult about?"

"The general situation. I want to get a grip on affairs, but I'm working in the dark. First of all: Ambal Isle, which Glay had no right to sell."

"No problem here. Return the payment and void the contract."

"Glay won't give me the money, and I don't have twelve thousand ozols of my own."

"A difficult situation," agreed Akadie. "Shira, of course, refused to sell. The deal was made only after his disappearance."

"Hmmm. What are you suggesting?"

"Nothing whatever. I'm supplying facts from which you can draw whatever inferences you like."

"Who is Lute Casagave?"

"I don't know. Superficially he seems a gentleman of quiet tastes, who takes an amateur's interest in local genealogy. He's compiling a conspectus of the local nobility, or so he tells me. His motives might well be other than pure scholarship, it goes without saying. Might he be trying to establish a claim upon one or another of the local titles? If so, interesting events will be forthcoming . . . Hmm. What else do I know of the mysterious Lute Casagave? He claims to be a Bole from Ellent, which is Alastor 485, as you're no doubt aware. I have my doubts."

"How so?"

"I am an observant man, as you know. After my little lunch at his manor, I consulted my references. I found that, oddly enough, the great majority of Boles are left-handed. Casagave is right-handed. Most Boles are devoutly religious and their place of perdition is the Black Ocean at the South Pole of Ellent; submarine creatures house the souls of the damned. On Ellent, to eat wet food is to encompass within oneself a clutch of vile influences. No Bole eats fish. Yet Lute Casagave quite placidly enjoyed a stew of sea-spider, and afterward a fine grilled duck-fish, no less than I. Is Lute Casagave a Bole?" Akadie held out his hands. "I don't know."

"But why should he pretend to a false identity? Unless—"

"Exactly. Still, the explanation may be quite ordinary. Perhaps he is an emancipated Bole. Over-subtlety is an error as gross as innocence."

"No doubt. Well, this to the side. I still can't give him his money because Glay won't return it. Do you know where it is?"

"I do." Akadie darted a side-glance toward Glinnes. "I must remark that this is Class Two information and I must calculate your fee accordingly."

"Quite all right," said Glinnes. "If it seems exorbitant you can always recalculate. Where is the money?"

"Glay paid it to a man named Junius Farfan, who lives in Welgen."

Glinnes frowned off across Ambal Broad. "I've heard that name before."

"Quite likely. He is secretary of the local Fanschers."

"Oh? Why should Glay give him the money? Is Glay a Fanscher as well?"

"If not, he is on the brink. So far, he does not affect the mannerisms and idiosyncrasies."

Glinnes had a sudden insight. "The odd gray clothes? The shorn hair?"

"These are overt symbols. The movement has naturally provoked an angry reaction, and not unreasonably. The precepts of Fanscherade directly contradict conventional attitudes and must be considered anti-social."

"This means nothing to me," Glinnes grumbled. "I've never heard of Fanscherade till today."

Akadie spoke in his most didactic voice: "The name derives from old Glottisch: *Fan* is a corybantic celebration of glory. The thesis appears to be no more than an insipid truism: life is a commodity so precious that it must be used to best advantage. Who could argue otherwise? The Fanschers engender hostility when they try to implement the idea. They feel that each person must establish exalted goals, and fulfill them if he can. If he fails, he fails honorably and has satisfaction in his striving; he has used his life well. If he wins—" Akadie made a wry gesture. "Who in this life ever wins? Death wins. Still—Fanscherade is at its basis a glorious ideal."

Glinnes made a skeptical sound. "Five trillion folk of Alastor, all striving and straining? There'd be peace for no one."

Akadie gave a smiling nod. "Understand this: Fanscherade is not a policy for five trillion. Fanscherade is one single outcry of wild despair, the loneliness of a single man lost among an infinity of infinities. Through Fanscherade the one man defies and rejects anonymity; he insists upon his personal magnificence." Akadie paused, then made a wry grimace. "One might remark, parenthetically, that the only truly fulfilled Fanscher is the Connatic." He sipped his wine.

The sun had set. Overhead hung a high layer of frosty green cirrus; to south and north were wisps and tufts of rose, violet and citron. For a period the two men sat in silence.

Akadie spoke in a soft voice. "So then—that is Fanscherade. Few Fanschers comprehend their new creed; after all, most are children distressed by the sloth, the erotic excesses, the irresponsibility, the slovenly appearance of their parents. They deplore the cauch, the wine, the gluttonous feasts, all of which are consumed in the name of immediacy and vivid experience. Perhaps their principal intent is to establish a new and distinctive image for themselves. They cultivate a neutral appearance, on the theory that a person should be known not by the symbols he elects to display but by his conduct."

"A group of strident and callow malcontents!" growled Glinnes. "Where do they find the insolence to challenge so many persons older and wiser than themselves?"

"Alas!" sighed Akadie. "You'll find no novelty there."

Glinnes poured more wine into the mugs. "It all seems foolish, unnecessary, and futile. What do people want from life? We Trills have all the good things: food, music, merriment. Is this mischievous? What else is there to live for? The Fanschers are gargoyles screaming at the sun."

"On the face of it, the business is absurd," said Akadie. "Still—" He shrugged. "—There is a certain grandeur in their point of view. Malcontents—but why? To wrench sense from archaic nonsense; to strike the sigil of human will upon elemental chaos; to affirm the shining brilliance of one soul alone but alive among five trillion placcid gray corpuscles. Yes, it is wild and brave."

"You sound like a Fanscher yourself," snorted Glinnes.

Akadie shook his head. "There are worse attitudes, but no, not I. Fanscherade is a young man's game. I'm far too old."

"What do they think of hussade?"

"They consider it spurious activity, to distract folk from the true color and texture of life."

Glinnes shook his head in wonder. "And to think the Trevanyi girl called me a Fanscher!"

"What a singular notion!" said Akadie.

Glinnes turned Akadie a sharp glance but saw only an expression of limpid innocence. "How did Fanscherade start? I remember no such trend."

"The raw material has been long ready at hand, or so I would imagine. A certain spark of ideology was required, no more."

"And who then is the ideologue of Fanscherade?"

"Junius Farfan. He lives in Welgen."

"And Junius Farfan has my money!"

Akadie rose to his feet. "I hear a boat. It's Marucha at last." He went to the dock, followed by Glinnes. Along Ilfish Water came the boat behind its mustache of white water, across the edge of Ambal Broad and up to the dock. Glinnes took the line from Glay and made it fast to a bollard. Marucha stepped jauntily up to the dock. Glinnes looked in amazement at her clothes: a sheath of severe white linen, black ankle boots, and a black cloche cap, which, in suppressing her hair, accentuated her resemblance to Glay.

Akadie came forward. "I'm sorry I missed you. Still, Glinnes and I have had a pleasant conversation. We've been discussing Fanscherade."

"How very nice!" said Marucha. "Have you brought him around?"

"I hardly think so," said Akadie with a grin. "The seed must lie before it germinates."

Glay, standing to the side, looked more sardonic than ever. Akadie continued. "I have certain articles for you. These"—he handed Marucha a small flask—"are sensitizers; they place your mind in its most receptive state, and conduce to learning. Be sure to take no more than a single capsule or you will become hyperesthesic." He handed Marucha a parcel of books. "Here we have a manual of mathematical logic, a discussion of minichronics, and a treatise on basic cosmology. All are important to your program."

"Very good," said Marucha somewhat stiffly. "I wonder what I would like to give you?"*

"Something on the order of fifteen ozols would be more than ample," said Akadie. "But no hurry, of course. And now I too must be on my way. The dusk is far along."

Still, Akadie lingered while Marucha counted out fifteen ozols and placed them in his limp-fingered hand. "Goodnight, my friend." She and Glay went to the house. Glinnes asked, "And what will I have the pleasure of forcing upon you for the consultation?"

"Ah indeed, let me consider. Twenty ozol would be more than generous, if my remarks have been of help."

Glinnes paid over the money, reflecting that Akadie set a rather high price on his expertise. Akadie departed up Farwan Water toward Saur River, thence by Tethryn Broad and Vernice Water to his eccentric old manse on Sarpassante Island.

Inside the house on Rabendary Island lights glowed. Glinnes slowly walked up to the verandah, where Glay stood watching him.

"I've learned what you did with the money," said Glinnes. "You've given away Ambal Isle for sheer absurdity."

---

* The question "How much do I owe you?" is considered crass on Trullion, where easy generosity is the way of life.

48

"We've discussed the situation as much as necessary. I'll be leaving your house in the morning. Marucha wants me to stay, but I think I'll be more comfortable elsewhere."

"Do your dirty little mess and run, eh?" The brothers glared at each other, then Glinnes swung off and into the house.

Marucha sat reading the manuals Akadie had brought. Glinnes opened his mouth, then shut it again and went out to sit brooding on the verandah. Inside the house Glay and Marucha spoke in low tones.

# Chapter 6

★ ★ ★

In the morning Glay bundled up his belongings and Glinnes took him to Saurkash. Not a word was spoken during the trip. When he had stepped from the boat to Saurkash dock, Glay said, "I won't be far away, not for a while at any rate. Maybe I'll camp on the Commons. Akadie will know where to find me in case I'm needed. Try to be kind to Marucha. She's had an unhappy life, and now if she wants to play at girlhood, where's the harm in it?"

"Bring back that twelve thousand ozols and I might pay you some heed," said Glinnes. "Right now, all I expect of you is nonsense."

"The more fool you," said Glay, and went off up the dock. Glinnes watched him go. Then, instead of returning to Rabendary, he continued west toward Welgen.

Less than an hour's skim across the placid waterways brought him into Blacklyn Broad, with the great Karbashe River entering from the north, and the sea a mile or so to the south.

Glinnes tied the boat to the public dock, almost in the shadow of the hussade stadium, a structure of gray-green mena poles joined with black iron straps and brackets. He noticed a great cream-colored placard printed in red and blue:

49

Glinnes read the placard a second time, wondering where Lord Gensifer would assemble sufficient talent for a team of tournament quality. Ten years before, a dozen teams had played around the Fens: the Welgen Storm-devils, the Invincibles of the Altramar Hussade Club, the Voulash Gialospans* of Great Vole Island, the Gaspar Magnetics, the Saurkash Serpents—this last the somewhat disorganized and casual group for whom he and Jut and Shira had played—the Gorgets of the Loressamy Hussade Club, and various others of various quality and ever-shifting personnel. Competition had run keen; skilled players were sought after, cozened, subjected to a hundred inducements. Glinnes had no reason to doubt that a similar situation prevailed now.

Glinnes turned away from the stadium with a new thought itching at the back of his mind. A poor hussade team lost money, and unless subsidized, fell apart. A mediocre team might either win or lose, depending on whether it scheduled games below or above itself. But a successful aggressive team often earned substantial booty in the course of a year, which when divided might well yield twelve thousand ozols per man.

Glinnes walked thoughtfully to the central square. The structures seemed a trifle more weathered, the calepsis vines shading the arbor in front of the Aude de Lys Tavern were somewhat fuller and richer, and—now that Glinnes took the pains to notice—a surprising number of Fanscher uniforms and Fanscher-influenced garments were in evidence. Glinnes sneered in disgust for the faddishness of it all. At the center of the square, as before, stood the prutanshyr: a platform forty feet on a side, with a gantry above, and to the side a subsidiary platform or stand for the musicians who provided counterpoint to the rites of penitence.

---

* gialospans: literally, girl-denuders, in reference to the anticipated plight of the enemy sheirl.

Ten years had brought one or two new structures, most notable a new inn, The Noble Saint Gambrinus, raised on mena timbers above the ground-level beer-garden, where four Trevanyi musicians were playing for such folk who had elected to take early refreshment.

Today was market day. Costermongers had set up carts around the periphery of the square; they were uniformly of the Wrye race, a folk as separate and particular as the Trevanyi. Trills of Welgen and the countryside strolled at leisure past the barrows, examining and handling, haggling, occasionally buying. The country folk were distinguishable by their garments: the inevitable paray, with whatever other vestments fancy, convenience, whim, or aesthetic impulse dictated—oddments of this, trifles of that, gay scarves, embroidered vests, shirts emblazoned with odd designs, beads, necklaces, jangling bracelets, head-bands, cockades. Residents of the town wore clothes somewhat less idiosyncratic, and Glinnes noticed a sizable proportion of Fanscher suits, of good gray material, smartly tailored, worn with polished black ankle-boots. Some wore bucket-caps of black felt pulled tight over the hair. Some of those wearing this costume were older folk, self-conscious in their stylish finery. Certainly, reflected Glinnes, not all of these could be Fanschers.

A thin long-armed man in dark gray approached Glinnes, who stared in shock and scornful amusement. "You too? Is it possible!"

Akadie showed no embarrassment. "Why not? Where is the harm in a fad? I enjoy pretending I'm young again."

"Must you pretend to Fanscherade at the same time?"

Akadie shrugged. "Again: why not? Perhaps they over-idealize themselves; perhaps they carp too earnestly at the superstition and sensuality of the rest of us. Still"—he made a deprecatory gesture—"I am as you see."

Glinnes shook his head in disapproval. "Suddenly these Fanschers control the wisdom of the world, and their parents, who gave them birth, are shiftless and squalid."

Akadie laughed. "Fads come, fads go. They relieve the tedium of routine; why not enjoy them?" Before Glinnes could answer, Akadie changed the subject. "I expected to find you here. You're naturally looking for Junius Farfan, and it just so happens that I can point him out to you. Look yonder, past that horrid instrument, to the parlor under the Noble Saint Gambrinus. In the deep shade to the left a Fanscher sits writing in a ledger. That man is Junius Farfan."

"I'll go talk to him now."

"Good luck," said Akadie.

Glinnes crossed the square and, stepping into the beer-parlor, approached the table Akadie had indicated. "You are Junius Farfan?"

The man looked up. Glinnes saw a face classically regular, if somewhat bloodless and cerebral. The gray suit hung with austere elegance on his spare frame, which seemed all nerve, bone and sinew. A black cloth casque confined his hair and dramatized a square pale forehead and brooding gray eyes. His age was probably less than that of Glinnes himself. "I am Junius Farfan."

"My name is Glinnes Hulden. Glay Hulden is my brother. Recently he turned over to you a large sum, on the order of twelve thousand ozols."

Farfan signified assent. "True."

"I bring bad news. Glay derived this money illegally. He sold property that belonged not to him but to me. To cut to the bone of the matter, I must have this money back."

Farfan seemed neither surprised nor overly concerned. He gestured to a chair. "Sit down. Will you take refreshment?"

Glinnes, seating himself, accepted a mug of ale. "Thank you. And where is the money?"

Farfan gave him a dispassionate inspection. "Naturally you did not hope that I would hand over twelve thousand ozols in a bag."

"But I did hope so. I need the money to reclaim the property."

Farfan smiled in polite apology. "Your hopes cannot be realized, for I cannot return the money."

Glinnes put down the mug with a thump. "Why not?"

"The money has been invested; we have ordered the machinery to equip a factory. We intend to manufacture those goods which are now imported into Trullion."

Glinnes spoke in a voice hoarse with fury. "Then you had better get new money into your fund and pay me my twelve thousand ozols."

Farfan gave a grave assent. "If the money was indeed yours, I freely acknowledge the debt, and I will recommend that the money be repaid with interest from the first profits of our enterprises."

"And when will this be?"

"I don't know. We are hoping somehow to acquire a tract of land, by loan or donation or sequestration." Farfan grinned and his face became suddenly boyish. "Thereafter we must construct a plant, arrange for raw materials, learn appropriate techniques, produce and sell our goods, pay for the original stocks of raw materials, buy new stocks and supplies, and so forth."

Glinnes said, "This all takes an appreciable period of time."

Junius Farfan frowned up into the air. "Let us fix upon the interval of five years. If you will then be good enough to renew your claim, we can discuss the matter again, I hope to our mutual satisfaction. As an individual I sympathize with your plight," said Junius Farfan. "As secretary of an organization which desperately needs capital, I am only too happy to use your money; I conceive our need to be more urgent than yours." He closed the register and rose to his feet. "Good-day, Squire Hulden."

# Chapter 7

★ ★ ★

Glinnes watched Junius Farfan cross the square, moving around and out of sight behind the prutanshyr. He had achieved about as much as he had expected—nothing. Nevertheless, his resentment now included the suave Junius Farfan as well as Glay. However, it now became time to forget the lost money and try to find new. He looked into his wallet, though he already knew its contents: three thousand-ozol certificates, four hundred-ozol certificates, another hundred ozols in smaller paper. He therefore needed nine thousand ozols. His retirement pension amounted to a hundred ozols a month, more than ample for a man in his circumstances. He left The Noble Saint Gambrinus and crossed the square to the Welgen Bank, where he introduced himself to the chief officer.

"To be brief," said Glinnes, "my problem is this: I need nine thousand ozols to repossess Ambal Isle, which my brother incorrectly sold to a certain Lute Casagave."

"Yes, Lute Casagave; I recall the transaction."

"I wish to make a loan of nine thousand ozols, which I can repay at a rate of a hundred ozols per month. This is the fixed and definite sum I receive from the Whelm. Your money is perfectly safe and you are assured of repayment."

"Unless you die. Then what?"

Glinnes had not reckoned upon such a possibility. "There is always Rabendary Island, which I can propose for security."

"Rabendary Island. You are the owner?"

"I am the current squire," said Glinnes with a sudden sense of defeat. "My brother Shira disappeared two months ago. He is almost certainly dead."

"Very likely true. Still, we cannot deal in 'almosts' and 'very likelys.' Shira Hulden cannot be presumed dead until four years have passed. Until then you lack legal control of Rabendary Island. Unless, of course, you can prove his death."

Glinnes shook his head in vexation. "By diving down to consult the merlings? The situation is absurd."

"I appreciate the difficulties, but we deal in many absurdities; this is no more than an ordinary example."

Glinnes threw up his hands in defeat. He left the bank and returned to his boat, pausing only to re-read the placard announcing the formation of the Fleharish Broad Hussade Club.

As the boat drove toward Rabendary, Glinnes performed a number of calculations, all with the same purport: nine thousand ozols was a great deal of money. He reckoned the utmost income he might derive from Rabendary Island: perhaps two thousand ozols a year and insufficient by a factor of five. Glinnes turned his mind to hussade. A member of an important team might well gain ten thousand or even twenty thousand ozols a year if his team played often and consistently won. Lord Gensifer apparently planned the formation of such a team. Well and good, except that all the other teams of the region strained and strove to the same end, scheming, intriguing, making large promises, propounding visions of wealth and glory—all in order to attract talented players, who were not plentiful. The aggressive man might be slow and clumsy; the quick man might have poor judgment or a bad memory or insufficient strength to tub his opponent. Each position made its specific demands. The ideal forward was fast, agile, daring, sufficiently strong to cope with the opponents' rovers and guards. A rover must also be quick and

54

skillful; most urgently, he must be skillful with the buff—that padded implement used to thrust or trip the opponent from the ways or courses into the tanks. The rovers were the first line of defense against the thrusts of the forwards, and the guards were the last. The guards were massive powerful men, decisive with their buffs. Since they were not often required to trapeze, or leap the tanks, agility was not an essential attribute in a guard. The ideal hussade player comprised all these qualities; he was powerful, intelligent, cunning, nimble, and merciless. Such men were rare. How, then, did Lord Gensifer propose to recruit a tournament-quality team? At Fleharish Broad, Glinnes decided to find out and swung south toward the Five Islands.

Glinnes moored his boat beside Lord Gensifer's sleek offshore cruiser and leapt to the dock. A path led through a park to the manor. As he mounted the steps, the door slid aside. A footman in lavender and gray livery appraised him without warmth. A perfunctory bow expressed his opinion of Glinnes' status. "What is your wish, sir?"

"Be so good as to tell Lord Gensifer that Glinnes Hulden wants a few words with him."

"Will you come inside, sir?"

Glinnes stepped into a tall hexagonal foyer, which had a floor of gleaming gray and white stelt.* Overhead hung a chandelier of a hundred light-points and a thousand diamond prisms. In each wall a wainscot of white artica wood framed high narrow mirrors which cast back and forth the glitter of the chandelier.

The footman returned and conducted Glinnes to the library, where Thammas Lord Gensifer, wearing a maroon lounge suit, sat at his ease before a screen, watching a hussade game.**

---

* stelt: a precious material quarried from volcanic necks upon certain types of dead stars; a composite of metal and natural glass, displaying infinite variations of pattern and color.
** The hussade field is a gridiron of "runs" (also called "ways") and "laterals" above a tank of water four feet deep. The runs are nine feet apart, the laterals twelve feet. Trapezes permit the players to swing sideways from run to run, but not from lateral to lateral. The central moat is eight feet wide and can be passed at either end, at the center, or jumped if the player is sufficiently agile. The "home" tanks at either end of the field flank the platform on which stands the sheirl.

Players buff or body-block opposing players into the tanks, but may not use their hands to push, pull, hold, or tackle.

The captain of each team carries the "hange"—a bulb on a three-

"Sit down, Glinnes, sit down," said Lord Gensifer. "Will you take tea or perhaps a rum punch?"

"I'll have rum punch, please."

Lord Gensifer motioned to the screen. "Last year's finals at Cluster Stadium. The black and reds are the Hextar Zulans from Sigre. The greens are the Falifonics from Green Star. Marvelous play. I've watched the game four times now and each time I'm more amazed."

"I saw the Falifonics two or three years ago," said Glinnes. "I thought them agile and deft, and swift as lightning."

"They're still the same. Not large, but they seem to be everywhere at once. They have no great defense, but they don't need any with the attack they mount."

The footman served rum punch in frosted silver goblets. For a period Lord Gensifer and Glinnes sat watching the play: charges and shifts, feints and ploys, apparently reckless feats of agility, timing so exact as to seem bizarre coincidence. Patterns formed to calls from the captain, aggressions were launched and repulsed. Gradually the combinations began to favor the Falifonics. The Falifonic middle forwards swung to fork a Zulan rover and Zulan guards charged to protect; the Falifonic right wing slid through the gap thus opened, gained the platform, seized the gold ring at the sheirl's waist, and play came to a halt for the paying of ransom. Lord Gensifer turned off the screen. "The Falifonics won handily, as no doubt you know. Booty shared out at four thousand ozols a man . . . But you didn't come to talk hussade. Or did you?"

"As a matter of fact, yes. I happened to be in Welgen today and noticed mention of the new Fleharish Broad Club."

Lord Gensifer made an expansive gesture. "I'm the sponsor. It's something I've wanted to do for a long time, and fi-

---

foot pedestal. When the light glows the captain may not be attacked, nor may he attack. When he moves six feet from the hange, or when he lifts the hange to shift his position, the light goes dead; he may then attack and be attacked. An extremely strong captain may almost ignore his hange; a captain less able stations himself on a key junction, which he is then able to protect by virtue of his impregnability within the area of the live hange.

The sheirl stands on her platform at the end of the field between the home tanks. She wears a white gown with a gold ring at the front. The enemy players seek to lay hold of this gold ring; a single pull denudes the sheirl. The dignity of the sheirl may be ransomed by her captain for five hundred ozols, a thousand, two thousand, or higher, in accordance with a prearranged schedule.

nally I took the plunge. Welgen Stadium is our home field, and now all I've got to do is assemble a team. What about you? Are you still playing?"

"I played for my division," said Glinnes. "We took the sector championships."

"That sounds interesting. Why don't you try out with us?"

"I might just do so, but first I've got a problem you might help me work out."

Lord Gensifer blinked cautiously. "I'll be glad to, if I can. What's the problem?"

"As you probably know, my brother Glay sold Ambal Isle out from under me. He won't return the money; in fact, it's gone."

Lord Gensifer raised his eyebrows. "Fanscherade?"

"Exactly."

Lord Gensifer shook his head. "Silly young fool."

"My problem is this. I have three thousand ozols of my own. I need another nine thousand to pay off Lute Casagave and break the contract."

Lord Gensifer pursed his lips and fluttered his fingers. "If Glay had no right to sell, then Casagave had no right to buy. The matter would seem to be between Glay and Casagave, with you in legal possession."

"Unfortunately I have no legal possession unless I can prove Shira dead, which I can't. I need cold hard cash."

"It's a dilemma," Lord Gensifer agreed.

"Here is my proposal: suppose I were to play with you—could you advance me nine thousand ozols against booty?"

Lord Gensifer sat back in his chair. "That's a very chancy investment."

"Not if you can put together a good team. Though frankly I don't see where you'll get the personnel."

"They're on hand." Lord Gensifer sat up in his seat, his pink face alive with boyish excitement. "I've drawn up what I consider the strongest team that could be assembled from players of the region. Listen to this." He read from a paper. "Wings: Tyran Lucho, Lightning Latken. Strikes: Yalden Wirp, Gold Ring Gonniksen. Rovers: Nilo Basgard, Wild Man Wilmer Guff. Guards: Splasher Maveldip, Bughead Holub, Carbo Gilweg, Holbert Hanigatz." Lord Gensifer put down the paper and peered triumphantly at Glinnes. "What do you think of that team?"

"I've been away too long," said Glinnes. "I only know about half the names. I've played with Gonniksen and Carbo

Gilweg, and against Guff and maybe one or two others. They were good ten years ago and they're probably better now. Are all these men on your team?"

"Well—not officially. My strategy is this. I'll talk to each man in turn. I'll show him the team and ask how he'd like to be a part of it. How can I lose? Everyone wants to earn some big booty for a change. No one is going to turn me down. As a matter of fact, I've already made contact with two or three of the fellows and they've all shown great interest."

"Where would I fit in? And what about the nine thousand ozols?"

Lord Gensifer said cautiously, "As to your first question, you must remember that I haven't seen you play recently. For all I know, you've gone slow and sour . . . Where are you going?"

"Thank you for the rum punch," said Glinnes.

"Just a minute. No need to get temperamental. After all, I spoke only the plain truth. I haven't seen you for ten years. Still, if you played with the sector champions, no doubt you're in good shape. What is your position?"

"Anything but sheirl. With the 93rd I played strike and rover."

Lord Gensifer poured Glinnes more punch. "No doubt something can be arranged. But you must understand my position. I'm going after the best. If you're the best you'll play for the Gorgons. If you're not—well, we'll need substitutes. That's sheer common sense—nothing to get excited about."

"Well then, what about the nine thousand ozols?"

Lord Gensifer sipped his punch. "I should think that if all goes well, and if you are playing for the club, you should take nine thousand ozols in booty in a very short time."

"In other words—you won't advance me the money?"

Lord Gensifer held up his hands. "Do you imagine that ozols grow on trees? I need money as badly as anyone. In fact—well, I won't go into details."

"If you're all that short of money, how can you finance a treasure-box?"

Lord Gensifer airily flicked his fingers. "No difficulty there. Whatever funds are jointly available we'll use—your three thousand ozols as well. It's all for the common cause."

Glinnes could hardly believe his ears. "My three thousand ozols? You want me to advance the fund? While you take an owner's share of booty?"

Lord Gensifer, smiling, leaned back in his chair. "Why not? Each contributes his best and his most, and each of us profits. That's the only way to operate. There's no reason to be scandalized."

Glinnes replaced his goblet on the tray. "It's just not done. The players contribute their skills, the club funds the treasure-box. I wouldn't give you an ozol; I'd organize my own team first."

"Just a moment. Perhaps we can work out a procedure that will please us all. Frankly, I'm short of cash. You need twelve thousand ozols within the year; your three thousand is worthless without the other nine."

"Not exactly worthless. It represents ten years' service in the Whelm."

Lord Gensifer waved aside the remark. "Suppose that you advance three thousand ozols to the fund. The first three thousand ozols we earn will go to you; you'll have your money back, and then—"

"The other players wouldn't allow such an arrangement."

Lord Gensifer pulled at his lower lip. "Well, the money could come from the club's share of the booty—in other words, out of my personal purse."

"Suppose there isn't any purse; suppose we lose my three thousand ozols? Then what? Nothing!"

"We don't plan to lose! Think positive, Glinnes!"

"I'm thinking positively about my money."

Lord Gensifer heaved a deep sigh. "As I say, my own financial status is at the moment up in the air . . . Suppose that we make this arrangement. You advance three thousand ozols to the club treasury. We will at first try for five-thousand-ozol teams, which we should handily demolish, and build up the treasury to ten thousand ozols. We then schedule ten-thousand-ozol teams. At this point booty will be distributed and you will be repaid from the club's share—the work of a game or two. Thenceforth I will lend you half the club's share until you have your nine thousand ozols, which you can thereupon repay from your ordinary share."

Glinnes tried to calculate in his head. "I don't understand any of this. You've left me far behind."

"It's simple. If we win five ten-thousand-ozol games, you have your money."

"If we win. If we lose, I have nothing. Not even the three thousand that I have now."

59

Lord Gensifer flourished his list of names. "This team won't lose games, I assure you of that!"

"You don't have that team! You don't have a fund. You don't even have a sheirl."

"No lack of applicants there, my boy. Not for the Fleharish Gorgons! I've already talked to a dozen beautiful creatures."

"All certified, no doubt."

"We'll certify them, never fear! But what a ridiculous business! A naked virgin looks like any other naked girl. Who's to know the difference?"

"The team. Irrational, I agree, but hussade is an irrational game."

"I'll drink to that," declared Lord Gensifer rather boisterously. "Who cares a fig for rationality? Only Fanschers and Trevanyi!"

Glinnes drained his goblet and rose to his feet. "I must be on my way home and see to my personal Trevanyi. Glay gave them the freedom of Rabendary and they plundered in all directions."

Lord Gensifer nodded sagely. "You can't give a Trevanyi anything but what he'll take double for contempt . . . Well, to revert to the three thousand ozols, what is your decision?"

"I'll want to consider the matter very carefully indeed. As for that list of players—how many have actually committed themselves?"

"Well—several."

"I'll talk to them all and learn if they're really serious."

Lord Gensifer frowned. "Hmm. Let's think this over a bit. In fact, will you stay for a bite of dinner? I'm quite alone tonight, and I detest dining in solitude."

"That's very kind of you, Lord Gensifer, but I'm hardly dressed for dinner at a manor."

Lord Gensifer made a deprecatory motion. "Tonight we'll dine informally—although I could lend you formal kit, if you insisted."

"Well, no. I'm not that meticulous, if you're not."

"Tonight we'll dine as we are. Perhaps you'd like to watch more of the championship game."

"As a matter of fact, I would."

"Good. Rallo! Fresh punch! This has lost its zest."

The great oval dinner table was set for two. Lord Gensifer and Glinnes faced each other across the expanse of white

linen; silver and crystal glittered under the blaze of a chandelier.

"It may seem strange to you," said Lord Gensifer, "that I
can live in what might seem extravagant style and still be
strapped for cash. But it's simple enough. My income derives
from invested capital, and I've had reverses. Starmenters
looted a pair of warehouses and set my company back on its
heels. Strictly temporary, of course, but for the moment my
income just barely matches my outgo. Do you know of Bela
Gazzardo?"

"I've heard the name. A starmenter?"

"The villain who cut my income in half. The Whelm can't
seem to come to grips with him."

"Sooner or later he'll be taken. Only inconspicuous starmenters survive. When they attain reputation their number is
up."

"Bela Gazzardo's been starmenting for many years," said
Lord Gensifer. "The Whelm is always in a different sector."

"Sooner or later he'll be taken."

Dinner proceeded, a repast of a dozen excellent courses,
each accompanied by flasks of fine wine. Glinnes reflected
that life in a manor was not without its pleasant aspects, and
his fancy roamed the future, when he had earned twenty or
thirty thousand ozols, or a hundred thousand, and Lute Casagave had been expelled from Ambal Isle and the manse was
empty. Then, what an adventure to renew, redecorate, refur-
nish! Glinnes saw himself in stately garments entertaining a
throng of notables at a table like Lord Gensifer's . . .
Glinnes laughed at the thought. Who would he invite to his
dinner parties? Akadie? Young Harrad? Carbo Gilweg? The
Drossets? Though for a fact Duissane would look extraordinarily lovely in such surroundings. Glinnes' imagination included the rest of the family and the picture burst.

Dusk had long since waned when Glinnes finally climbed
into his boat. The night was clear; overhead hung a myriad
stars, magnified to the size of lamps. Elevated by the wine, by
the large prospects that Lord Gensifer had suggested, by the
halcyon beauty of starlight on calm black water, Glinnes sent
his boat scudding across Fleharish Broad and up Selma
Water. Under the glorious Trullion night his problems dis-
solved into wisps of unreasonable petulance. Glay and Fanscherade? A fad, an antic, a trifle. Marucha and her
foolishness? Let her be, let her be; what better occupation lay
open to her? Lord Gensifer and his crafty proposals? They

61

might just eventuate as Lord Gensifer hoped! But the absurdity of it all! Instead of borrowing nine thousand ozols, he had barely escaped with his own three thousand intact! Lord Gensifer's schemes no doubt derived from a desperate need of money, thought Glinnes. No matter how affable and how ostensibly candid, Lord Gensifer was still a man to be dealt with most carefully.

Up narrow Selma Water drifted the boat, past hushberry brakes and bowers of soft white lanting, then out upon Ambal Broad, where a small breeze shivered the star-reflections into a tinkling twinkling carpet. To the right stood Ambal Isle, surmounted by fanzaneel frond-clusters; they lay on the sky like splashes of black ink. And there ahead—Rabendary Island, dear Rabendary, and his home dock. The house showed no light. Was no one at home? Where was Marucha? Visiting friends, most likely.

The boat coasted up to the dock. Glinnes climbed up on the groaning old boards, made fast the boat, walked up the path to the house.

A creak of leather, a shuffle of steps. Shadows moved; dark shapes occulted the stars. Heavy objects struck down upon his head and neck and shoulders, thudding and jarring, grinding his teeth, grating his vertebrae, filling his nose with an ammoniacal reek. He fell to the ground. Heavy blows struck into his ribs, his head; the impacts rumbled and groaned like thunder and filled the total space of the world. He tried to roll away, to curl into a knot, but his senses wandered away.

The kicking ceased; Glinnes floated on a cloud of enervation. From far far away he noticed hands exploring his person. A harsh whisper rang in his brain: "Get the knife, get the knife." Further touches, then another flurry of kicks. From a great distance Glinnes thought to hear a trill of reckless laughter. Consciousness fragmented like droplets of mercury; Glinnes lay in a torpor.

Time passed; the carpet of stars slid across the sky. Slowly, slowly, from many directions, the components of consciousness began to wander back together.

Something strong and cold seized Glinnes' ankle, drew him down the path toward the water. Glinnes groaned and spread out his fingers to clutch the sod, without effect. He kicked with all his strength and struck into something pulpy. The grip on his ankle loosened. Glinnes painfully hunched up on hands and knees and crawled back up the path. The merling came after him and resumed its grip. Glinnes again kicked out and the merling croaked in annoyance.

Glinnes rolled weakly over. Under the Trullion starblaze man and merling confronted each other. Glinnes began to slide back on his haunches, a foot at a time. The merling hopped forward. Glinnes' back struck the steps leading up to the verandah. Underneath were fence-staves cut from prickle-bush. Glinnes turned and groped; his fingers touched one of the staves. The merling snatched and once more dragged him toward the water. Glinnes thrashed like a grounded fish, and breaking free, struggled back to the verandah. The merling uttered a dismal croak and jumped forward; Glinnes grasped a stave and thrust it at the creature's groin; it sagged away. Glinnes hunched himself up on the stairs, stave ready; the merling dared approach no further. Glinnes crawled into the house, forced himself to stand erect. He tottered to the light-switch, and brought glow into the house. He stood swaying. His head throbbed, his eyes refused to focus. Breathing tore at his ribs; conceivably several were broken. His thighs ached where his attackers had sought to make pulp of his crotch, failing only for the poor illumination. A new and sharper pang struck him; he felt for his wallet. Nothing. He looked down at his boot scabbard; his marvelous proteum knife was gone.

Glinnes sighed in fury. Who had done this? He suspected the Drossets. Recalling the tinkle of merry laughter, he was certain.

# Chapter 8

### ★ ★ ★

In the morning Marucha had not yet arrived home; Glinnes presumed that she spent the night with a lover. Glinnes was happy that she was not on hand; she would have analyzed every aspect of his folly, for which he was not in the mood.

Glinnes lay on the couch, aching in every bone, sweating with hatred for the Drossets. He staggered into the bathroom, examined his purple face. In the cabinet he found a pain-relieving potion, with which he dosed himself, then limped back to the couch.

He dozed off and on throughout the morning. At noon the telephone chime sounded. Glinnes stumbled across the room and spoke into the mesh, without showing his face to the screen. "Who's calling?"

"This is Marucha," came his mother's clear voice. "Glinnes—are you there?"

"Yes, I'm here."

"Well then, show yourself; I detest speaking to persons I can't see."

Glinnes fumbled around with the vision-push. "The button seems to be stuck. Can you see me?"

"No, I cannot. Well, it doesn't matter. Glinnes I've come to a decision. Akadie has long wanted me to share his home, and now that you are back and presently will be bringing a woman into the house, I have agreed to the arrangement."

Glinnes only half restrained a mournful chuckle. How his father Jut would have roared in wrath! "My best wishes for your happiness, mother, and please convey my respects to Akadie."

Marucha peered into the screen. "Glinnes, your voice sounds strange. Are you well?"

"Yes, indeed—just a bit hoarse. After you've settled yourself I'll come over for a visit."

"Very well, Glinnes. Do take care of yourself, and please don't be too stern with the Drossets. If they want to stay on Rabendary, where is the harm in it?"

"I'll certainly consider your advice, mother."

"Good-by Glinnes." The screen faded.

Glinnes heaved a deep sigh and winced for the zig-zags of pain across his ribs. Were any broken? He explored with his fingers, prodding the most tender areas, and could come to no decision.

He took a bowl of porridge out on the verandah and ate a dreary meal. The Drossets, of course, had departed, leaving a litter of rubbish, a pile of dead foliage, a dispirited outhouse of branches and fronds to mark the site of their camp. Three thousand four hundred ozols they had earned by their night's work, as well as the pleasure of punishing their persecutor. The Drossets were well-pleased today.

Glinnes went to the telephone and called Egon Rimbold,

the medical practitioner in Saurkash. He explained something of his difficulties and Rimbold agreed to pay him a visit.

Limping out to the verandah, Glinnes lowered himself into one of the old string chairs. The view as always was placid. Pearl-colored haze obscured the distance; Ambal seemed a floating fairy island. His mind drifted . . . Marucha, ostensibly disdainful of aristocratic ritual, had become a hussade princess, risking the poignant humiliation—or was it glory?—of public exposure in the hope that she might make an aristocratic marriage. She had settled for the Squire of Rabendary, Jut Hulden. Perhaps at the back of her mind had lurked the image of Ambal Manor, where nothing could have persuaded Jut to live . . . Jut was dead; Ambal had been sold and Marucha now found nothing on Rabendary to keep her . . . To regain Ambal Isle he could repay twelve thousand ozols to Casagave and tear up the contract. Or he could prove Shira's death, whereupon the transaction became illegal. Twelve thousand ozols were hard to come by, and a man taken down to the merling's dinner table left few traces . . . Glinnes hunched around to look along the path. There: where the Drossets had waited behind the prickleberry hedge. There: where they had beaten him. There: the marks he had scratched into the sod. Not far beyond lay the placid surface of Farwan Water.

Egon Rimbold arrived in his narrow black runabout. "Instead of returning from wars," said Rimbold, "it appears that you've been through them."

Glinnes told him what had occurred: "I was beaten and robbed."

Rimbold looked across the meadow. "I notice that the Drossets are gone."

"Gone but not forgotten."

"Well, let's see what we can do for you."

Rimbold worked to good effect, using the advanced pharmacopoeia of Alastor and pads of adhesive constrict. Glinnes began to feel like a relatively sound man.

Packing his instruments, Rimbold asked, "I suppose you reported the attack to the constabulary?"

Glinnes blinked. "To tell the truth, the idea never occurred to me."

"It might be wise. The Drossets are a rough lot. The girl is as bad as the rest."

"I'll see to her as well as the others," said Glinnes. "I don't know how or when, but none will escape."

Rimbold made a gesture counseling moderation, or at least caution, and took his leave.

Glinnes reexamined himself in the mirror and took a glum satisfaction in his improved appearance. Returning to the verandah, and lowering himself gingerly into a chair, he considered how best to revenge himself on the Drossets. Threats and menaces might provide a temporary satisfaction, but when all was considered, they served no useful purpose.

Glinnes became restless. He limped here and there around the property and was dismayed by the neglect and dilapidation. Rabendary was disreputable even by Trill standards; Glinnes once again became angry at Glay and Marucha. Did they feel no friendliness whatever for the old home? No matter; he would set things straight, and Rabendary would be as he remembered it from his childhood.

Today he was too lame to work. With nothing better to do, he gingerly stepped into his boat and drove up Farwan Water to the Saur River, then over the top of Rabendary to Gilweg Island and the rambling old home of his friends the Gilwegs. The rest of the day was given to that typical Trill festivity which the Fanschers considered shiftless, untidy and dissolute. Glinnes became somewhat intoxicated; he sang old songs to the music of concertinas and guitars; he romped with the Gilweg girls and made himself so agreeable that the Gilwegs volunteered to come to Rabendary on the very next day to help clean up the Drosset camp.

The subject of hussade was broached. Glinnes mentioned Lord Gensifer and the Fleharish Gorgons. "So far the team is no more than a list of important names. Still, what if all became Gorgons? Stranger things have happened. He wants me at strike and I'm inclined to give it a try, if only for the sake of money."

"Bah," said Carbo Gilweg. "Lord Gensifer doesn't know wet from dry as far as hussade is concerned. And where will he find the ozols? Everyone knows that he lives from hand to mouth."

"Not so!" declared Glinnes. "I took a meal with him, and I can vouch that he stints himself very little."

"That may be, but operating an important team is another matter. He'll need uniforms, helmets, a respectable treasury—it amounts to five thousand ozols or more. I doubt if he can give substance to the idea. Who is to be his captain?"

Glinnes reflected. "I don't believe he specified a captain."

"There's a sticking point. If he recruits a reputable captain, he'll attract players more skeptical than yourself."

"Don't think me so innocent! I gave him nothing but an expression of interest."

"You'd be better off with our good old Saurkash Tanchinaros," declared Ao Gilweg.

"For a fact, we could use a pair of good forwards," said Carbo. "Our back line, if I say so myself, is as good as any, but we can't get our own men past the moat. Join the Tanchinaros! We'll sweep Jolany Prefecture clean."

"How much is your treasure?"

"We can't seem to push past a thousand ozols," Carbo admitted. "We win one, then lose one. Frankly, we've got uneven quality. Old Neronavy isn't the most inspiring captain; he never stirs from his hange, and he only knows three plays. I could go down the lineup, but it wouldn't mean much."

"You've just persuaded me to the Gorgons," said Glinnes. "I remember Neronavy from ten years ago. I'd rather have Akadie for captain."

"Apathy, torpor," said Ao Gilweg. "The group needs stirring up."

"We haven't had a pretty sheirl for two years," said Carbo. "Jenlis Wade—bland as a dead cavout. She just looked puzzled when she lost her gown. Barsilla Cloforeth—too tall and hungry. When they stripped her no one even bothered to look. Barsilla marched off in disgust."

"We have pretty sheirls here"—Ao Gilweg jerked his thumb at his daughters Rolanda and Berinda—"except that they prefer to play something other than hussade with the boys. Now they can't quite qualify."

Afternoon became avness, avness became dusk, dusk became dark, and Glinnes was persuaded to spend the night.

In the morning Glinnes returned to Rabendary and began to clear the site of the Drosset camp. A peculiar circumstance gave him pause. A hole had been dug two feet into the ground on the site of the fire. The hole was empty. Glinnes could form no sensible conjecture to account for such a hole, at the precise center of the old fire-site.

At noon the Gilwegs arrived, and two hours later every evidence of the Drosset presence had been expunged.

Meanwhile the Gilweg women prepared the best meal possible, disparaging Marucha's larder, which they considered austere. They had never cared much for Marucha to begin with; she gave herself too many airs.

The Gilwegs now knew every detail of Glinnes' troubles. They offered an amplitude of sympathy and as much conflicting advice. Ao Gilweg, the head of the family, had spoken to Lute Casagave on several occasions. "A canny character, seething with schemes! He's not out there on Ambal Isle for his health!"

"It's the usual way with off-world folk," his wife Clara declared. "I've seen many, all overwrought and anxious, fussy and fastidious. Not one knows how to live a normal life."

"Casagave is either bashful or blind," said Carbo. "If you pass his boat he never so much as lifts his head."

"He fancies himself a great noble," said Clara with a sniff. "He's far too good for us ordinary folk. We've never tasted a drop of his wine, that's for sure."

Clara's sister, Currance, asked, "Have you seen his servant? There's a sight for you! I believe he's half Polgonian ape, or some such mixture. That one will never set foot in my house, so much I swear."

"True," declared Clara. "He has the look of a villain. And never forget: birds of a feather flock together! Lute Casagave is undoubtedly as bad as his servant!"

Ao Gilweg held up his hands in remonstration. "Now, now! A moment for sensible thought! Nothing has been proved against either of these men; in fact, they're not even accused!"

"He sequestered Ambal Isle! Isn't that enough?"

"Perhaps he was misled, who knows? He might well be a just and innocent man."

"A just and innocent man would relinquish his illegal occupancy!"

"Exactly! Perhaps Lute Casagave is that man!" Ao turned to Glinnes. "Have you discussed the matter with Lute Casagave himself? I thought not."

Glinnes looked skeptically toward Ambal Isle. "I suppose I could speak to him. But one stark fact remains: even a just man would want his twelve thousand ozols, which I am not prepared to supply."

"Refer him to Glay, to whom he paid the money," Carbo advised. "He should have assured a clear title before he closed the bargain."

"It's a strange circumstance, strange indeed . . . Unless he knew for a fact that Shira was indeed dead, which leads into a set of macabre speculations."

"Bah!" declared Ao Gilweg. "Take the bull by the horns; go speak to the man. Tell him to vacate your property and go for his money to Glay, the man to whom he paid it."

"By the Fifteen Devils, you're right!" exclaimed Glinnes. "It is absolutely clear and obvious—he hasn't a leg to stand on! I'll make this clear to him tomorrow."

"Remember Shira!" spoke Carbo Gilweg. "He may be a man without restraint!"

"Best to carry a weapon," Ao Gilweg advised. "Nothing to induce humility as well as an eight-bore blaster."

"At the moment I have no weapon," said Glinnes. "Those Trevanyi villains gleaned my belongings like a rumblesnout sucking bugs from a box. Still, I doubt if I'll need weapons; if Casagave, as I hope, is a reasonable man, we'll quickly reach an understanding."

Between Rabendary dock and Ambal Isle lay only a few hundred yards of still water, a trip that Glinnes had made uncounted times. Never had it seemed so long.

Ambal Isle showed no activity; only Casagave's gray runabout indicated his presence. Glinnes moored his boat, jumped up on the dock as jauntily as his still-aching ribs permitted. As etiquette demanded, he touched the bell-button before starting up the walk.

Ambal Manor was much like Gensifer Manor: a tall white structure of extravagant complexity. Bays projected from every wall; on fluted pilasters rested the roof: four milk-glass domes and a central golden spire. No smoke issued from the chimney; no sound could be heard from within. Glinnes touched the doorell.

A minute passed. There was movement behind a bay window; then the door opened and Lute Casagave looked forth—a man considerably older than Glinnes, thin-legged, stoop-shouldered, in a loose off-worlder's suit of gray gabardine. Silver hair hung beside a sallow face, which included a long bony nose, long gaunt cheeks, eyes like chips of cold stone. Casagave's face expressed a stern and alert intelligence, but it did not seem the face of a man who might contribute twelve thousand ozols to the cause of abstract justice.

Casagave spoke neither greeting nor question but stared silently forth, waiting for Glinnes to define the reason for his presence.

Glinnes said politely, "I'm afraid I have some bad news for you, Lute Casagave."

"You may address me as Lord Ambal."

Glinnes' mouth went slack. "'Lord Ambal'?"

"This is how I choose to be known."

Glinnes shook his head dubiously. "That's all well and good; your blood may be the noblest of Trullion. Still, you can't be Lord Ambal, because Ambal Isle is not your property. That's the bad news to which I referred."

"Who are you?"

"I am Glinnes Hulden, Squire of Rabendary, and I own Ambal Isle. You gave my brother Glay money for property he neglected to own. It's an unpleasant situation. I certainly don't intend to charge you rent for your time here, but I'm afraid you'll have to find another residence."

Casagave's eyebrows contracted; his eyes became slits. "You talk nonsense. I am Lord Ambal, the sanguineal descendant to that Lord Ambal who illegally sought to dispose of the ancestral property. The original transaction was invalid; the Hulden title was never good to begin with. Be grateful for your twelve thousand ozols; I was not obliged to pay anything."

"Now then!" cried Glinnes. "The sale was made to my great-grandfather. It was recorded with the registrar at Welgen and cannot be invalidated!"

"I'm not so sure of that," said Lute Casagave. "You are Glinnes Hulden? This means nothing to me. Shira Hulden is the man from whom I bought the property, with your brother Glay acting as his agent."

"Shira is dead," said Glinnes. "The sale was fraudulent. I suggest that you make representations to Glay for your money."

"Shira is dead? How do you know?"

"He is dead, probably murdered and dragged off by the merlings."

"'Probably'? Probably has no legal standing. My contract is sound unless you can prove otherwise, or unless you die, when the question becomes moot."

"I don't plan to die," said Glinnes.

"Who does? The event comes on us all willy-nilly."

"Do you threaten me now?"

Casagave merely gave a dry chuckle. "You are trespassing on Ambal Isle; you have ten seconds to remove yourself."

Glinnes' voice shook with rage. "The shoe is on the other

foot. I provide you three days, and three days only, to get off my property."

"And then?" Lute Casagave's voice was sardonic.

"Never mind what then. Get off Ambal Isle or you'll learn."

Casagave gave a shrill whistle. Footsteps thudded; behind Glinnes appeared a man seven feet tall, weighing perhaps three hundred pounds. His skin was the color of teak; black hair clung to his head like fur. Casagave jerked his thumb toward the dock. "Either in your boat or into the water."

Glinnes, still sore from a previous beating, did not care to risk another. He turned on his heel and stalked down the path. Lord Ambal? What a travesty! So this had been the motivation for Casagave's researches.

The boat took Glinnes out upon the water. He slowly circled Ambal Isle; never had it seemed so lovely. What if Casagave ignored the three-day deadline—as he was sure to do? Glinnes gave his head a dreary shake. Force would bring him afoul of the constabulary—unless he could prove Shira's death.

# Chapter 9

★ ★ ★

Akadie lived in a quaint old manse on a point of land known as Rorquin's Tooth overlooking Clinkhammer Broad, several miles northwest of Rabendary. Rorquin's Tooth was a jut of weathered black stone, perhaps the stump of an ancient volcano, now overgrown with jard, fire-blossom, and dwarf pomanders; at the back rose a copse of sentinellos. Akadie's manse, the folly of a long-forgotten lord, raised five towers to the sky, each of different height and architectural order. One was roofed with slate, another with tile, a third with green glass, the fourth with lead, the fifth with the artificial material spandex. Each supported at its summit a study, with special appurtenances and outlooks to suit one or another of Akadie's moods. Akadie recognized and enjoyed each of his own quirks and made a virtue of inconsistency.

In the early morning, while the haze still swirled in wisps, Glinnes drove his boat north up Farwan Water and the Saur, then west along narrow weed-choked Vernice Water into Clinkhammer Broad. Reflected double upon the smooth water stood Akadie's five-towered manse.

Akadie had only just arisen from his bed. His hair was rumpled into wisps; his eyes were barely half-open. Nevertheless he gave Glinnes an affable good-morning. "Please do not expound your business before breakfast; the world is not yet in focus."

"I came to see Marucha," said Glinnes. "I am not in need of your services."

"In that case, talk as you will."

Marucha, always an early riser, seemed taut and peevish, and greeted Glinnes without effusiveness. She served Akadie a breakfast of fruit, tea and buns, and poured Glinnes tea.

"Ah!" said Akadie, "the day begins, and once again I will concede that a world exists beyond the confines of this room." He sipped his tea. "And how go your affairs?"

"As well as could be expected. My troubles have not disappeared at a snap of the fingers."

"Sometimes," Akadie observed, "a person's troubles are only those which he creates for himself."

"This is absolutely true in my case," said Glinnes. "I strive to recover my property and protect what is left, and in so doing I stimulate my enemies."

Marucha, working in the kitchen, showed elaborate disdain for the conversation.

Glinnes went on. "The basic culprit is of course Glay. He worked a world of mischief, then walked away from the mess. I consider him a poor excuse for a Hulden, and for a brother."

Marucha could no longer contain her tongue. "I doubt if he cares whether he's a Hulden or not. As far as brotherhood is concerned the relationship extends in both directions. You are not helping him in his work, let me remind you."

"It costs too much," said Glinnes. "Glay can afford gifts of twelve thousand ozols because the money never belonged to him. I saved only thirty-four hundred ozols, which Glay's cronies the Drossets took from me. I now have nothing."

"You have Rabendary Island. That is a great deal."

"At last you acknowledge Shira's death."

Akadie held up his hand. "Now then! Let us take our tea

up to the South Vantage. Come along up the stairs, but take care; the treads are narrow."

They mounted into the lowest and most spacious tower, which afforded a view over all of Clinkhammer Broad. Akadie had hung antique gonfalons about the dark paneling; a collection of eccentric red stoneware pots stood in a corner. Akadie put teapot and cups on the withe table and motioned Glinnes to pull up one of the fan-backed old withe chairs. "When I enticed Marucha into the house I did not expect a complement of family dissensions as well."

"Perhaps this morning I am a trifle out of sorts," Glinnes admitted. "The Drossets waylaid me in the dark, thrashed me soundly, and took all my money. For this reason I can't sleep of nights; my insides seethe and boil and twist with rage."

"An exasperation, to say the least. Are you planning countermeasures?

Glinnes gave him an incredulous glare. "I plan nothing else! But nothing seems sensible. I could kill one or two Drossets, end up on the prutanshyr, and still lack my money. I could drug their wine and search their camp while they slept, but I have no such drug, and even if I had, how could I be sure that all had drunk the wine?"

"These feats are easier planned than accomplished," said Akadie. "But allow me a suggestion. Do you know the Glade of Xian?"

"I have never visited the place," said Glinnes. "It is the Trevanyi burial ground, so I understand."

"It is much more than that. The Bird of Death flies from the Vale of Xian, and the dying man hears its song. Trevanyi ghosts walk in the shade of the great ombrils, which grow nowhere else in Merlank. Now—and here is the point!—if you located the Drosset crypt and secured one of the death-urns, Vang Drosset would sacrifice his daughter's chastity to get it back."

"I am uninterested—or let us say, barely interested—in his daughter's chastity. I merely require my money. Your idea has merit."

Akadie made a deprecatory gesture. "You are very kind. But the proposal is as inept and hallucinatory as any of the others. The difficulties are insuperable. For instance, how could you learn the location of the crypt except from Vang Drosset? If he loved you well enough to confide this basic secret of his existence, why would he deny you your ozols and the accommodation of his daughter as well? But assume you so beguiled Vang Drosset that he told his secret and you went to the Vale of Xian. How would you evade the Three Crones, not to mention the ghosts?"

"I don't know," said Glinnes.

The two men sat in silence, sipping tea. After a moment Akadie asked, "Have you made the acquaintance of Lute Casagave?"

"Yes. He refuses to leave Ambal Isle."

"Predictably. He would at least want his twelve thousand ozols back."

"He claims to be Lord Ambal."

Akadie sat up in his chair, eyes dancing with speculation. Here, for Akadie, was a truly fascinating concept. Somewhat regretfully, he shook his head and settled back into the chair. "Unlikely. Very unlikely. And irrelevant in any case. I fear that you must resign yourself to the loss of Ambal Isle."

"I can't resign myself to losing anything!" cried Glinnes in a passion. "A hussade game, Ambal Isle: it's all the same. I'll never give up; I must have what is due me!"

Akadie held up his hand. "Calm yourself. I will consider at leisure and who knows what will occur? The fee is fifteen ozols."

"Fifteen ozols!" demanded Glinnes. "For what? All you did was tell me to be calm."

Akadie made a suave gesture. "I gave you that negative advice which often is as valuable as a positive program. For instance, suppose you asked me: 'How can I leap from here to Welgen in a single bound'? I could utter one word, 'Impossible!' to save you a great deal of useless exercise; and thus justify a fee of twenty or thirty ozols."

Glinnes smiled grimly. "In the matter at hand, you save me no useless exercise; you have told me nothing I don't know already. You must consider this a social call."

Akadie shrugged. "It is of no consequence."

The two men returned to the lower floor, where Marucha sat reading a journal published in Port Maheul: *Interesting Activities of the Elite.*

"Good-by, mother," said Glinnes. "Thank you for the tea."

Marucha looked up from the journal. "You're more than welcome, of course." She began to read once more.

As Glinnes drove back across Clinkhammer Broad, he wondered why Marucha disliked him, though in his heart he knew the answer well enough. Marucha did not dislike Glinnes; she disliked Jut and his "gross behavior"—his carousing, bellowed songs, rude amorousness, and general lack of elegance. In short, she considered her husband a boor. Glinnes, though far more gracious and easy than his father, reminded her of Jut. There could never be real warmth between them. Good enough, thought Glinnes; he wasn't especially fond of Marucha either . . .

Glinnes turned the boat into Zeur Water, which bounded the Prefecture Commons on the northeast. On impulse he slowed and turned into the shore. Nosing his boat through the reeds, he made it fast to the crook of a casammon tree, and clambered up the bank to where he could look across the island.

Three hundred yards away, beside a copse of black candlenuts, the Drossets had pitched their three tents—the same rectangles of orange, dirty maroon and black that had offended Glinnes' eyes on Rabendary. On a bench Vang Drosset sat hunched over a fruit of some kind—a melon, or perhaps a *cazaldo*. Tingo, wearing a lavender headkerchief, squatted beside the fire, chopping up tubers and throwing them into the caldron. The sons Ashmor and Harving were not in evidence, nor was Duissane.

Glinnes watched for five minutes. Vang Drosset finished the *cazaldo* and flung the husk at the fire. Then, hands on knees, he turned and spoke to Tingo, who continued her work.

Glinnes jumped down the bank to his boat and drove home at full speed.

An hour later he returned. During Glay's sojourning with the Trevanyi he had used their costume; these garments Glinnes now wore, as well as a Trevanyi turban. A young cavout lay on the floor of the boat, head muffled and legs tied. The boat also carried three empty cartons, several good iron pots, and a shovel.

Glinnes took the boat to where he had previously run it ashore. He climbed up the bank and observed the Drosset camp through binoculars.

The caldron simmered over the fire. Tingo was nowhere to be seen. Vang Drosset sat on the bench carving a dako burl. Glinnes stared intently. Would Vang Drosset be using his knife? Chips and shavings effortlessly departed the dako, and Vang Drosset approvingly examined the knife from time to time.

Glinnes brought the cavout up from the boat and, removing the muffle, tethered the creature by one hind leg so that it might wander a few yards out upon the common.

Glinnes concealed himself behind a clump of hushberry, where he muffled the lower part of his face in the loose tail of the turban.

Vang Drosset carved the dako. He paused, stretched his arms, and noted the cavout. He watched it a moment, then, rising to his feet, scrutinized the entire common. No one in sight. He wiped the knife and tucked it into his boot. Tingo Drosset put her head from the tent; Vang Drosset had a word with her. She came forth and looked dubiously at the cavout. Vang Drosset set off across the common, walking with an air of furtive purpose. Ten yards from the cavout he seemed to see it for the first time, and halted as if in wonder. He noticed the tether and traced it to the casammon tree. He took four quiet steps forward, craning his neck. He saw the boat and stopped short, while his eyes performed an inventory of its contents. A shovel, several useful pots, and what might those cartons contain? He licked his lips, looked sharply right and left. Peculiar. Probably the work of a child. Still, why not take a look in the cartons? Certainly no harm in a look.

Vang Drosset walked cautiously down the bank, and he never knew what struck him. Glinnes, fury surging in his veins, leapt forth and almost tore Vang Drosset's head off with a pair of tremendous blows over each ear. Vang Drosset fell to the ground. Glinnes pushed his face into the mud, tied his hands behind his back, lashed his knees and ankles with a length of rope he had brought for the purpose. Then he gagged and blindfolded Vang Drosset, who was now uttering stertorous moans.

He brought the knife from Vang Drosset's black boot: his own. A delight to have the keen blade once more in his possession! He searched Vang Drosset's garments, slicing them with the knife to facilitate examination. Vang Drosset's purse held only twenty ozols, which Glinnes appropriated. He pulled off Vang Drosset's boots and sliced open the soles. He found nothing and threw the boots away.

Vang Drosset carried no large sum of money on his person. Glinnes gave him a kick in the ribs for disappointment. He looked across the commons to observe Tingo Drosset on her way to the outhouse. Glinnes hoisted the cavout to his shoulder, concealing his face, and marched across the commons. He reached the maroon tent just as Tingo Drosset had completed her errand. He looked into the maroon tent.

Empty. He walked to the orange tent. Empty. He stepped inside. Tingo Drosset spoke to his back: "Looks to be a good beast. But don't take it inside! What's the matter with you? Slaughter it down by the water."

Glinnes put down the animal and waited. Tingo Drosset, expostulating over the strange behavior of her husband, entered the tent. Glinnes threw his turban over her head and bore her to the ground. Tingo Drosset squawked and cursed at this unexpected act of her husband's.

"Another sound from you," growled Glinnes, "I'll slit your throat ear to ear! Lie quiet if you know what's good for you!"

"Vang! Vang!" screeched Tingo Drosset. Glinnes thrust the tail of the turban into her mouth.

Tingo was squat and sturdy and caused Glinnes considerable exertion before she lay helplessly tied, blindfolded and gagged. Glinnes' hand smarted from a bite. Tingo Drosset's head ached from the retaliatory blow. Not likely that Tingo Drosset would carry the family money, but stranger things had happened. Glinnes gingerly examined her garments while she groaned and grunted, thrashed and jerked in horrified outrage, expecting the worst.

He searched the black tent, then the orange tent, in a corner of which Duissane had ranged a few trinkets and keepsakes, and last the maroon tent. He found no money, nor had he expected to; the Trevanyi habit was to bury their valuables.

Glinnes seated himself on Vang Drosset's bench. Where would he bury money, were he Vang Drosset? The location must be convenient to hand and unmistakably identified by some sort of indicator: a post, a rock, a bush, a tree. The spot would be somewhere within the immediate field of vision; Vang Drosset would like to keep the hiding place under his benign surveillance. Glinnes looked here and there. Directly in front of him the caldron hung over the fire, with a rude table and a pair of benches to the side. Only a few feet away the ground had been seared by the heat of another fire. The old fire-site seemed a few steps more convenient than the spot where the caldron now hung. No explanation for the peculiar habits of the Trevanyi, thought Glinnes. At the camp on Rabendary . . . The thought trailed off as Glinnes recalled the camp on Rabendary Island, with the ground freshly dug on the site of the campfire.

Glinnes nodded sagely. Just so. He rose to his feet and walked to the fire. He moved tripod and caldron, and using an old broken-hafted spade, thrust the fire aside. The baked soil below yielded easily. Six inches below the surface the spade scraped on a black iron plate. Glinnes tipped up the iron to reveal a cake of dry clay, which he also removed. The cavity below held a pottery jar. Glinnes drew forth the jar. It contained a bundle of red and black hundred-ozol notes. Glinnes nodded complacently and tucked all in his pocket.

The cavout, now grazing, had defecated. Glinnes scraped the droppings into the pottery jar, replaced it in the cavity, and arranged all as before, with the fire burning under the caldron. To casual inspection, nothing had been disturbed.

Shouldering the cavout, Glinnes strode back across the common to where he had left his boat. Vang Drosset had been struggling to free himself, to no avail, and had only rolled himself down the slope into the mud at the water's edge. Glinnes smiled with indulgent amusement, and with all Vang Drosset's wealth in his pocket forbore kicking the contorted shape. He tethered the cavout in the stern of the boat and cast off. A hundred yards along the shore a giant casammon tree sprawled its twisted branches over the water. Glinnes drove the boat through the reeds to one of the crooked roots, made fast the painter, then climbed from the root into the branches. Through a gap in the foliage he could see the Drosset camp, which appeared quiet.

Glinnes made himself comfortable and counted the money. In the first bundle he reckoned three thousand-ozol certificates, four hundreds, and six tens. Glinnes chuckled in satisfaction. He removed the band from the second bundle, which was wound around a golden fob: fourteen hundred-ozol certificates. Glinnes paid them no heed, staring instead at the golden fob, eery chills tickling his back. The fob he remembered well; it had belonged to his father. There: ideograms for the name Jut Hulden. And below, a second set of ideograms: Shira Hulden.

There were two possibilities: the Drossets had either robbed Shira alive, or they had robbed him dead. And these were the boon comrades of his brother Glay! Glinnes spat toward the ground.

He sat now on the branch, his brain roiling with excitement and horrified disgust. Shira was dead. The Drossets could never have taken his money otherwise. This was now his conviction.

He sat watching and waiting. His euphoria waned and also his horror; he sat passively. An hour passed and part of another. Up from the dock on Ilfish Water came three persons: Ashmor, Harving, and Duissane. Ashmor and Harving went directly to the orange tent; Duissane stood still, apparently hearing a sound from Tingo. She ran into the maroon tent and instantly pushed her head out to call her brothers. She disappeared once more into the tent. Ashmor and Harving joined her. Five minutes later they slowly emerged in voluble conversation. Tingo, apparently none the worse for her experience, came forth. She pointed across the common. Ashmor and Harving set off, and in due course found and released Vang Drosset. The three returned across the common, the sons talking and gesticulating. Vang Drosset hobbling on bare feet, holding his tattered clothing close about himself. At the camp he looked all about, and especially he studied the fire. Apparently it had not been disturbed.

He went into the maroon tent. The sons stood arguing with Tingo, who was now making hysterical expostulations, pointing across the common. Vang Drosset came forth from the maroon tent, once more fully clad. He marched up to Tingo and cuffed her; she drew back bawling in anger. He came for her again; she seized a stout branch and stood her ground; Vang Drosset turned gloomily away. He went to look more closely at the campfire, bent his head sharply and saw embers and ashes where Glinnes had shifted the fire. He gave a hoarse call, audible to Glinnes in the tree. Jerking the tripod aside, he kicked the fire flying, and with his bare fingers tore up the iron plate. Then the clay block. Then the pottery jar. He looked within. He looked up at Ashmor and Harving, who stood by expectantly.

Vang Drosset raised his arms high in a magnificent gesture of despair. He dashed the pot to the ground; he jumped up and down on the shards; he kicked the fire and sent the brands flying; he held aloft his knotted arms and raved curses to all directions of the compass.

Now was the time to depart, thought Glinnes. He slipped down from the tree, stepped into his boat, and drove back to Rabendary Island. A highly satisfactory day. The Trevanyi garments had guarded his identity; the Drossets might suspect, but they could not know. At this moment all the Trevanyi of the region were suspect, and the Drossets would sleep little this night as they debated the culpability of each.

Glinnes prepared himself a meal and ate out on the verandah. Afternoon became avness, that melancholy dying-time of day, when all the sky and far spaces became suffused with the color of watered milk.

The chime of the telephone provided a sudden discord. Glinnes went within to find the face of Thammas Lord Gensifer looking forth from the screen. Glinnes touched the vision push button. "Good afternoon, Lord Gensifer."

"A good afternoon to you, Glinnes Hulden! Are you ready to play hussade? I don't mean at this very instant, of course."

Glinnes responded with a cautious question of his own. "I take it your plans have matured?"

"Yes. The Fleharish Gorgons are now organized and ready to begin practice. I have your name penciled in at right strike."

"And who is left strike?"

Lord Gensifer looked down at his list. "A very promising young man by the name of Savat. You two should make a brilliant combination."

"Savat? I've never heard of him. Who are the wings?"

"Lucho and Helsing."

"Hmm. None of these names are familiar. Are these the players you originally had in mind?"

"Lucho, of course. As for the others—well, that list was always tentative, to be amended whenever something better could be arranged. As you well know, Glinnes, some of these established players are fairly inflexible. We're better off with people willing and anxious to learn. Enthusiasm, zest, dedication! These are the qualities that make for winning!"

"I see. Who else has signed up?"

"Iskelatz and Wilmer Guff are the rovers—how does that sound? You won't find two better rovers in the prefecture. The guards—Ramos is a crackerjack—and Pylan, who is also very good. Sinforetta and 'Bump' Candolf are not quite so mobile, but they are solid; no one will drive them aside. I'll play captain and—"

"Eh? What's this? Did I hear you correctly?"

Lord Gensifer frowned. "I'll play captain," he said in a measured voice. "And that more or less is the team, except for substitutes."

Glinnes was silent a moment or two. Then he asked, "What about the fund?"

"The fund will be three thousand ozols," said Lord Gensifer primly. "For the first few games we'll play a conservative fifteen hundred ozols, at least until the team jells."

"I see. When and where will you practice?"

"At Saurkash field, tomorrow morning. I take it then that you'll definitely play with the Gorgons?"

"I'll certainly come down tomorrow and we'll see how things go. But let me be candid, Lord Gensifer. A captain is the most important man on the team. He can make us or break us. We need an experienced captain. I doubt if you have that experience."

Lord Gensifer became haughty. "I have made a thorough study of the game. I've gone through Kalenshenko's *Hussade Tactics* three times; I've mastered the *Ordinary Hussade Manual*; I've explored all the latest theories, such as Counterflow Principle, the Double Pyramid System, Overvallation—"

"All this may be true, Lord Gensifer. Many people can theorize about the game, but the reflexes are ultimately important, and unless you've played a great deal—"

Lord Gensifer said stiffly, "If you'll do your best, everyone else will do theirs. Is there anything more? . . . At the fourth gong, then." The screen went dead.

Glinnes growled in dismay. For half a broken ozol he'd tell Lord Gensifer to play captain, forward, rover, guard, and sheirl together. Lord Gensifer as captain indeed!

At least he had his money back, with compensation for the beating. Almost five thousand ozols: a tidy sum, which he ought to put in a safe place.

Glinnes sealed the money in a pottery jar like that the Drossets had used. He buried it in the back yard.

An hour later a boat issued from Ilfish Water and came across Ambal Broad. Within sat Vang Drosset and his two sons. As they passed the Rabendary dock, Vang Drosset rose to his feet and scrutinized the Hulden boat with eyes like needles. Glinnes had removed all the goods with which he had tempted Vang Drosset; the boat was undistinguishable from a hundred others. Glinnes sat on the verandah, feet on the rail. Vang Drosset and his sons looked from the boat to Glinnes, eyes full of suspicion; Glinnes returned the gaze impassively.

The Drosset boat continued up Farwan Water, the Drossets muttering among themselves and looking back toward Glinnes. There went the men who had killed his brother, thought Glinnes.

# Chapter 10

## ★ ★ ★

Lord Gensifer, wearing a new maroon and black uniform, stood on a bench and addressed his players. "This is an important day for all of us, and for the history of hussade in Jolany Prefecture! Today we start to mold the most efficient, adroit, and ruthless team ever to ravage the hussade fields of Merlank. Some of you are proficient already, with reputations; others are still unknown—"

Glinnes, considering the fifteen men around him, reflected that the proportion of these two sorts was on the order of one in eight.

"—but by dint of dedication, discipline, and sheer"—here Lord Gensifer used the word *kercha'an:* effort conducing to superhuman feats of strength and will—"we will sweep all before us! We'll expose the fundament of every virgin between here and Port Jaime! We'll carry booty home in buckets; we'll be rich and famous, one and all! . . .

"But first the toil and sweat of preparation. I have diligently researched the theory of hussade; I know Kalenshenko word for word. Everyone agrees: defeat your opponent's strength and you've got the gold ring in your grasp. That means we must out-leap and out-swing the best forwards around; we've got to tub the sternest guards of Jolany; we've got to out-think the craftiest strategists of Trullion! . . .

"Now to work. I want the forwards to criss-cross the tanks, buffing* three procedures at each station. Establish a rhythm, you forwards! The rovers will go through standard drill, and the guards as well. We've got to master the fundamentals! I'd like to think that instead of two rovers and four guards, we have six agile powerful rovers all over the back stations, capable at any time of ramming home the piston." Lord Gensifer here alluded to the tactic of a strong team sweeping a

---

* buff: a three-foot padded club, used to thrust opponents into the tanks.

weaker team ahead of it up the field. "All to work! Let's drill like men inspired!"

So the practice began, with Lord Gensifer running here and there, praising, criticizing, castigating, stimulating his team with shrill *ki-yik-yik-yiks*.

Twenty minutes later Glinnes had gauged the quality of the team. Left wing Lucho and right rover Wilmer Guff had been components of that hypothetical team Lord Gensifer had proposed to Glinnes, and were both excellent players—deft, sure, aggressive. Left rover Iskelatz also seemed a sound player, if of a self-contained, even surly, disposition. Iskelatz clearly disliked strenuous practice and preferred to reserve his best energies for the game itself, a trait which almost immediately exasperated Lord Gensifer. Left strike Savat and right wing Helsing were young men, alert, active, but somewhat raw, and during buff-drill Glinnes continually feinted them off balance. Guards Ramos, Pylan, and Sinforetta were, respectively, slow, inept, and overweight; only left middle guard "Bump" Candolf combined sufficient mass, strength, cleverness and agility to qualify as an able athlete. A hussade truism asserted that a poor forward might defeat a poor guard but a good guard would restrain a good forward. A team lived by its forwards and died by its guards—so stated another aphorism of the game. Glinnes foresaw a number of long afternoons unless Lord Gensifer were able to strengthen his back-field.

The Gorgons, then, in their present phase, fielded a fair front line, a sound center, and a weak back-field. Lord Gensifer's capacity as captain was difficult to assess. The ideal captain, like the ideal rover, could play at any station of the field, though some captains, like old Neronavy of the Tanchinaros, never left the protection of their hanges.

In regard to Lord Gensifer, Glinnes reserved judgment. He seemed quick and strong enough, if somewhat overweight and sluggish on the swings . . .

Lord Gensifer uttered one of his *ki-yik-yik-yiks*. "You forwards there! Zest now, let's see those feet twinkle; are you a quartet of bears? Glinnes, must you caress Savat so lovingly with your buff? If he can't block you let him feel it! And you guards—let's see you prance! Knees bent, like angry animals! Remember, every time they take hold of that gold ring it costs us money . . . Better . . . Let's run through a few plays. First the Center Jet Series from the the Lantoun System . . ."

The team drilled for two hours in an amiable spirit, then halted for lunch at The Magic Tench. After lunch Lord Gensifer diagrammed a group of formations he had conceived himself, variations on the difficult Diagonal Sequences. "If we can master these patterns, we thrust irresistibly against both wings and rovers; then when they collapse inward we plunge down either the right or left land."

"All very well," said Lucho, "but notice, you leave the wing lanes unprotected, and there's not a feather to prevent a counter-plunge down our own outside lanes."

Lord Gensifer frowned. "The rovers must swing to the side in such a case. Timing here is essential."

The team ran rather languidly through Lord Gensifer's deployments, for the warm time of day had arrived and all were tired after the morning's efforts. Finally Lord Gensifer, half exasperated, half rueful, dismissed the team. "Tomorrow, same time; but come expecting a workout. Today was a vacation. I know only one way to field a team, and that's drill!"

Three weeks the Gorgons practiced, with uneven results. Certain of the players became bored; certain others growled and muttered at Lord Gensifer's chivvying. Glinnes considered Lord Gensifer's repertory of plays far too complicated and chancy; he felt the back-field to be too weak to allow an effective attack. The rovers were forced to protect the guards, and the forwards were therefore limited in their range. Attrition took a toll. Left rover Iskelatz, who was competent but too casual to please Lord Gensifer, resigned from the team, as did right wing Helsing, in whom Glinnes discerned the potentialities for excellence. The replacements were both weaker men. Lord Gensifer dropped Pylan and Sinforetta, the two most sluggish guards, and recruited a pair only slightly better, both of whom, so Glinnes learned from Carbo Gilweg, had been unable to win places with the Saurkash Tanchinaros.

Lord Gensifer entertained the team at Gensifer Manor and introduced the Gorgon sheirl, Zuranie Delcargo from the village Puzzlewater, so named for the nearby hot sulfur springs. Zuranie was pallidly pretty, if thin, and shy to the point of speechlessness. Her personality aroused Glinnes to wonder—what force or ambition could impel such a girl to risk public exposure? Whenever she was addressed, she jerked her head away so that long blonde hair fell across her face, and she spoke only three words during the course of the evening. She displayed not an inkling of sashei, that wild and gallant élan which inspires a team to transcend its theoretical limitations.

Lord Gensifer took the occasion to announce the schedule of forthcoming games, the first of which would take place two weeks hence at Saurkash Stadium, against the Voulash Gannets.

A day or two later Zuranie came to watch the practice. Rain had fallen during the morning and a raw wind blew out of the south. The players were glum and peevish. Lord Gensifer ran up and down the field like a great bumbling insect, expostulating, wheedling, crying *"Ki-yik-yik-yik!"* to no effect. Huddling from the wind beside the pump-man's hut, Zuranie watched the sluggish maneuvers with foreboding and despondency. At last she made a timid motion to Lord Gensifer. He jogged across the field. "Yes, sheirl?"

Zuranie spoke in a petulant voice: "Don't call me sheirl; I don't know why I ever thought I'd want to do this. Really! I could never never stand on that place, with all those people watching me. I think I would absolutely die. Please, Lord Gensifer, don't be angry, but I simply can't."

Lord Gensifer raised his eyes to the scudding gray clouds, not far overhead. "My dear Zuranie! Of course you'll be with us! We play the Voulash Gannets in two days! You'll be famous and glorified!"

Zuranie made a helpless motion. "I don't want to be a famous sheirl; I don't want all my clothes pulled off—"

"That only happens to the losing sheirl," Lord Gensifer pointed out. "Do you think the Gannets can beat us, with Tyran Lucho and Glinnes Hulden and me and Bump Candolf ranging the stations? We'll sweep them back like chaff; we'll tank them so often they'll think they are fish!"

Zuranie was only partially reassured. She gave a tremulous sigh and said no more. Lord Gensifer, at last understanding that no useful purpose could be served by prolonging the practice, called a halt. "Same time tomorrow," he told the team. "We've got to put snap into our lateral movement, especially in the back court. You guards, you've got to range the field! This is hussade, not a tea party for you and your toy animals. Tomorrow at the fourth chime."

The Voulash Gannets were a young team lacking all reputation; the players seemed striplings. The Gannet captain was Denzel Warhound, a lanky tow-headed youth with the wise sly eyes of a mythical creature. The sheirl was a buxom round-faced girl with a flying mop of dark curls; in the pregame march about the field she conducted herself with full-blooded enthusiasm, strutting, bouncing, waving her arms, and the Gannets loped along beside her, barely able to contain their nervous activity. By contrast, the Gorgons seemed stately and dour, with sheirl Zuranie a frail asthenic wraith. Her evident despair caused Lord Gensifer an exasperation he did not dare to express for fear of demoralizing her completely. "Brave girl; there's a brave girl!" he declared as if consoling a sick animal. "It won't be all that bad; you'll see I'm right!" But Zuranie's apprehensions were not dispelled.

Today the Gorgons wore their maroon and black uniforms for the first time. The helmets were especially dramatic, molded of a dull-rose metalloid, with black fleurettes for cheek-pieces. Black spikes bristled from the scalps; the eyeholes cunningly simulated the pupils of great staring eyes; the noses split to become black plush maws, from which hung lank red tongues. Some of the team thought the costume extravagant; a few disliked the flapping tongues; most were apathetic. The Gannets wore a brown uniform with an orange helmet, distinguished only by a crest of green feathers. Contrasting the mettlesome Gannets with the splendid but sluggish Gorgons, Glinnes felt impelled to discuss tactics with Lord Gensifer.

"Notice the Gannets if you will; they're like colt kevals, full of vigor and nonsense. I've seen such teams before, and we can expect aggressive, even rash, play. Our job is to make them beat themselves. We'll want to use our traps to cut off their forwards so that our guards and rovers can double on them. If we use our weight, we've got a chance to defeat them."

Lord Gensifer raised his eyebrows in displeasure. "A chance to defeat them? What nonsense is this? We'll sweep them up and down the field like a dog chasing chickens! We shouldn't even be playing them except that we need the practice."

"Still, I advise a careful game. Let them make the mistakes, or they might make capital of ours."

"Bah, Glinnes; I believe you're past your prime."

"To the extent that I'm not playing for fun. I want to earn money—nine thousand ozols, to be exact, and I want to win."

"Do you think your need is unique?" demanded Lord Gensifer in a voice thick with rage. "How do you think I financed the treasure-box? Bought the uniforms? Paid team expenses? I drained myself bloodless."

"Very well," said Glinnes. "You need money; I need money. So let's win, by playing the game we're best able to play."

"We'll win, never fear!" declared Lord Gensifer, once again bluff and hearty. "Do you think I'm a tyro? I know the game up one side and down the other. Now enough of this wailing; I declare, you're as timid as Zuranie. Notice the crowd—a good ten thousand people. That'll add ozols to the booty!"*

Glinnes nodded gloomily. "If we win." He noticed a man sitting alone in a box at the bottom of the Elite tier; Lute Casagave, with binoculars and camera. The gear was not unusual; many devotees of the game recorded the denuding of the sheirl in music and image. Notable collections of such events existed. Nonetheless Glinnes was surprised to find in Lute Casagave so lively an interest in hussade. He seemed not the type for frivolity.

The field judge went to the microphone; the music dwindled away; a hush came over the crowd. "Sportfolk of Saurkash and Jolany Prefecture! Today a match between the gallant Voulash Gannets, and their sheirl Baroba Felice, and the indomitable Gorgons of Thammas Lord Gensifer, with the lovely sheirl Zuranie Delcargo! The teams pledge the inviolable dignity of their sheirls with all their valor and two treasures of fifteen hundred ozols. May the winners enjoy glory and the losers take pride in their fortitude and the tragic purity of their sheirl! Captains, approach!"

Lord Gensifer and Denzel Warhound came forward. A toss of the coin gave first call to the Gorgons; open transmission for the Gorgons would be signalized by the green light, with the red light for the Gannets.

"The penalities will be called with rigor," stated the field judge. "There must be neither kicking nor pulling. No verbal interchanges. I will not tolerate buff-clinging. A blow must fall cleanly. The team on defense must utter no distracting sounds. I am experienced in these matters, as are the monitors; we will be vigilant. A player in the foul tank must clasp the hand of his rescuer; a desultory wave or gesture will not

* Half of the gate receipts were customarily divided between the competing teams in the proportion of three parts to the winning team, one part to the losers.

be sufficient. Have you any questions? Very good, gentlemen. Dispose your forces and may the glory of your sheirls impel you both to noble feats. The green light to the Gorgons; the red light to the Gannets!"

The team deployed to their stations; the Trevanyi orchestra played traditional music as the captains conducted the sheirls to their respective pedestals.

The music stopped. The captains went out to their hanges and now came that electric moment before the first flash of light. The spectators were silent; the players strained with tension; the sheirls stood eager and palpitant, each willing with all her heart's intensity that the detested virgin at the other end of the field be the one to be bared and humiliated.

A gong! The signal lights flashed green. For twenty seconds the Gorgon captain might call plays, while the Gannets must act or react in silence. Lord Gensifer deployed the first phase of the Jet Stream Attack: a wedge-shaped driving tactic of strikes and wings up the middle, with rovers covering the side lanes. Lord Gensifer clearly had ignored Glinnes' advice. Cursing under his breath, Glinnes moved forward; unopposed, he jumped the moat, as did left strike Savat. The Gannet forwards had all slid aside; now they leapt the moat to attack Sarkado, the Gorgons' left rover. Glinnes met the Gannet left rover; the two feinted with buffs, prodded and pushed; the Gannet rover gave way. Glinnes' instincts told him exactly when to turn to meet the rush of the Gannet right rover. Glinnes struck him across the neck while he was still off balance and toppled him into the tank. He struck water with a most satisfactory splash.

Another splash: a Gannet guard had tanked Chust, the right wing.

Lord Gensifer's voice came sharp: *"Ki-yik-yik-yik!* Thirteen-thirty! Go then, Glinnes; Lucho, watch the rover! *Yik ki-yik!"*

The green light changed to red; now Denzel Warhound called signals and brought his hange to the moat. The middle guards jumped forward, two against Glinnes; he engaged them, hooked and thrust with such effect that they confused each other. Glinnes swung to Way 3, which was open to the pedestal, but the guards recovered; one ran to cover the mouth of Way 3. The center guards meanwhile swung behind Glinnes. He tanked one; Savat tanked the other; both turned to race for the Gannet pedestal, with only two guards left to halt them. The light changed to green; Lord Gensifer bawled desperate orders. A gong! Glinnes looked back to see a Gannet forward on the pedestal with Zuranie's gold ring in his hand. Play halted; Lord Gensifer grudgingly paid ransom to Denzel Warhound.

The teams returned to their respective territories. Lord Gensifer spoke in irritation: "Execution: that's the word! We're falling over our own feet. They're actually no match for us; they caught us by a fluke."

Glinnes restrained the old maxim: *In hussade no flukes.* He said, "Let's advance at them across the field, station by station; don't let them get back to the guards!" For the Gannets had gained the pedestal by a simple feint and whirl past the inept Ramos.

Lord Gensifer ignored Glinnes. "The Jet Stream again, and this time let's do it right! Rovers, guard the side alleys; wings, blast up the center behind the strikes. We won't let these ninny-boys tank us again!"

The team deployed; the gong sounded and the green light gave the offensive to the Gorgons. "Thirteen-thirty, *ki-yik!*" cried Lord Gensifer. "Right at 'em all the way to the belly-ring."

Again the Gannet forwards slid aside to allow Savat and Glinnes across the moat. This time, however, they swung behind Glinnes and, to his intense annoyance, tripped him. He might still have held his own except for the rover swinging in upon the trapeze to hurl him into the tank.

Glinnes above all else hated to be tanked; the process was cold and wet and injured his self-esteem. Disconsolately he waded back under the ways and squelched up the ladder to the Gorgons' base area. He surfaced at an appropriate time, engaging a Gannet wing who already had worked his way almost to the pedestal. In a wet fury, Glinnes dazed him with thrusts and feints and toppled him head over heels into the tank.

Green light on. "Forty-five twelve," cried Lord Gensifer. Glinnes groaned—Lord Gensifer's most complicated play, the Grenade, or double diagonal. No choice but to run the play; he would do his best. The forwards came together at the moat, and finding no opposition at the center bridge, sprang across in different directions, followed by the rovers. The single faint hope of success, thought Glinnes, was to drive upon the Gannet sheirl before the startled Gannets could reach Sheirl Zuranie. The Gannet guards shifted to hold the end of the way; two rovers were tanked, a Gannet and a

Gorgon; and now Lord Gensifer ordered two guards across the moat, just as the light turned red.

Denzel Warhound stood by his hange, inviolate, grinning in total composure. He called his signals. Both Gorgon guards were intercepted and tanked. Glinnes, Savat, and the wings, recognizing disaster, raced back to guard the pedestal. Glinnes reached base area just in time to drive a Gannet forward back from the pedestal and into the tank; Lucho did the same to another, but almost the whole Gannet team was storming the base area. The tanked guards surfaced, wet and angry, and by dint of fury and superior weight bore the Gannets back.

Green light. Lord Gensifer's call: "Forty-five twelve; we've got 'em now, lads; the way is clear! Go! go!"

Glinnes, furious over the call, disengaged and ran Lord Gensifer's pattern along with the other forwards. The light but agile Gannet guards broke back and kept pace with them . . . A gong. By some miracle of stealth and agility (more likely by someone's sheer ineptitude, thought Glinnes) one of the Gannet rovers had gained the pedestal and seized the gold ring at Zuranie's waist.

With trembling fingers Lord Gensifer paid another ransom. In conference his voice was hoarse with emotion. "You men aren't executing. We can't win if everyone walks around like sleepwalkers! We've got to take the game to these fellows! Why, they're hardly more than boys! This time let's make the play go. Double diagonal again, and everyone do his duty!"

The gong, the green light, Lord Gensifer's encouraging "*Ki-yik*," and the Gorgons deployed in Lord Gensifer's double diagonal.

A double gong, signifying a foul. Lord Gensifer himself had clutched the buff of a Gannet rover and was consigned to the foul tank up at the back of the Gannet base, where he hunched in sullen fury. Glinnes, the right forward, became acting captain.

The gong sounded, and the light was still green. Glinnes had no need to call a play. He gestured left and right; the wings and forwards advanced to the moat. The light went red. The Gannets, elated by their two-ring score, feinted at the left and sent two forwards across at the right side-way, with a rover leaping the moat. The rover and one of the forwards were tanked; the other forward retreated, and Denzel Warhound called back his attack until the tanked man returned to action. Green light. Lord Gensifer, in the foul tank, made urgent gestures appealing for rescue; Glinnes studiously looked the other way. He pointed the rovers to the side-ways, summoned the two middle guards forward. Red light. The Gannets massed on the left but forebore to cross the moat; the crafty Denzel Warhound preferred to bide his time until he could catch the Gorgons in disequilibrium.

Green light. Glinnes sent the Gorgon forward across the moat and brought the middle guards up to the center bridge—a slow exertion of mass and pressure upon a faster but lighter team. Two Gorgon wings were tanked, and two Gannet strikes. The Gorgons had established a solid line on the Gannet side of the field, and all the while Lord Gensifer beckoned frantically for rescue. The Gorgons pressed slowly up the ways, using their weight and experience to advantage, compressing the Gannets into their base area. Three Gannets were tanked, one after the other, then two more. Then the gong sounded. Tyran Lucho had gained the pedestal, his hand on the gold ring. Grim and disapproving, Lord Gensifer came up from the foul tank and took ransom from the Gannet captain.

The teams returned to base deployment. Lord Gensifer, angry from his long confinement in the foul tank, declared, "Rash, too rash tactics! When a team is two rings down, the guards should never move so far past the moat—that's one of Kalenshenko's first dictums!"

"We took their ring," said Lucho, the most outspoken man on the team. "That's the important matter."

"Regardless," said Lord Gensifer in a steely voice, "we will continue to play a sound basic game. They have the light; we'll use the Number 4 Feint."

Lucho was not to be silenced. "Let's simply mass on the moat. We don't need traps or feints or fancy tactics—simply basic play!"

"This is a hussade game," declared Lord Gensifer, "not a gang-fight. We'll show 'em tactics to make their heads swim."

The Gannets charged the moat with reckless verve; Denzel Warhound clearly intended to forestall the Gorgon tactics of the previous period. Gannets leaped the moat all across the field, while Denzel Warhound planted his hange on the center bridge, from which he could be dislodged only by Lord Gensifer. Right wing Cherst tanked the Gannet rover and was tanked in turn; Glinnes was forced to guard the right side-way.

Green light. "Forty-five-twelve!" cried Lord Gensifer. "This time, lads! Show them class!"

"I think we'll be showing them something else," Glinnes told Wilmer Guff. "Namely, Zuranie."

"He's the captain."

"So then—here we go."

Denzel Warhound might have been anticipating this exact play. His forwards returned to trap Glinnes, and again he was tanked by a swinging rover; Lucho met a similar fate on the opposite side. Together they made the best possible haste to the ladder, only to hear the Trevanyi orchestra break into the *Ode to Beauty Jubilant*.

"And there we have it," said Glinnes.

They surfaced in time to see Denzel Warhound on the pedestal, his hand on the gold ring. Zuranie looked up into the sky with a dazed expression. "Where is your money? Five hundred ozols will save your shierl; five hundred ozols for her pride—is this so dear?"

"I'd pay it," Glinnes remarked to Wilmer Guff, "except that it would be money thrown away. Lord Gensifer would run me back and forth through his double-diagonal till I drowned."

The music surged loud—stately cadences which tickled the hair at the nape of the neck and brought a dryness to the mouth. From the crowd came a soft sound, a fluting of exaltation. Zuranie's face was frozen in a white mask—impossible to guess her emotions. The music halted. A low-voiced gong sounded—once, twice, three times—and the captain pulled the ring. Zuranie's gown came away; her shrinking flesh was exposed on the pedestal.

At the opposite end of the field Sheirl Baroba Felice performed an impromptu jig of delight and jumped down into the arms of the Gannets, who now departed the field.

Lord Gensifer silently brought a black velvet cloak to cover Zuranie; the Gorgons also departed the field.

In the dressing room Lord Gensifer bravely broke the silence.

"Well, men, this wasn't our day—so much is clear. The Gannets are a far better team than is supposed; their speed was a bit too much for us. Everybody out to Gensifer Manor. We won't call it a victory celebration, but we'll test the color of some good Sokal wine . . ."

At Gensifer Manor, Lord Gensifer regained his composure.

He circulated affably among those of his aristocratic friends who had visited the Saurkash Stadium to watch him at his latest fad. Around the loaded buffets, under the glitter of the antique chandeliers, beside the magnificent collection of Rol Star gonfalons, the banter played back and forth.

"Never expected such speed from you, Thammas, till you went to denude that bouncy little Gannet sheirl!"

"Ha ha! Yes, I'm a real pacer where the ladies are concerned!"

"We've long known Thammas to be a great sportsman, but why oh why did the Gorgons take their only ring while he sat in the tank?"

"Resting, Jonas, only resting. Why work when you can sit in nice cool water?"

"Good group, Thammas, good group. Your lads do you credit. Keep them up to snuff."

"Oh I will, sir, I will. No fear of that."

The Gorgons themselves stood somewhat stiffly to the side, or perched on the delicate jadewood furniture, sipping wines they had never before tasted, giving monosyllabic answers to the questions put by Lord Gensifer's friends. Lord Gensifer finally came up and spoke to them, by now in a benign mood. "Well then—no recriminations, no reproaches. I'll state only the obvious: I see room for improvement, and by the stars"—here Lord Gensifer raised his arms to the ceiling in the posture of an outraged Zeus—"we'll achieve it. From the forwards, I'll have more snap and dash. From the rovers, decisive buffing, quicker reactions! Did your feet hurt today, rovers? So it seemed. From the guards, more ferocity, more dependability. When the enemy confronts our guards, I want them to think only of home and mother. Any remarks?"

Glinnes looked off and up into the air and thoughtfully sipped pale-green Sokal wine from his goblet.

Lord Gensifer continued. "Our next opponents are the Tanchinaros; we meet them in two weeks at Saurkash Stadium. I'm sure that events will go differently. I've watched them; they're slow as Dido's one-legged grandmother. We'll simply stroll around them to the pedestal. We'll take their money and bare their sheirl, and be off and gone like Welshmen."

"Speaking of money," drawled Candolf, "how much is our treasure after today's fiasco? Also, who is our sheirl?"

"The treasure will be two thousand ozols," said Lord Gensifer coldly. "The sheirl might be any of several delightful creatures anxious to share our ascendancy."

Lucho said, "The Tanchinaros are slow up front, but with guards like Gilweg, Etzing, Barreu, and Shamoran, the forwards could play in wheel chairs."

Lord Gensifer waved the remark aside. "A good team plays it own game and forces the enemy to react. The Tanchinaro guards are only flesh and bone. We'll tank them so often they'll think they're tanchinaros* in sheer reality!"

"A toast to this!" called out Chaim, Lord Shadrak. "To eleven dripping-wet Tanchinaros and their bare-bottomed sheirl!"

# Chapter 11

## ★ ★ ★

After Lord Gensifer's party, Glinnes went to spend the night with Tyran Lucho, who lived on Altramar Island, a few miles east of Five Islands, with the South Ocean a quarter mile south across a lagoon and a line of sand spits. A white beach was the Lucho front yard. Glinnes and Tyran arrived to find a star-watch in progress. Over a pair of soft red fires crabs, crayfish, sea-bulbs, pentabrachs, sourweed and a mix of smaller sea-stuffs grilled and sizzled. Kegs of beer had been broached; a table supported coarse crusty loaves, fruits and conserves. Thirty folk of all ages ate, drank, sang, played guitars and mouth-calliopes, romped in the sand, addressed themselves to someone they intended to lure up the beach later in the evening. Glinnes felt instantly at ease, in contrast to the restraint he had felt at Lord Gensifer's party, where the jocularity had been on a more formal level. Here were those Trills despised by Fanscherade—undisciplined, frivolous, gluttonous, amorous, some unkempt and dirty, others merely unkempt. Children played erotic games, and adults as well; Glinnes observed several noticeably under the influence of cauch. Each person wore those garments he deemed ap-

---

* tanchinaro: a black and silver fish of the Far South Ocean.

propriate; a stranger might have thought himself at a fancy-dress charade. Tyran Lucho, conditioned and disciplined by hussade, used garments and manners less flamboyant; still, like Glinnes, he relaxed gratefully upon the sand with a mug of beer and a chino-leaf of grilled sea-meats. The party was nominally a "star-watch"; the air was soft and the stars hung close like great paper lanterns. But a mood of revelry was on the group and there would be small pondering of the stars this night.

Tyran Lucho had played with teams of reputation. On the field he was regarded as a taciturn man of great skill and almost alone in his ability to break down the field through an apparently impervious front of opponents—dodging, feinting, swinging from way to way, or swinging out and snapping himself back, a trick which sometimes persuaded opponents to the ludicrous act of tanking themselves. Along with Wild Man Wilmer Guff, Lucho had been represented on Lord Gensifer's original dream-team. Glinnes settled himself beside Lucho and the two discussed the day's game. "Essentially," said Glinnes, "we're sound forward—with the exception of Clubfoot Chust—and pitifully weak back-field."

"True. Savat has excellent potential. Unfortunately, Tammi confuses him and he doesn't know whether to run forward or back."

"Tammi" was the team's jocular term for Thammas Lord Gensifer.

"Agreed," said Glinnes. "Even Sarkado is at least adequate, though he's really too indecisive to make a good team."

"To win," said Lucho, "we need a back-field, but even more urgently we need a captain. Tammi doesn't know which direction he's going."

"Unfortunately it's his team."

"But it's our time and our profit!" declared Lucho with a vehemence that surprised Glinnes. "Also our reputation. It does a man no good to play with a set of buffoons."

"First of all," said Glinnes, "a man tends to relax his own standards of play."

"I've been thinking the matter over. I left the Poldan Avengers so that I could live at home, and I thought perhaps Lord Gensifer could field a team. But he'll never do so if he insists on running the team as if it were his private toy."

"Still, he's captain; who'd play his position? What about you?"

Lucho shook his head. "I don't have the patience. What about you?"

"I prefer to play strike. Candolf is pretty sound."

"He's possible, in a pinch. But I've got a better man in mind—Denzel Warhound."

Glinnes considered. "He's smart and he's quick, and he doesn't mind contact. He'd be a good one. How strong a Gannet is he?"

"He wants to play. The Gannets don't have a home stadium; theirs is a very makeshift operation. Warhound would switch if a good opportunity came up."

Glinnes emptied his mug of beer. "Tammi would lay an egg if he knew what we're talking about . . . Who is the pretty girl in the white smock? I ache to see her so lonely."

"She's second cousin to my brother's wife. Her name is Thaio and she's very sympathetic."

"I'll just go ask her if she wants to be a sheirl."

"She'll say that up till the age of nine this was her dearest ambition."

The game between the Gorgons and Tanchinaros occurred on the afternoon of a beautiful warm day, with the sky a hemisphere of milkglass. The Tanchinaros were immensely popular in Saurkash, and the stadium was crowded far beyond capacity. Out of idle curiosity Glinnes looked along the line of boxes; there as before sat Lute Casagave, again with his camera. Odd, thought Glinnes.

The teams formed in ranks for the parade and the sheirls came forth: for the Tanchinaros, Filene Sadjo, a fresh-faced fisherman's daughter from Far Spinney; for the Gorgons, Karue Liriant, a tall dark-haired girl with a ripe and sumptuous figure, evident even under the classic folds of her white gown. Lord Gensifer had kept her identity a mystery until a team meeting three days before the game. Karue Liriant had not tried to make herself popular—a bad omen in itself. Still, Karue Liriant was only the least factor disruptive of morale. The left side guard Ramos, annoyed by Lord Gensifer's criticisms, had quit the team. "It's not that I'm so expert," he told Lord Gensifer, "it's just that you're so much worse. I should be *ki-yik-yik-yikking* at you rather than you *ki-yikking* at me."

"Off the field with you!" barked Lord Gensifer. "If you hadn't quit I would send you down in any case."

"Bah," said Ramos. "If you sent down all those complaining you'd be playing by yourself."

The question of replacement arose during post-practice refreshment. "Here's an idea to help the team," Lucho told Lord Gensifer. "Suppose you were to play guard, as you're well able to do; you're big enough and obstinate enough. Then I know a man who'd make us a very able captain indeed."

"Oh?" said Lord Gensifer frostily. "And who is this paragon?"

"Denzel Warhound, now with the Gannets."

Lord Gensifer took pains to control his voice. "It might be simpler and less disruptive merely to recruit a new guard."

Lucho had no more to say. The new guard appeared at the next practice session, a man even less capable than Ramos.

The Gorgons, therefore, came to play the Tanchinaros in less than an optimum frame of mind.

After circling the field, the two teams pulled down their helmets to accomplish that always startling metamorphosis of men into heroic demiurges, each assuming in some degree the quality of the mask. For the first time Glinnes saw the Tanchinaro masks; they were striking affairs of silver and black, with red and violet plumes—the Tanchinaros made a fine display as they took the field. As expected, the Tanchinaros were strong and massive. "A team of ten guards and a fat old man," as Carbo Gilweg had expressed it. The "fat old man" was Captain Nilo Neronavy, who never left the protective radius of his hange, and whose plays were as forthright as Lord Gensifer's were intricate and confusing. Glinnes anticipated no difficulties in defense; the Tanchinaro forwards were inept on the trapeze, and the swift Gorgon front line could play them one at a time. Offense was a different matter. Glinnes, had he been captain, would have drawn them in and out—to one side, then another—until a path flickered open for a lightning lunge by one of the forwards. He doubted if Lord Gensifer would use this strategy, or even if he could control the team well enough to orchestrate the quick feints and ploys.

The Gorgons won the green light. The gong sounded; the light flashed green; the game was on. "Twelve-ten, *ki-yik!*" cried Lord Gensifer, thrusting the forwards and rovers to the moat with the guards advancing two stations. "Thirteen-eight!"—a thrust at the side passages by wings and rovers, with strikes ready to jump the moat. So far, so good. The next call almost on the instant should be, "Eight-thirteen," signifying rovers across and forwards in a feint to the left. The rovers crossed the moat; the Tanchinaro forwards hesitated, and now there was time for a swift attack on the Tanchinaro right wing. But Lord Gensifer vacillated; the forwards recovered, the rovers recrossed the moat, and the light shone red.

So the game went for fifteen minutes. Two Tanchinaro forwards were tanked on offense but were able to return to the field before the Gorgons could exploit the advantage. Lord Gensifer became impatient and tried a new tactic—precisely that play which Glinnes had used to score against the Gannets, and which was quite inappropriate against the Tanchinaros. As a result, all four forwards, a rover, and Lord Gensifer himself were tanked, and the Tanchinaros marched down the field to an easy ring. Lord Gensifer paid over a thousand ozols ransom.

The teams regrouped. "I know one way to win the game," Lucho told Glinnes. "Keep Tammi in the foul tank."

"Very well," said Glinnes. "The 'Sheer Stupidity' play. Tell Savat; I'll tell Chust."

Green light; Lord Gensifer set his team into motion. Two seconds before the light changed the entire Gorgon front line moved out in an apparently senseless direction. In astounded reaction Lord Gensifer bellowed counterplays well after the light had flashed red. The game halted while Lord Gensifer, not entirely unaware of what had happened, hunched himself down in the foul tank.

Glinnes, as right strike, assumed control. During red light the Tanchinaros tried to storm the moat. By dint of precise timing, the Gorgon forwards tanked both Tanchinaro strikes and the wings retreated. Green light. Glinnes put his ideas into effect. He called plays in a series. The front surged back and forth; then the Gorgon forwards and rovers were across. The Tanchinaro rovers were tanked, but the Tanchinaro guards remained—an inexorable bulwark. Glinnes called up his own two center guards; eight men drove down the center; the Tanchinaro guards were forced to mass. Glinnes crossed behind, thrust Carbo Gilweg into the tank as a friendly gesture, and seized the gold ring.

Lord Gensifer came sulkily forth from the tank, speaking no word to anyone, and collected a thousand ozols from Nilo Neronavy.

The teams took positions. Red light. The Tanchinaros

massed on their own left side, hoping to tempt some reckless Gorgon across the moat. Glinnes caught Lucho's eyes; both knew the other's intent and both crossed, both raced up the center lanes at a speed to confound a team ostensibly on offense. Behind came the wings and the rovers. A flurry of feints and swings and the Gorgons were in the back court engaging the guards. Wild Man Wilmer Guff, the rover, slid past and grabbed the ring.

"That's another way to win," Lucho crowed to Glinnes. "We attack during off-light, when Tammi can't argue."

The teams regrouped. Red light again. Nilo Neronavy employed the strategy best suited to the Tanchinaro abilities: a grinding advance up the field. Both Lucho and Chust were tanked; Savat and Glinnes were driven back. The Tanchinaros brought all guards to the moat. Green light. Lord Gensifer called, "Twenty-two!", a simple play as good as any, sending the forwards pell-mell toward the Tanchinaro backcourt. The Tanchinaro guards retreated; the Gorgons could not win past. Carbo Gilweg engaged Glinnes; the two struggled with their buffs—up, back, hook, parry. Gilweg lowered his head, drove forward; Glinnes tried to dodge but could not avoid Gilweg's buff. Into the tank. Gilweg looked down at him. "How's the water?"

Glinnes made no reply. The gong had sounded. One or another of the Tanchinaros had taken a ring.

The teams took a five-minute rest period. Lord Gensifer moved austerely off to the side; Lucho nevertheless went to offer him counsel. "They'll be playing Big Push again for certain. In fact they won't wait; during green light they'll push. We've got to break down their center before they get their line across."

Lord Gensifer made no reply.

The teams once more took the field. Green light. Lord Gensifer brought his men up to the moat. The Tanchinaros had assumed a hedgehog formation, daring the Gorgons to attack, a situation where the agile Gorgon forwards, swinging the trapeze, might well tank isolated Tanchinaros—or might be tanked. Lord Gensifer refused to attack. Red light. The Tanchinaros remained in defensive formation. Green light. Lord Gensifer still restrained his men, a policy unwise only in that it indicated uncertainty. Glinnes called to him, "Let's go over; we can always come back!"

Lord Gensifer stood stonily silent.

Red light. The Tanchinaros came forward, all eleven

men—"the sheirl guarding the pedestal," as the saying went. As before, they thrust past the moat, with only the guards on Tanchinaro territory.

Green light. Lord Gensifer called for a feint to right and an attack on the Tanchinaros who had gained a foothold on the left. In the scrimmage two men from each team were tanked, but meanwhile the Tanchinaros had thrust far down the Gorgon right wall, and the ineffectual new guard was tanked.

The light went red. The Tanchinaros, foot by foot, thrust toward the Gorgon pedestal, where Karue Liriant waited, showing no apparent distress.

Green light. Lord Gensifer was faced with a dire situation. His forwards held the center but Tanchinaro guards and rovers coming down the center lanes cramped and constrained them. Glinnes attacked the Tanchinaro strike; from the corner of his eye he thought to see a free course downfield, if he could only feint one of the guards out of position.

Red light. Glinnes swung away from the Tanchinaro strike. He raced to the moat and across. He was free; he was clear! Carbo Gilweg, making a desperate effort, dove out to hook Glinnes with his buff; both fell into the moat.

Gong—three times. The game was won.

The field judge summoned Lord Gensifer and called for ransom, which was denied. The music became exalted and sad, a music golden as sunset, with rhythm like a beating heart and chords sweet with human passion. For the third time the field judge called for ransom; for the third time Lord Gensifer ignored the call. The Tanchinaro strike pulled the ring; the gown fell away from Karue Liriant. Naked and unconcerned, she faced the audience; in fact, she showed a slight smile, Casually she preened herself, tilting up on one toe, looking over first one shoulder, then the other, while the crowd blinked in wonder at this unfamiliar demonstration.

An odd speculation came to Glinnes' mind. He peered at her. Karue Liriant was pregnant? The possibility occurred to others as well; a murmur rose in the stands. Lord Gensifer hurriedly brought up a cloak and escorted his still-smiling sheirl from the pedestal. Then he turned to the team. "There will be no party tonight. I now have the unpleasant duty of punishing insubordination. Tyran Lucho, you may regard yourself as at liberty. Glinnes Hulden, your conduct—"

Glinnes said, "Lord Gensifer, spare me your criticism. I resign from the team. Playing conditions are impossible."

Ervil Savat, the left strike, said, "I resign as well."

"And I," said Wilmer Guff, the right rover, one of the strong players who had carried the brunt of the load. The remainder of the team hesitated. If they all resigned they might find no other organized team on which to play. They held their tongues in a troubled silence.

"So be it," said Lord Gensifer. "We are well rid of you. All have been headstrong—and you, Glinnes Hulden, and you, Tyran Lucho, have sedulously sought to undermine my authority."

"Only that we might score a ring or two," said Lucho. "But no matter—good luck to you and your Gorgons." He removed his mask and handed it over to Lord Gensifer. Glinnes did likewise, then Ervil Savat and Wilmer Guff. Bump Candolf, the single effective guard, could see no future playing on the team as it was presently constituted, and he also gave his mask to Lord Gensifer.

Outside the dressing room, Glinnes told his four comrades, "Tonight, all to my house, for what in effect will be our victory party. We're free of that mooncalf Tammi."

"Basically a sound notion," said Lucho. "I'm in the mood for a jug or two, but there'll be more merriment along Altramar Beach, and we'll find a sympathetic audience."

"As you wish. My verandah is quiet of late. No one sits there but myself, and maybe a merling or two during my absence."

Along the way to the dock the five met Carbo Gilweg with two other Tanchinaro guards, all in high spirits. "Well played, Gorgons, but today you encountered the desperate Tanchinaros."

"Thank you for the consolation," said Glinnes, "but don't call us Gorgons. We no longer enjoy this distinction."

"What's all this? Did Lord Gensifer give up his wild scheme of directing a hussade team?"

"He gave up on us, and we gave up on him. The Gorgons still exist, or so I suppose. All Tammi needs is a new front line."

"By an odd coincidence," said Carbo Gilweg, "that's all the Tanchinaros need too . . . Where are you bound?"

"Out to Lucho's in Altramar, for our private victory party."

"Better yet, visit the Gilwegs for a more authentic version."

"I think not," said Glinnes. "You won't want our long faces at the feast."

"On the contrary! I have a special reason for inviting you. In fact, let's stop into The Magic Tench for a mug of beer."

The eight men seated themselves around a round table, and the serving girl brought forth eight ample goblets.

Gilweg frowned into his foam. "Let me develop an idea—an obvious and excellent idea. The Tanchinaros, like Lord Gensifer, need a front line. It's no secret; everybody admits the fact. We're a team of ten guards and a beer keg."

"That's all very well and I see your point," said Glinnes, "but your forwards, whether they're really guards or not, are sure to object."

"They have no right to object. The Tanchinaros are an open club; anyone can join, and if he cuts the mustard he plays. Think of it! For the first time in memory, the miserable Saurkash Tanchinaros a real team!"

"The idea has appeal." Glinnes looked at his fellows. "How do you others feel?"

"I want to play hussade," said Wilmer Guff. "I like to win. I am in favor of the scheme."

"Count me in," said Lucho. "Perhaps we'll have a chance to play the Gorgons."

Savat agreed to the proposal, but Candolf was dubious. "I'm a guard. There's no place for me on the Tanchinaros."

"Don't be too sure," said Gilweg. "Our left wing guard is Pedro Shamoran, and he's got a bad leg. There'll be a shuffle of places, and maybe you can even play left rover; you're certainly quick enough. Why not try?"

"Very well; why not?"

Gilweg drained his mug. "Good then. It's settled! And now we can all celebrate the Tanchinaro victory!"

# Chapter 12

★ ★ ★

When Glinnes arrived home late the following morning he found a strange boat tied to his dock. No one sat on the verandah, and the house was empty. Glinnes went outside to look around and saw three men sauntering across the meadow: Glay, Akadie, and Junius Farfan. All three wore neat garments of black and gray, the uniform of Fanscherade. Glay and Farfan spoke earnestly together; Akadie walked somewhat apart.

Glinnes went forward to meet them. Akadie put on a half-sheepish smile in the face of Glinnes' scornful amazement. "I never thought you'd involve yourself in this rubbish," snorted Glinnes.

"One must move with the times," said Akadie. "Indeed, I find the garments a source of amusement." Glay turned him a cool glance; Junius Farfan merely laughed.

Glinnes waved his hand to the verandah. "Seat yourselves! Will you drink wine?"

Farfan and Akadie took a goblet of wine; Glay gave a curt refusal. He followed Glinnes into the house where he had spent his childhood and stood looking about the room with the eyes of a stranger. He turned and preceded Glinnes from the house.

"I have a proposition for you," said Glay. "You want Ambal Isle." He looked toward Junius Farfan, who laid an envelope on the table. "You shall have Ambal Island. There is the money to dislodge Casagave."

Glinnes reached for the envelope; Glay pushed it away. "Not so fast. When Ambal is again your property you can go to live there if you choose. And I get the use of Rabendary."

Glinnes looked at him in astonishment. "Now you want Rabendary! Why can't we both live here as brothers, and work the land together?"

Glay shook his head. "Unless you changed your attitudes, there would only be dissension. I don't have energy to waste. You take Ambal; I'll take Rabendary."

"This is the most marvelous proposition I have ever heard," said Glinnes, "when both belong to me."

Glay shook his head. "Not if Shira is alive."

"Shira is dead." Glinnes went out to his hiding place, uncovered the pot, and removed the golden fob, which he brought back to the verandah. He tossed it on the table. "Remember this? I took it from your friends the Drossets. They killed and robbed Shira and threw him to the merlings."

Glay glanced at the fob. "Did they admit it?"

"No."

"Can you prove you took it from the Drossets?"

"You have heard me tell you."

"That's not enough," said Glay curtly.

103

Glinnes slowly turned his head and stared into Glay's face. Slowly he rose to his feet. Glay sat rigid as a steel post. Akadie said hurriedly, "Of course your word is sufficient, Glinnes. Sit down."

"Glay can withdraw his remark and then withdraw himself."

Akadie said, "Glay meant only that your word is legally insufficient. Am I right, Glay?"

"Yes, yes," said Glay in a bored voice. "Your word is sufficient, as far as I am concerned. The proposal remains the same."

"Why the sudden yearning to return home to Rabendary?" asked Glinnes. "Are you giving up your fancy dress party?"

"To the contrary. On Rabendary we will found a Fanscherade community, a college of dynamic formulations."

"By the stars," marveled Glinnes. "Formulations. To what purpose?"

Junius Farfan said in a soft voice, "We intend to found an academy of achievement."

Glinnes looked out over Ambal Broad in bemusement. "I admit to perplexity. Alastor Cluster is thousands of years old; men by the trillions fill the galaxy. Great mentors here, there, everywhere across the whole pageant of existence, have propounded problems and solved them. Everything conceivable has been achieved and all goals attained—not once, but thousands of times over. It is well known that we live in the golden afternoon of the human race. Hence, in the name of the Thirty Thousand Stars, where will you find a fresh area of knowledge that must urgently be advanced from Rabendary meadow?"

Glay made an impatient motion, as if at Glinnes' embarrassing stupidity. Junius Farfan, however, responded politely. "These concepts are naturally familiar to us. It can easily be demonstrated, however, that the scope of knowledge, and hence achievement, is unlimited. A boundary between the known and the unknown always exists. In such a situation, opportunity is also unlimited for any number of folk whatever. We do not pretend or even hope to extend knowledge across new borders. Our academy is only precursory: before we explore new fields we must delineate the old, and define the areas where achievement is possible. This is a tremendous work in itself. I expect to work my life out only as a precursor. Even so, I will have given this life meaning. I invite you,

104

Glinnes Hulden, to join Fanscherade and share our great aim."

"And wear a grey uniform and give up hussade and star-watching? By no means. I don't care whether I achieve anything or not. As for your college, if you laid it down on the meadow you'd spoil my view. Look at the light on the water yonder; look at the color in the trees! Suddenly it seems as if your talk of 'achievement' and 'meaning' is sheer vanity—the pompous talk of small boys."

Junius Farfan laughed. "I'll agree to 'vanity,' along with arrogance, egocentricity, elitism, whatever you wish. No one has claimed otherwise, any more than Jan Dublays claimed mortification of the flesh when he wrote *The Rose in the Gargoyle's Teeth*."

"In other words," said Akadie gently, "Fanscherade deftly turns the force inherent in human vice to presumably useful ends."

"Abstract discussions are entertaining," remarked Junius Farfan, "but we must keep ourselves focused upon dynamic, rather than static, processes. Do you agree to Glay's proposal?"

"That Rabendary be turned into a Fanscherade madhouse? Of course not! Have you people no soul? Look out over this landscape! There's ample human achievement in the universe, but not nearly enough beauty. Establish your academy somewhere out on the lava beds, or back of the Broken Hills. Not here."

Junius Farfan rose to his feet. "We'll bid you good-day." He picked up the envelope. Glinnes reached forward; Glay's hand clamped his wrist. Farfan placidly tucked the envelope in his pocket.

Glay drew back with a wolfish grin. Glinnes leaned forward, muscles tense. Junius Farfan watched him soberly. Glinnes relaxed. Farfan's gaze was steady and sure, and disconcerting.

Akadie said, "I'll stay here with Glinnes; he'll ferry me home after a bit."

"As you will," said Farfan. He and Glay went to their boat, and after a last appraisal of Rabendary Meadow, the two departed.

"There's something downright insolent about that proposal," said Glinnes through gritted teeth. "Do they take me for a dunderhead, to be fleeced so easily?"

"They are absolutely sure in their purpose," said Akadie.

"Perhaps you mistake assurance for insolence . . . Agreed, the qualities sometimes converge. Still, neither Glay nor Junius Farfan is an insolent man. Farfan indeed is extraordinarily bland. Glay would appear somewhat remote, but still, all in all, a true-hearted fellow."

Glinnes could hardly control his indignation. "When they cheat me from eight directions and steal my property? Your concepts need reexamination."

Akadie signified that the matter lacked consequence. "I looked in at the hussade game yesterday. I must say that I was greatly diverted, though the play was not altogether precise. Hussade is intensely an interaction between personalities; no one game is ever like another. I might even believe that the masks are unconsciously recognized as a necessity, to prevent personalities from dominating the game."

"In hussade anything might be true. I know that I can't abide Lord Gensifer's personality, to such effect that I'll be playing with the Tanchinaros."

Akadie nodded sagely. "I chanced to meet Lord Gensifer this morning, in Voulash of all places, at the Placid Valley Inn. Over a cup of tea he mentioned that he had released several players for insubordination."

"Insubordination?" Glinnes snorted. "More accurately, for outright disgust. What did he want in Voulash? Mind you, the question is casual. I don't care to pay a fee."

Akadie spoke with dignity. "Lord Gensifer was discussing hussade with some of the Voulash Gannets. I believe that he induced several of them to join the Gorgons."

"Well indeed! So Lord Gensifer refuses to quit?"

"On the contrary. He seethes with dedication. He claims that he has been beaten only by flukes and sluggishness, and never by the opposition."

Glinnes laughed scornfully. "Whenever Lord Gensifer sat in the foul tank we were able to score. When he called plays, we were chased all over the field."

"Will you fare better with old Neronavy? He's not noted for imaginative play."

"Quite true. I think we could do better." Glinnes ruminated a moment. "Would you care to ride over to Voulash again?"

"I have nothing better to do," said Akadie.

Denzel Warhound lived in a cabin between two vast myrsile trees, at the head of Placid Valley. He had not yet been apprised of Lord Gensifer's visit to Voulash, but he displayed neither surprise nor rancor. "The Gannets were a part-time proposition; I'm surprised the team held together as well as it did. Just a moment." He went to the telephone and spoke several minutes with someone whose face Glinnes could not see, then returned to the porch. "Both strikes, both wings and a rover—all Gorgons now. The Gannets have flown for the last time this year, I assure you."

"As a matter of possible interest," said Glinnes, "the Tanchinaros could make good use of an aggressive captain. Neronavy is not as alert as he might be. With a clever captain, the Tanchinaros might well win considerable money."

Denzel Warhound pulled at his chin. "The Tanchinaros are an open club, I believe?"

"As open as the air."

"The idea has appeal, quite decidedly."

# Chapter 13

★ ★ ★

The transition of the Tanchinaros from "ten guards and a fat old man" to a balanced and versatile team was not achieved without disgruntlement. The irascible Nilo Neronavy refused to concede the superior skills of Denzel Warhound. When the reverse was demonstrated he stormed from the field, accompanied by the displaced forwards and the sheirl, his niece. An hour later, in the arbor of The Magic Tench, Neronavy and his group declared themselves the nucleus of a new team, to be known as the Saurkash Fishkillers, and went so far as to challenge Lord Gensifer, who chanced to be passing by, to a match with his Gorgons. Lord Gensifer agreed to consider the offer.

The Tanchinaros, suddenly awake to their potentialities, drilled with care, developing precision, coordination, and a repertory of basic plays. Their first opponents would be the Raparees from Galgade in the East Fens. The Raparees would play for no more than fifteen hundred ozols, which in any event was about the capability of the Tanchinaro treasury. And who for sheirl? Perinda, the club manager, introduced several lackluster candidates, whom the team found unsuitable.

"We're a Class A team," declared Denzel Warhound. "Maybe better—so get us a Class A sheirl. We won't settle for any old slab of merling bait."

"I have a girl in mind," said Perinda. "She is absolutely first class—*sashei*, beauty, enthusiasm—except for one or two small points."

"Ah indeed? She is the mother of nine children?"

"No. I'm sure she's virgin. After all, she's Trevanyi, which is one of the small flaws I mentioned."

"Aha," said Glinnes. "And her other flaws?"

"Well—she seems rather emotional. Her tongue has a life of its own. All in all, she is a very spirited person—an ideal sheirl."

"Aha! And her name—conceivably Duissane Drosset?"

"Quite correct. Do you have objection?"

Glinnes pursed his lips, trying to define his precise attitude toward Duissane Drosset. No question as to her verve and *sashei*—she would certainly provide impetus for the team. He said, "I have no objection."

If Duissane was abashed to find Glinnes on the team, she gave no signal of the fact. She came alone to the practice field—independent conduct indeed for a Trevanyi girl. She wore a dark brown cloak, which the south wind pressed against her slight figure, and seemed very appealing, almost innocent. She had little to say but watched the Tanchinaros at their exercises wtih apparently intelligent attention, and the team performed with a considerable increment of energy.

Duissane accompanied the team to the arbor of The Magic Tench, where they usually took after-practice refreshment. Perinda seemed distrait, and when he introduced Duissane formally he somewhat pointedly described her as "one of our candidates."

Savat cried out, "So far as I'm concerned, she's our sheirl. Let's have no more of this 'candidate' talk."

Perinda cleared his throat. "Yes, yes, of course. But one or two matters have come up, and we traditionally choose our sheirls after full discussion."

"What remains to be discussed?" demanded the guard Etzing. He asked Duissane, "Are you prepared to serve us loyally as our sheirl, and take the bad with the good and the good with the bad?"

Duissane's luminous gaze, wandering over the group, seemed to rest an instant upon Glinnes. But she said, "Yes, certainly."

"Well then!" cried Etzing. "Shall we acclaim her?"

"A moment, just a moment!" said Perinda, slightly flushed. "As I say, one or two small points remain to be discussed."

"Such as what?" bawled Etzing. "Let's hear them!"

Perinda puffed out his cheeks, pink with embarrassment. "We can discuss the matter another time."

Duissane asked, "What are these small points? Discuss them now, for all of us. Perhaps I can explain whatever needs explaining. Go on," she commanded, as Perinda still hesitated. "If allegations have been made I want to hear them." And again it seemed as if her gaze rested a long instant upon Glinnes.

"'Allegations' is too strong a word," stammered Perinda. "Just hints and rumors in regard to—well, your virginity. The condition seems to be doubtful, even though you are Trevanyi."

Duissane's eyes flashed. "How could anyone dare say such a thing about me? It is all so unjust and cowardly! Luckily I know my enemy, and I will never forget his antagonism!"

"No, no!" cried Perinda. "I won't say from where the rumor came to me. It's only that—"

"You wait here!" Duissane told them. "Do not depart until I return. If I must be distrusted and humiliated, allow me at least a contravention." She swept furiously from the arbor, almost colliding with Lord Gensifer and one of his cronies, Lord Alandrix, on their way into the bower.

"Stars!" exclaimed Lord Gensifer. "And who might she be? And at whom is she so enraged?"

Perinda spoke in a subdued voice. "My lord, she is a candidate for Tanchinaro sheirl."

Lord Gensifer laughed in great satisfaction. "She's made the wisest move of her life, fleeing the engagement. Truth to tell, she's a delicious little thing. I wouldn't mind pulling her ring myself."

"Almost certainly the opportunity will never arise," said Glinnes.

"Don't be too sure! The Gorgons are a different team now that changes have been made."

"I imagine that you can get a game with us, if the booty is adequate."

"Indeed. How much do you consider adequate?"

"Three thousand, five thousand, ten thousand—as much as you like."

"Bah. The Tanchinaros can't raise two thousand ozols, let alone ten thousand."

"Whatever booty the Gorgons put up, we'll match it."

Lord Gensifer nodded judiciously. "Something just might come of this. Ten thousand ozols, you say."

"Why not?" Glinnes looked around the arbor. All the Tanchinaros present knew as well as he did that the treasury contained three thousand ozols at the most, but only Perinda betrayed uneasiness.

"Very good," said Lord Gensifer briskly. "The Gorgons accept the challenge, and in due course we'll make the necessary arrangements." He turned to go, just as Duissane Drosset marched back into the arbor. Her golden-red curls were somewhat disarranged; her eyes glowed with equal parts of triumph and rage. She glared towards Glinnes and thrust a document at Perinda. "There! I must suffer inconvenience merely to quiet the spiteful tongues of vipers. Read! Are you satisfied?"

Perinda scrutinized the document. "This appears to be a document asserting the purity of Duissane Drosset, and the attestor is none other than Doctor Niameth. Well then, the unfortunate matter is settled."

"Not so fast," called Glinnes. "What is the date on the document?"

"What a degraded creature you are!" stormed Duissane. "The document is dated today!"

Perinda concurred, and added dryly, "Doctor Niameth did not note the precise hour and minute of his examination, but I suppose this is carrying exactitude too far."

Lord Gensifer said, "My dear young lady, don't you think you might fare better with the Gorgons? We are a courteous group, the exact opposite of these rude Tanchinaros."

"Courtesy wins no hussade games," said Perinda. "If you want to be snatched naked at your first game, go with the Gorgons."

Duissane flicked Lord Gensifer an appriasing glance. Half-regretfully she shook her head. "I've only permission for the Tanchinaros. You'd have to supplicate my father."

Lord Gensifer raised his eyes to the ceiling, as if imploring

110

one or another of the deities to witness the graceless demands put upon him. He bowed low. "My best regards." With another salute to the Tanchinaros he left the arbor.

Perinda looked at Glinnes. "Your badinage is all very well, but where will we find ten thousand ozols?"

"Where will Lord Gensifer find ten thousand ozols? He tired to borrow money from me. Who knows what a month or two will bring? Ten thousand ozols may seem a trivial sum."

"Who knows, who knows?" muttered Perinda. "Well then, back to Duissane Drosset. Is she our sheirl or is she not?"

No one protested; perhaps, with Duissane looking from face to face, no one dared. And so it was arranged.

The game with the Galgade Reparees went with almost embarrassing ease. The Tanchinaros were surprised to find their tactics so effective. Either they were six times more powerful than they had assumed, or the Raparees were the weakest team of Jolany Prefecture. Three times the Tanchinaros thrust the length of the field, their formations supple and decisive, the Raparees always seeming to find two Tanchinaros upon them, their sheirl in constant travail, while Duissane stood composed and cold, even somewhat stern, the white robe enhancing her frail charm. The Raparees, dejected and outclassed, paid three ransoms and resigned the field with their sheirl not denuded, to the displeasure of the crowd.

After the game the Tanchinaros assembled at The Magic Tench. Duissane held somewhat aloof from the conviviality, and Glinnes, chancing to look to the side, struck full into the lowering gaze of Vang Drosset. Almost immediately he conducted Duissane from the premises.

A week later the Tanchinaros fared up the Scurge River to Erch on Little Vole Island to play the Erch Elements, with almost the same results. Lucho had been shifted to left strike, the better to work in tandem with Glinnes Hulden, and Savat played right wing with adequate accuracy. Still, there were relatively weak areas in the deployment, which a skillful team would exploit. Gajowan, the left wing, was light and somewhat diffident, and Rolo, the left rover, was rather too slow. During the game with the Elements, Glinnes noticed Lord Gensifer in one of the middle boxes. He also noted Lord Gensifer's eyes turned often toward Duissane, though in this

111

regard he was not alone, for Duissane projected an irresistible fascination. In the white gown, her Trevanyi background was forgotten; she seemed an entrancing confection—wistful, tart, gay, tragic, reckless, cautious, wise, foolish. Glinnes thought to see other attributes as well; he could never look at her without hearing a tinkle of laughter through the starlit darkness.

The next game, with the Hansard Dragons, pointed up the soft spot in the Tanchinaros' left wall, when the Dragons twice drove deep along the Tanchinaro left flank. In each case they were halted by the guards, then defeated by a thrust against the sheirl from the right, and the Tanchinaros won the game in three successive skirmishes. Again Lord Gensifer sat in one of the middle boxes, with several men strange to Glinnes, and after the game he appeared at The Magic Tench, where he renewed his challenge to the Tanchinaros. Each side would offer a treasury of ten thousand ozols, so Lord Gensifer stipulated, and the game must take place four weeks from the present date.

Somewhat dubiously, Perinda accepted the challenge. As soon as Lord Gensifer had departed, The Tanchinaros began to speculate as to what devious scheme Lord Genisfer had in mind. As Gilweg put it, "Not even Tammi could hope to win with his present team."

"He thinks he'll storm our left side," said Etzing dourly. "They almost got away with it today."

"He wouldn't speculate ten thousand ozols on that theory," said Glinnes. "I smell a whole set of startling antics, such as an entire new team—the Vertrice Karpouns, the Port Angel Scorpions—wearing Gorgon uniforms for the day."

"That must be what he's got in mind," Lucho agreed. "Tammi would think it a fine joke to beat us with such a team."

"The ten thousand ozols wouldn't hurt his feelings either."

"Such a team would rip open our left side as if it were a melon," predicted Etzing, and he glanced across the arbor to where Gajowan and Rolo listened with glum expressions. For these two, the conversation could have only a single implication: by the inexorable logic of competition, two-thousand-ozol players had no place on a ten-thousand-ozol team.

Two days later a pair of new men joined the Tanchinaros. The first, Yalden Wirp, had been represented on Lord Gensifer's original dream-team; the second, Dion Sladine, while playing with an obscure team from the Far Hills, had attracted Denzel Warhound's respectful attention. The vulnerable left flank of the Tanchinaros had been not only strengthened but converted into a source of dynamic potential.

# Chapter 14

★ ★ ★

Rolo and Gajowan were persuaded to remain with the club in the capacity of substitutes and utility players, and in a game with the Wigtown Devisers, two weeks before the challenge match with the Gorgons, they played their old positions. The Devisers, a team of good reputation, lost a hard-fought ransom before they discovered the soft left side. They began to hurl probes and thrusts at the vulnerable area, and several times gained the back court, only to fail before the mobile and massive Tanchinaro guards. For almost ten minutes the Tanchinaros defended their territory, apparently lacking offensive force, while Lord Gensifer watched from his box, occasionally leaning to mutter a comment to his friends.

The Tanchinaros finally won, if sluggishly, by the usual three successive takes. Duissane as yet had never known a hand on her ring.

The Tanchinaro treasury was now well in excess of ten thousand ozols. The players speculated upon the possibilities of wealth. Several options were open. They could regard themselves as a two-thousand-ozol team and try to play teams of such quality. For this they would find scheduling difficult, if not impossible. They might rate themselves a five-thousand-ozol team and play in this category, risking not too much, gaining moderately. Or they might rank themselves a team of the first quality, and play ten-thousand-ozol teams— to gain both wealth and that ineffable quality known as *isthoune*. If the *isthoune*\* became sufficiently intense, they might declare themselves a team of championship quality and

---

\* *isthoune*: exalted pride and confidence; *mana;* the emotion which compels heroes to reckless feats; a word essentially untranslatable.

113

engage to prove themselves against any team of Trullion or elsewhere, for any treasure within their capabilities.

The day of the challenge match began with a thunderstorm. Lavender lightning spurted from cloud to cloud and occasionally struck down at the hills, shivering one or another of the tall menas with incandescent electric ague. At noon the storm drifted over the hills and hung there muttering and grumbling.

The Tanchinaros were first on the field and were announced to a pulsing crowd of sixteen thousand folk: "The dynamic and inexorable Tanchinaros of the Saurkash Hussade Club, in their usual uniforms of silver, blue and black, who vow to defend forever the honor of their precious and exalted sheirl Duissane! The personnel includes the captain: Denzel Warhound; the strikes: Tyran Lucho and Glinnes Hulden; the wings: Yalden Wirp and Ervil Savat; the guards . . ." So down the roster. "And now appearing on the field, in their striking uniforms of maroon and black, the new and utterly determined Gorgons, under the wise captaincy of Thammas Lord Gensifer, who champion the indescribable charm of their sheirl Arelmra. Strikes . . ."

Precisely as Glinnes had expected, Lord Gensifer brought on the field a team totally different from that which the Tanchinaros had previously defeated. These present Gorgons carried themselves with competence and purpose; they were clearly no strangers to victory. Only one man did Glinnes recognize as a local: the captain, Lord Gensifer. His scheme was, of course, immediately transparent, and would seem to have for its purpose the winning of a quick ten thousand ozols. Hussade sportsmanship was loose and chancy; the game depended much upon feints, tricks, intimidation, any sort of deception. Hence, Lord Gensifer's stratagem did him neither credit nor shame, though it made for a game in which certain niceties might be overlooked.

From the orchestra came music—the traditional *Marvels of Grace and Glory*—as the sheirls were escorted to their pedestals. The Gorgon sheirl, Arelmra, a stately dark-haired girl, evinced no great surge of that warm propulsive immediacy known as *emblance*. Lord Gensifer, so Glinnes noted, seemed placid and bland. His aplomb dwindled a trifle when he noticed the changes at wing and rover; then he shrugged and smiled to himself.

The teams took their places. The music of horns, drums

and flutes sounded—the poignant *Sheirls Softly Hopeful for Glory*.

The captains met at the center bridge with the field judge. Denzel Warhound took occasion to comment, "Lord Gensifer, your team is rife with strange faces. Are they all local folk?"

"We are all citizens of Alastor. We are local folk, all five trillion of us," said Lord Gensifer largely. "And your own team? All inhabit Saurkash?"

"Saurkash or the environs."

The field judge tossed up the rod. The Gorgons were awarded green and the game began. Lord Gensifer called his formation and the Gorgons moved forward—intent, keen, assured. The Tanchinaros instantly sensed a team of high quality.

The Gorgons feinted to the Tanchinaro right, then hurled a brutal assault at the left. Strong shapes in maroon and black, the masks leering in mindless glee, thrust against the silver and black. The Tanchinaro left side gave only enough to encapsulate a group of Gorgons and press them against the moat. The light went red. Warhound tried to close a trap around a pair of advanced Gorgons, but the Gorgon rovers came forward and opened an escape route. Patterns shifted; formations thrust and pulled, testing first one individual, then another. After about ten minutes of indecisive play, Lord Gensifer incautiously strayed from his hange. Glinnes leapt the moat, engaged Lord Gensifer and toppled him into the tank.

Lord Gensifer emerged wet and furious, which had been Glinnes' intent; the Gorgons were now hindered by the fervor of his play-calling. The Tanchinaros made a sudden center lunge of classic simplicity; Ervil Savat leapt up on the pedestal and seized Arelmra's ring. Her patrician features drooped in annoyance; clearly she had expected no such invasion of her citadel.

Lord Gensifer stonily paid over five thousand ozols, and the field judge called a five-minute rest period.

The Tanchinaros conferred. "Tammi seethes with blue fury," said Lucho. "This isn't at all what he had in mind."

"Let's tank him again," Warhound suggested.

"My idea precisely. This is a good team, but we can get at them through Tammi."

"But stealth!" Glinnes warned. "So that they don't guess

what we're up to! Tank Tammi by all means, but as if it were a casual by-blow."

Play resumed. Lord Gensifer came forth ominous in his wrath and the Gorgons themselves seemed to share his fury. Play moved up and down the field, fluid and fast. During red light, Warhound thrust out his left wing, which abruptly veered to come at Lord Gensifer, who raced back for the protection of his hange, but vainly—he was intercepted and tanked. For an instant an avenue lay open for the Tanchinaro forwards, and Warhound sent them pell-mell down the field. Lord Gensifer came mad-eyed up the ladder, just in time to pay a second ransom, and his ten thousand ozols were gone.

The Gorgons thoughtfully took counsel together. Warhound called over to the referee, "What does that other team call itself on ordinary occasions?"

"Didn't you know? They're the Stilettos from Rufous Planet, on exhibition tour. You're playing a good team today. They've already beaten Port Angel Scorpions and the Jonus Infidels—with their own captain, needless to say."

"Well then," said Lucho generously, "let's give them all a fine bath, to keep them humble. Why victimize poor Tammi alone?"

"Bravo! We'll send them back to Rufous clean and tidy!"

Red light. The Tanchinaros vaulted the moat to find the Gorgons in a Stern Redoubt formation. With two scores to the good, the Tanchinaro guards were able to play somewhat more loosely than usual. They advanced to the moat, then crossed—a procedure which showed an almost insulting disregard for the enemy's offensive capability. A sudden flurry of action, a melee; into the tank splashed Gorgons and Tanchinaros. On the ways, maroon and black strove with silver, blue and black; metals fangs glinted into ghoulish black grins. Figures swayed, toppled; captains uttered hoarse calls, almost unheard over the sounds of the crowd and the skirling music. Arelmra stood with hands clenched against her chest. Her detachment had vanished; she seemed to cry and groan, though her voice could not be heard through the din. The Tanchinaro guards burst into the ranked Gorgons, and Warhound, ignoring his hange, sprang past to snatch the golden ring.

The white gown fluttered away; Arelmra stood nude while passionate music celebrated the defeat of the Gorgons and the tragedy of the sheirl's humiliation. Lord Gensifer brought

116

her a robe and conducted her from the field, followed by the despondent Gorgons. Duissane was lifted by exultant Tanchinaros and carried to the Gorgon pedestal, while the orchestra played the traditional *Scintillating Glorifications*. Overcome with emotion, Duissane threw up her arms and cried out in joy. Laughing and crying, she kissed the Tanchinaros, until she confronted Glinnes, and then she drew back and marched off the field.

The Tanchinaros presently assembled at The Magic Tench, to hear the congratulations of their well-wishers.

"Never a team with such decision, such impact, such finesse!"

"The Tanchinaros will make Saurkash famous! Think of it!"

"Now what will Lord Gensifer do with his Gorgons?"

"Maybe he'll try the Tanchinaros with the Solelamut Select, or the Green Star Falifonics."

"I'd put my ozols on the Tanchinaros."

"Tanchinaros!" cried Perinda. "I've just come from the telephone. There's a fifteen-thousand-ozol game for us in two weeks—if we want it."

"Naturally we want it! Who with?"

"The Vertrice Karpouns."

The arbor became silent. The Karpouns were reckoned one of the five best teams of Trullion.

Perinda said, "They know nothing of the Tanchinaros, except that we've won a few games. I think they expect an easy fifteen thousand ozols."

"Avaricious animals!"

"We're as avaricious as they—perhaps worse."

Perinda continued. "We would play at Welgen. In addition to the treasure—should we win—we would take a fifth of the gate. We might well share out a treasure of close to forty thousand ozols—close to three thousand apiece."

"Not bad for an afternoons work!"

"That's only if we win."

"For three thousand ozols I'll play alone and win."

"The Karpouns," said Perinda, "are an absolutely proficient team. They've won twenty-eight straight games and their sheirl has never been touched. As for the Tanchinaros—I don't think anybody knows how good we are. The Gorgons today were an excellent team, handicapped by an indecisive captain. The Karpouns are as good or better, and we might well lose our money. So—what's the vote? Shall we play them?"

"For a chance at three thousand ozols I'd play a team of real karpouns."*

# Chapter 15

★ ★ ★

Welgen Stadium, largest of Jolany Prefecture, was occupied to its fullest capacity. The aristocracy of Jolany, Minch, Straveny, and Gulkin Prefectures filled the four pavilions. Thirty thousand common folk hunched on benches in the ordinary sections. A large contingent had arrived from Vertrice, three hundred miles west; they occupied a section decorated with orange and green, the Karpoun colors. Overhead hung twenty-eight orange and green gonfalons, signifying the twenty-eight successive Karpoun victories.

For an hour the orchestra had been playing hussade music: victory paeans of a dozen famous teams, traditional laments and exaltations; the *War Song of the Miraksian Players*, which chilled the nerves and constricted the viscera; the haunting sad-sweet *Moods of Sheirl Hralce;* then, five minutes before game time, the *Glory of Forgotten Heroes.*

The Tanchinaros came on the field and stood by the east pedestal, their silver masks tilted up and back. A moment later the Karpouns appeared beside the west pedestal. They wore dark green jerkins and trousers of striped dark green and orange; like the Tanchinaros, they wore their masks tilted back. The teams somberly examined each other across the length of the field. Jehan Aud, the Karpoun captain, veteran of a thousand games, was known to be a tactical genius; no detail escaped his eye; for every permutation of the action he instinctively brought to bear an optimum response. Denzel Warhound was young, innovative, lightning-swift. Aud knew the sureness of experience; Warhound seethed with a multiplicity of schemes. Both men were confident. The Karpouns

---

* karpoun: a feral tiger-like beast of the Shamshin Volcanoes.

had the advantage of long association. The Tanchinaros put against them a raw surge of vitality and élan, in a game where these qualities carried great weight. The Karpouns knew that they would win. The Tanchinaros knew that the Karpouns would lose.

The teams waited while the orchestra played *Thresildama*, a traditional salute to the competing teams.

The captains appeared with the sheirls; the orchestra played *Marvels of Grace and Glory*. The Karpoun sheirl was a marvelous creature named Farero, a flashing-eyed blonde girl, radiant with *sashei*. In accordance with some mystical process, when she stepped upon the pedestal she transcended herself, to become her own archetype. Duissane, likewise, became an intensified version of herself: frail, wistful, indomitably courageous, suffused with gallant derring-do and her own distinctive *sashei*, as compelling as that of the sublime Farero.

The players drew down their masks; the flashing silver Tanchinaros looked across at the cruel Karpouns.

The Karpouns won the green light and the first offensive deployment. The teams took their positions on the field. The music altered, each instrument performing a dozen modulations to create a final golden chord. Dead silence. The forty thousand spectators held their breath.

Green light. The Karpouns struck forward in their celebrated "Tidal Wave," intending to envelop and smother the Tanchinaros out of hand. Across the moat leapt the forwards; behind came the rovers and, close behind, the guards, ferociously seeking contact.

The Tanchinaros were prepared for the tactic. Instead of falling back, the four guards charged forward and the teams collided like a pair of stampeding herds, and the melée was indecisive. Some minutes later Glinnes won free and gained the pedestal. He looked Farero the Karpoun sheirl full in the face, and seized her ring. She was pale with excitement and disconcerted; never before had an enemy laid hands on her ring.

The gong sounded; Jehan Aud somewhat glumly paid over eight thousand-ozol certificates. The teams took a rest period. Five Tanchinaros had been tanked and five Karpouns; the honors were even. Warhound was jubilant. "They're a great team, no question! But our guards are unmovable and our forwards are faster! Only in the rovers do they show superiority, and not much there!"

"What will they try next time?" asked Gilweg.

"I suppose more of the same," said Warhound, "but more methodically. They want to pin our forwards and bring their strength to bear."

Play resumed. Aud now used his men conservatively, thrusting and probing, hoping to trap and tank a forward. The crafty Warhound, seeing how the land lay, purposely restrained his forces, and finally outwaited Aud. The Karpouns tried a sudden slash down the center; the Tanchinaro forwards slid to the side and let them pass, then jumped the moat. Lucho climbed the pedestal and seized Farero's ring.

Seven thousand ozols were paid as ransom.

Warhound told the team, "Don't relax! They'll be at their most dangerous! And they haven't won twenty-eight games by luck. I expect a 'Tidal Wave.'"

Warhound was correct. The Karpouns stormed the Tanchinaro citadel with all their forces. Glinnes was tanked; Sladine and Wilmer Guff were tanked. Glinnes returned up the ladder in time to tank a Karpoun wing only ten feet from the pedestal; then he was tanked a second time, and before he could return to the field the gong sounded.

For the first time Duissane had felt a hand at her gold ring. Warhound furiously paid back eight thousand ozols.

Glinnes had never played a more grueling game. The Karpouns seemed tireless; they bounded across the field, vaulting and swinging as if the game had only commenced. He could not know that to the Karpouns the Tanchinaro forwards seemed unpredictable flickers of silver and black, wild as devils, so unnaturally agile that they seemed to run on air, while the Tanchinaro guards loomed over the field like four inexorable Dooms.

Up and down the field moved the battle; step by step the Tanchinaros thrust against the Karpoun pedestal, the forwards wicked and remorseless, driving, bumping, swinging, thrusting. The roar of the crowd faded to the back of consciousness; all reality was compressed into the field, the runs and ways, the waters glinting in the sunlight. A heavy cloud passed briefly over the sun. Almost at this instant Glinnes saw a path open through the orange and green. A trap? With the last energy of his legs he darted forward, around, over and through. Orange and green yelled hoarsely; the Karpoun masks, once so sage and austere, seemed contorted in pain. Glinnes gained the pedestal, seizing the gold ring at Farero's waist, and now he must pull the ring and lay the blue-eyed maiden bare before forty thousand exalted eyes. The music soared, stately and tragic; Glinnes' hand twitched and hesitated; he did not dare to shame this golden creature . . .

The dark cloud was not a cloud. Three black hulls settled upon the field, blotting out the light of afternoon. The music stopped short; from the public-address came a poignant cry: "Starmenters! Take—" The voice broke off in a gabble of words, and a new harsh voice spoke: "Keep your seats. Do not move or stir about."

Glinnes nontheless took Farero's arm, jerked her from the pedestal, down the ladder to the tank under the field. "What are you doing?" she gasped, pulling back in horror.

"I'm trying to save your life," said Glinnes. "The starmenters would never leave you behind, and you'd never see your home again."

The girl's voice quavered. "Are we save under here?"

"I wouldn't think so. We'll leave by the outlet sump. Hurry—it's at the far end."

They splashed through the water at best speed, under the ways, past the center moat. And now down the other ladder came Duissane, her face pinched and white with fear. Glinnes called to her, "Come alone—we'll leave by the sump; perhaps they'll neglect to guard it."

At the corner of the tank the water flowed out and down a flume into a narrow little waterway. Glinnes slid down the flume and jumped to a ledge of ill-smelling black mud. Next came Duissane, clutching the white gown about herself. Glinnes pulled her over to the mud-bank; she lost her footing and sat back into the muck. Glinnes could not restrain a grin. "You did that on purpose!" she cried in a throbbing voice.

"I did not!"

"You did!"

"Whatever you say."

Farero came down the flume; Glinnes caught her and pulled her over to the ledge. Duissane struggled to her feet. The three looked dubiously along the channel, which meandered out of sight under arching hushberries and pipwillows. The water seemed dark and deep; a faint scent of merling hung in the air. The prospect of swimming or even wading was unthinkable. Moored across the way was a crude little canoe, evidently the property of a couple of boys who had gained illicit entry to the field through the sump.

Glinnes clambered over the flume to the canoe, which was

121

half full of water and wallowed precariously under his weight. He bailed out a few gallons of water, then dared delay no longer. He pushed the boat across the water. Duissane stepped in, then Farero, and the water rose almost to the gunwales. Glinnes handed the bailing bucket to Duissane, who went scowling to work. Glinnes paddled cautiously out into the waterway. Behind them, from the stadium, came the rasp of the announcement system: "Those folk in Pavilions A,B,C, and D will file to the south exits. Not all will be taken; we have an exact list of those we want. Be brisk and make no trouble; we'll kill anyone who hinders us."

Unreal! thought Glinnes. An outrageous avalanche of events: excitement, color, passion, music, and victory—now fear and flight, with two sheirls. One hated him. The other, Farero, examined him from the side of her magnificent seablue eyes. Now she took the bucket from Duissane, who sulkily scraped the mud from her gown. What a contrast, thought Glinnes: Farero was rueful but resigned—indeed, she probably preferred flight through the sump to nudity on the pedestal; Duissane obviously resented every instant of discomfort and seemed to hold Glinnes personally responsible.

The waterway curved. A hundred yards ahead gleamed Welgen Sound, with South Ocean beyond. Glinnes paddled more confidently; they had escaped the starmenters. A massive raid! And no doubt long planned for a time when all the wealthy folk of the prefecture came together. There would be captives taken for ransom, and girls taken for solace. The captives would return crestfallen and impoverished; the girls would never be seen again. The stadium vaults would yield at least a hundred thousand ozols and the treasures of the two teams would supply another thirty thousand, and even the Welgen banks might be plundered.

The waterway widened and meandered away from the shore across a wide mud flat pimpled with gas craters. To the east ran Welgen Spit, on the other side of which lay the harbor; to the west the shore extended into the late afternoon haze. Under the open sky Glinnes felt exposed—unreasonably so, he told himself; the starmenters could not now afford the time to pursue them, even should they deign to note the wallowing canoe. Farero had never ceased to bail. Water entered through several leaks, and Glinnes wondered how long the boat would stay afloat. The shuddering black slime of the mudflats was uninviting. Glinnes made for the nearest of the wooded islets which rose from the sound, a hummock of land fifty yards across.

The boat rocked upon an ocean swell and shipped water. Farero bailed as fast as possible, Duissane scooped with her hands, and they reached the islet just as the canoe sank under them. With enormous relief Glinnes pulled the canoe up the little apron of beach. Even as he stepped ashore, the three starmenter ships rose into view. They slanted up into the southern sky and were gone, with all their precious cargo.

Farero heaved a sigh. "Except for you," she told Glinnes, "I'd be aboard one of those ships."

"I would also be up there, except for myself," snapped Duissane.

Aha, thought Glinnes, here is a source for her annoyance: she feels neglected.

Duissane jumped ashore. "And what will we do out here?"

"Somebody will be along sooner or later. In the meantime, we wait."

"I don't care to wait," said Duissane. "Once the boat is bailed out we can row back to shore. Must we sit shivering on this miserable little spot of land?"

"What else do you suggest? The boat leaks and the water swarms with merling. Still, I might be able to mend the leaks."

Duissane went to sit on a chunk of driftwood. Whelm ships streaked in from the west, circled the area, and one dropped down into Welgen. "Too late, much too late," said Glinnes. He bailed the canoe dry and wadded moss into such cracks as he could find. Farero came to watch him. She said, "You were kind to me."

Glinnes looked up at her.

"When you might have pulled the ring, you hesitated. You didn't want to shame me."

Glinnes nodded and went back to work on the boat.

"This may be why your sheirl is angry."

Glinnes looked sideways toward Duissane, who sat scowling across the water. "She is seldom in a good humor."

Farero said thoughtfully, "To be sheirl is a very strange experience; one feels the most extraordinary impulses . . . Today I lost, but the starmenters saved me. Perhaps she feels cheated."

"She's lucky to be here, and not aboard one of the ships."

"I think that she is in love with you and jealous of me."

Glinnes looked up in astonishment. "In love with me?" He

turned another covert glance toward Duissane. "You must be wrong. She hates me. I've ample evidence of this."

"It may well be. I am no expert in these affairs."

Glinnes rose from his work, studied the canoe with gloomy dissatisfaction. "I don't trust that moss—especially with the avness wind coming from the land."

"Now that we're dry it's not unpleasant. Though my people must be worried, and I'm hungry."

"We can find shore food," said Glinnes. "We'll have a fine supper—except that we lack fire. Still—a plantain tree grows yonder."

Glinnes climbed the tree and tossed fruit down to Farero. When they returned to the beach, Duissane and the canoe were gone. She was already fifty yards distant, paddling for that waterway by which they had left the stadium. Glinnes gave a bark of sardonic laughter. "She is so in love with me and so jealous of you that she leaves us marooned together."

Farero, flushing pink, said, "It is not impossible."

For a period they watched the canoe. The offshore breeze gave Duissane difficulty. She stopped paddling and bailed for a moment or two; the moss evidently had failed to stanch the leaks. When again she began to paddle she rocked the canoe, and while clutching at the gunwale, lost the paddle. The offshore breeze blew her back, past the isle where Glinnes and Farero stood watching. Duissane ignored them.

Glinnes and Farero climbed upon the central hummock and watched the receding canoe, wondering whether Duissane might be swept out to sea. She drifted among the islets and the canoe was lost to sight.

The two returned to the beach. Glinnes said, "If we had a fire we could be quite comfortable, at least for a day or so . . . I don't care for raw sea-stuff."

"Nor I," said Farero.

Glinnes found a pair of dry sticks and attempted to rub up a fire, without success. He threw the sticks away in disgust. "The nights are warm, but a fire is pleasant."

Farero looked here, there, everywhere but directly at Glinnes. "Do you think that we'll be here so long?"

"We can't leave till a boat comes past. It might be an hour; it might be a week."

Farero spoke in something of a stammer. "And will you want to make love to me?"

Glinnes studied her for a moment, and reaching out,

touched her golden hair, "You are beautiful beyond words. I would take joy in becoming your first lover."

Farero looked away. "We are alone . . . My team today was defeated, and I won't be sheirl again. Still—" She stopped speaking, then pointed and said in a soft flat voice, "Yonder passes a boat."

Glinnes hesitated. Farero made no urgent movements. Glinnes said reluctantly, "We must do something about silly Duissane and the canoe." He went to the water's edge and shouted. The boat, a power skiff driven by a lone fisherman, altered course, and presently Glinnes and Farero were aboard. The fisherman had come in from the open sea and had noticed no drifting canoe; quite possibly Duissane had gone ashore on one of the islets.

The fisherman took his boat around the end of the spit and into Welgen dock. Farero and Glinnes rode in a cab to the stadium. The driver had much to say regarding the starmenter raid. "—never an exploit to match it! They took the three hundred richest folk of the region and at least a hundred maidens, poor things, who'll never be put up for ransom. The Whelm came too late. The starmenters knew precisely who to take and who to ignore. And they timed their operation to the second and were gone. They'll earn fortunes in ransom!"

At the stadium Glinnes bade Sheirl Farero a muted farewell. He ran to the dressing room, slipped off his Tanchinaro uniform, and resumed his ordinary clothes.

The cab carried him back to the dock, where Glinnes hired a small runabout. He drove around the spit, out into Welgen Sound. The flat light of avness painted sea, sky, islets and shore in pallid and subtle colors to which no name could be applied. The silence seemed surreal; the gurgle of water under the keel was almost an intrusion.

He passed the islet where he had originally landed with Farero and Duissane, and went beyond, out into the area where the canoe had drifted. He circled the first of the islets but saw no sign either of canoe or Duissane. The next three islets were also vacant. The sea spread vast and calm beyond the three little islets yet to be investigated. On the second of these he spied a slender figure in a white gown, waving frantically.

When Duissane recognized the man who drove the boat, she abruptly stopped waving. Glinnes leapt ashore and pulled the boat up the beach. He secured the bow line to a crooked root, then turned and looked about. The flat low line of the mainland was dim in the inconclusive light. The sea heaved slow and supple, as if constricted under a film of silk. Glinnes looked at Duissane, who had maintained a cold silence. "What a quiet place. I doubt if even the merlings swim out this far."

Duissane looked at the boat. "If you came out to get me, I am now ready to leave."

"There's no hurry," said Glinnes. "None whatever. I brought bread and meat and wine. We can bake plantains and quorls* and maybe a curset.** We'll have a picnic while the stars come out."

Duissane compressed her lips petulantly and looked off toward the shore. Glinnes stepped forward. He stood only a foot away from her—as close as he had ever been. She looked up at him without warmth, her tawny-gray eyes shifting, or so it seemed to Glinnes, through a dozen moods and emotions. Glinnes bent his head, and putting an arm around her shoulders, kissed her lips, which were cold and unresponsive. She pushed him away with a thrust of her hands, and seemed suddenly to recover her voice. "You're all alike, you Trills! You reek with cauch; your brain is a single lecherous gland. Do you aspire only to turpitude? Have you no dignity, no self-respect?"

Glinnes laughed. "Are you hungry?"

"No. I have a dinner engagement and I will be late unless we leave at once."

"Indeed. Is that why you stole the canoe?"

"I stole nothing. The canoe was as much mine as yours. You seemed content to ogle that insipid Karpoun girl. I wonder that you're not still at it."

"She feared that you would be offended."

Duissane raised her eyebrows high. "Why should I think twice, or even once, about your conduct? Her concern embarrasses me."

"It is no great matter," said Glinnes. "I wonder if you would gather firewood while I fetch plantains?"

Duissane opened her mouth to refuse, then decided that such an act was self-defeating. She found a few dry twigs, which she tossed haughtily down upon the beach. She scrutinized the boat, which was pulled far up on the beach, and be-

---

* quorls: a type of mollusk living in beach sand.
** curset: a crab-like sea insect.

yond her strength to float. The starting key had been removed from the lock.

Glinnes brought plantains, kindled a fire, dug up four fine quorls, which he cleaned, rinsed in the sea and set to baking with the plantains. He brought bread and meat from the boat, and spread a cloth on the sand. Duissane watched from a distance.

Glinnes opened the flask of wine and offered it to Duissane.

"I prefer to drink no wine."

"Do you intend to eat?"

Duissane touched the tip of her tongue to her lips. "And then what do you plan?"

"We will relax on the beach and star-watch, and who knows what else?"

"Oh you are a despicable person; I want nothing to do with you. Untidy and gluttonous, like all the Trills."

"Well, at least I'm not worse. Settle yourself; we'll eat and watch the sunset."

"I'm hungry, so I'll eat," said Duissane. "Then we must go back. You know how Trevanyi feel about indiscriminate amorousness. Also, never forget—I am the Tanchinaro sheirl, and a virgin!"

Glinnes made a sign to indicate that these considerations were of no great cogency. "Changes occur in all our lives."

Duissane stiffened in outrage. "Is this how you plan to soil the team's sheirl? What a scoundrel you are, who so sanctimoniously insisted upon purity and then told such vicious lies about me."

"I told no lies," declared Glinnes. "I never even told the truth—how you and your family robbed me and left me for the merlings, and how you laughed to see my lying for dead."

Duissane said somewhat feebly, "You got only what you deserved."

"I still owe your father and your brothers a knock or two," said Glinnes. "As for you, I am of two minds. Eat, drink wine, fortify yourself."

"I have no appetite. None whatever. I do not think it just that a person should be so ill-treated."

Glinnes gave no answer and began to eat.

Presently Duissane joined him. "You must remember," she told him, "that if you carry out your threat, you will have betrayed not only me but all your Tanchinaros, and befouled yourself as well. Then, you will be faced with an accounting of another sort, from my family. They will dog you to the end of time; never will you know a moment's peace. Thirdly, you will gain all my contempt. And for what? The relief of your gland. How can you use the word 'love' when you really plan revenge? And this of a most paltry kind. As if I were an animal, or something without emotion. Certainly—use me, if you wish, or kill me, but bear in mind my utter contempt for all your disgusting habits. Furthermore—"

"Woman," roared Glinnes, "be kind enough to shut your mouth. You have blighted the day and the evening as well. Eat your meal in silence and we will return to Welgen." Scowling, Glinnes hunched down upon the sand. He ate plantains, quorls, meat, and bread; he drank two flasks of wine, while Duissane watched from the corner of her eye, a peculiar expression on her face, half-sneer, half-smirk.

When he had eaten, Glinnes leaned back against a hummock and mused for a time upon the sunset. With absolute fidelity the colors were reflected in the sea, except for an occasional languid black cusp in the lee of a swell.

Duissane sat in silence, arms clasped around her knees.

Glinnes lurched to his feet and thrust the boat into the water. He signaled Duissane. "Get in." She obeyed. The boat returned across the sound, around the point of the spit, and up to the Welgen dock.

A large white yacht floated beside the jetty, which Glinnes recognized to be the property of Lord Gensifer. Lights glowed from the portholes, signifying activity aboard.

Glinnes looked askance at the yacht. Would Lord Gensifer be hosting a party tonight, after the starmenter raid? Strange. But then, the ways of the aristocrats always had been beyond his comprehension. Duissane, to his amazement, jumped from the boat and ran to the yacht. She climbed the gangplank and vanished into the salon. Glinnes heard Lord Gensifer's voice: "Duissane, my dear young lady, whatever—" The remainder of his sentence was muffled.

Glinnes shrugged and returned the boat to the rental depot. As he walked back down the dock, Lord Gensifer hailed him from the yacht. "Glinnes! Come aboard for a moment, there's a good fellow!"

Glinnes sauntered indifferently up the gangway. Lord Gensifer clapped him on the back and conducted him into the salon. Glinnes saw a dozen folk in fashionable garments, apparently aristocratic friends of Lord Gensifer, and also Akadie, Marucha, and Duissane, who now wore over her sheet white gown a red cloak, evidently borrowed from one of the ladies present. "Here then is our hero!" declared Lord Gensifer. "With cool resource he saved two lovely sheirls from the sarmenters. In our great grief we at least can be thankful for this boon."

Glinnes looked in wonder about the salon. He felt as if he were living a particularly absurd dream. Akadie, Lord Gensifer, Marucha, Duissane, himself—what a strange mix of people!

"I hardly know what happened today," said Glinnes, "beyond the bare fact of the raid."

"The bare fact is about all anyone knows," said Akadie. He seemed unusually subdued and neutral, and careful in his choice of words. "The starmenters knew exactly who they wanted. They took exactly three hundred folk of substance, and about two hundred girls as well. The three hundred are to be ransomed for a minimum of a hundred thousand ozols apiece. No ransom prices have been set on the girls, but we will do our best to buy them back."

"Then they've already been in communication?"

"Indeed, indeed. The plans were carefully made, and each person's financial capacity was carefully gauged."

Lord Gensifer said with facetious self-deprecation, "Those left behind have suffered a loss of prestige, which we keenly resent."

Akadie went on. "For reasons apparently good and sufficient, I have been appointed collector of the ransom, for which effort I am to receive a fee. No great amount, I assure you—in fact, five thousand ozols will requite my work."

Glinnes listened, dumbfounded. "So the total ransom will be three hundred times a hundred thousand, which is—"

"Thirty million ozols—a good day's work."

"Unless they end up on the prutanshyr."

Akadie made a sour face. "A barbaric relict. What benefit do we derive from torture? The starmenters come back regardless."

"The public is edified," said Lord Gensifer. "Think of the kidnaped maidens—one of whom might have been my good friend Duissane!" He placed his arm around Duissane's shoulders and gave her a mock-fraternal squeeze. "Is, then, the revenge too severe? Not to my way of thinking."

Glinnes blinked and gaped back and forth between Lord Gensifer and Duissane, who seemed to be smiling at a secret

129

joke. Had the world gone mad? Or was he in truth living a preposterous dream?

Akadie formed a quizzical arch with his eyebrows. "The starmenters' sins are real enough; let them suffer."

One of Lord Gensifer's friends asked, "By the way, which particular band of starmenters is responsible?"

"There has been no attempt at anonymity," said Akadie. "We have attracted the personal attention of Sagmondo Bandolio—Sagmondo the Stern—who is as wicked as any."

Glinnes knew the name well; Sagmondo Bandolio had long been the quarry of the Whelm. "Bandolio is a terrible man," said Glinnes. "He extends no mercy."

"Some say he is a starmenter only for sport," Akadie remarked. "They say he has a dozen identities about the cluster, and that he could live forever on the fortunes he has gained."

The group mused in silence. Here was evil on a scale so fast that it became awesome.

Glinnes said, "Somewhere in the prefecture is a spy, someone intimate with all the aristocrats, someone who knows the exact level of every fortune."

"That statement must be reckoned accurate," said Akadie.

"Who could it be?" pondered Lord Gensifer. "Who could it be?"

And all persons present considered the matter, and each formed his private speculation.

# Chapter 16

★ ★ ★

The Tanchinaros, by defeating the Karpouns, had done themselves a disservice. Since Sagmondo Bandolio and his starmenters had taken their treasure, the team was without resources, and because of their demonstrated abilities, Perinda could schedule no thousand-ozol or two-thousand-ozol games. And now they lacked the treasure to challenge any teams in the ten-thousand-ozol class.

A week after the Karpoun game the Tanchinaros met at

Rabendary Island, and Perinda explained the sorry state of affairs. "I've found only three teams willing to play us, and not one will risk their sheirl for less than ten thousand ozols. Another matter: we lack a sheirl. Duissane seems to have caught the interest of a certain lord, which naturally was her ambition. Now neither she nor Tammi choose to risk the exposure of her precious hide."

"Bah!" said Lucho. "Duissane never loved hussade in the first place."

"Naturally not," said Warhound. "She's Trevanyi. Have you ever seen a Trevanyi play hussade? She's the first Trevanyi sheirl I've ever known."

"Trevanyi play their own games," said Gilweg.

"Like 'Knives and Gullets,'" said Glinnes.

"And 'Trills and Robbers.'"

"And 'Merling, Merling, Who's Got the Cadaver.'"

"And 'Hide and Sneak.'"

Perinda said, "We can always recruit a sheirl. Our problem is money."

Glinnes said grudgingly, "I'd put up my five thousand ozols if I thought I'd get it back."

Warhound said, "I could scrape up a thousand, one way or another."

"That's six thousand," said Perinda. "I'll put in a thousand—or rather, I can borrow a thousand from my father . . . Who else? Who else? Come then, you miserly mud-thumpers, bring out your wealth."

Two weeks later the Tanchinaros played the Ocean Island Kanchedos, at the great Ocean Island Stadium, for a twenty-five thousand-ozol purse, with fifteen thousand hazarded by each team and ten thousand by the stadium. The new Tanchinaro sheirl was Sacharissa Simone, a girl from Fal Lal Mountain—pleasant, naive and pretty, but lacking in that imponderable quality *sashei*. There was likewise general doubt as to her virginity, but no one wanted to make an issue of the matter. "Let's all of us have a night with her," grumbled Warhound, "and resolve the question to everybody's satisfaction."

Whatever the reason, the Tanchinaros played sluggishly and committed a number of startling errors. The Kanchedos won an easy three-ring victory. Sacharissa's possibly innocent body was displayed in every detail to thirty-five thousand spectators, and Glinnes found himself with only three or four

131

hundred ozols in his purse. In a state of stupefied depression he returned to Rabendary Island, and flinging himself down in one of the old string chairs, he spent the evening staring across the broad at Ambal Isle. What a chaotic mess he had made of his life! The Tanchinaros—impoverished, humiliated, on the verge of fragmentation. Ambal Isle—now farther from his grasp than ever. Duissane, a girl who had worked a curious enthrallment upon him, had now fixed her ambitions upon the aristocracy, and Glinnes, previously only lukewarm, now roiled at the thought of Duissane in another man's bed.

Two days after the catastrophic game with the Kanchedos, Glinnes rode the ferry into Welgen to find a buyer for twenty sacks of his excellent Rabendary musk-apples, a matter soon arranged. With an hour to wait for the return trip, Glinnes stopped for a bite of lunch at a small restaurant half indoors, half out under the shade of a fulgeria arbor. He drank a pot of beer and gnawed at bread and cheese, and watched the folk of Welgen move about their affairs . . . Here passed a group of true Fanschers—sober young folk, erect and alert, frowning into the distance as if absorbed in concepts of great portent . . . And here came Akadie, walking quickly, with his head lowered, his Fanscher-style jacket flapping out to the sides. Glinnes called out as he passed, "Akadie! Drop yourself in a chair; take a pot of beer!"

Akadie halted as if he had struck an invisible obstruction. He peered into the shade to isolate the source of the voice, glanced over his shoulder, and ducked hastily into a chair beside Glinnes. His face was pinched; his voice when he spoke was sharp and nervous. "I think I've put them aside, or at least I hope so."

"Oh?" Glinnes looked along the way Akadie had come. "Who have you put aside?"

Akadie's response was typically oblique. "I should have refused the commission; it has brought me only anxiety. Five thousand ozols! When I am dogged by avaricious Trevanyi, awaiting only a moment of carelessness. What a farce. They can take their thirty million ozols, together with my paltry five thousand, and fabricate the most expensive bumstopper in the marveling memory of the human universe."

"In other words," said Glinnes, "you have collected the thirty million ozols ransom?"

Akadie gave a peevish nod. "I assure you, it is not real money; that is to say, the five thousand ozols which becomes my fee represents five thousand spendable ozols. I carry thirty

132

million ozols in this case"—here he nudged a small black case with a silver clasp—"but it seems like so much wadded paper."

"To you."

"Precisely." Akadie peered over his shoulder once again. "Other folk are less adept in abstract symbology, or more accurately, they use different symbols. These tokens to me are fire and smoke, pain and fear. Others perceive an entirely different set of referrents: palaces, space-yachts, perfumes and pleasures."

"In short, you fear that the money will be stolen from you?"

Akadie's nimble mind had far outdistanced a categorical response. "Can you imagine the vicissitudes liable to the man who withheld thirty million ozols from Sagmondo Bandolio? The conversation might go in this fashion: Bandolio: 'I now require of you, Janno Akadie, the thirty million ozols entrusted to your care.' Akadie: 'You must be brave and forebearing, since I no longer have the money.' Bandolio: . . . Alas. My imagination falters. I can conceive no further. Would he be cold? Would he rave? Would he utter a negligent laugh?"

"If indeed you are robbed," said Glinnes, "one small benefit will be the gratification of your curiosity."

Akadie acknowledged the remark with only a sour sideglance. "If I could surely identify someone, or something; if I knew precisely whom or what to avoid . . ." He left the sentence unfinished.

"Have you noticed any specific threat? Or are you just nervous?"

"I am nervous, to be sure, but this is my usual state. I loathe discomfort, I dread pain, I refuse even to acknowledge the possibility of death. All these circumstances now seem to hover close."

"Thirty million ozols is an impressive sum," said Glinnes wistfully. "Personally, I need only twelve thousand of them."

Akadie pushed the case toward Glinnes. "Here you are; take whatever you require and explain the lack to Bandolio . . . But no." He jerked the case back once more. "I am not allowed this option."

"I am puzzled on one account," said Glinnes. "Since you are so anxious, why do you not simply place the money in a bank? Yonder, for instance, is the Bank of Welgen, twenty seconds from where we sit."

Akadie sighed. "If only it were that easy . . . My instructions are to keep the money ready at hand, for delivery to Bandolio's messenger."

"And when does he come?"

Akadie rolled his eyes up toward the fulgeria. "Five minutes? Five days? Five weeks? I wish I knew."

"It seems somewhat unreasonable," said Glinnes. "Still, the starmenters work by the systems they find most useful. And think! A year from today the episode will provide you many a merry anecdote."

"I can think only of this moment," grumbled Akadie. "This case sits in my lap like a red-hot anvil."

"Who exactly do you fear?"

Even at his most fretful, Akadie could not resist a didactic analysis. "Three groups hotly yearn for ozols: the Fanschers, that they may buy land, tools, information and energy; the noble folk, in order to refurbish their flaccid fortunes; and the Trevanyi, who are naturally avaricious. Only moments ago I discovered two Trevanyi walking unobtrusively behind me."

"This may or may not be significant," said Glinnes.

"All very well to deprecate." Akadie rose to his feet. "Are you returning to Rabendary? Why not ride out with me?"

They walked to the dock and in Akadie's white runabout set off eastward along the Inner Broad. Between the Lace Islands, across Ripil Broad they sped, past Saurkash, then along narrow Athenry Water and out upon Fleharish Broad, where they observed a rakish black and purple craft darting back and forth at great speed.

"Speaking of Trevanyi," said Glinnes, "notice who joyrides with Lord Gensifer."

"I noticed her." Akadie thoughtfully stowed his black case under the stern seat.

Lord Gensifer drove his boat through a sportive caracole, projecting a long feather of spume into the air, then rushed hissing forward to overtake Akadie and Glinnes. Akadie, murmuring an objurgation, allowed his boat to coast to a standstill; Lord Gensifer drew up alongside. Duissane, wearing a charming pale-blue gown, glanced sidewise with an expression of sulky boredom but made no other acknowledgment. Lord Gensifer was in one of his most expansive moods. "And where are you bound this lovely afternoon, with such a pair of hangdog looks about you? Off to rob Lord Milfred's duck preserve, or so I'd wager." Lord

Gensifer here made waggish allusion to an ancient joke of the district. "What a pair of rogues, to be sure."

Akadie replied in his most polished voice. "I fear we have more important concerns, beautiful day or not."

Lord Gensifer made an easy gesture to signify that the course of his little joke was run. "How does your collection progress?"

"I took in the last moneys this morning," said Akadie stiffly. The subject was clearly one he did not care to pursue, but Lord Gensifer tactlessly continued. "Just hand me over a million or two of those ozols. Bandolio would hardly feel the difference."

"I'd be pleased to hand you over the whole thirty million," said Akadie, "and you could settle accounts with Sagmondo Bandolio."

"Thank you," said Lord Gensifer, "but I think not." He peered into Akadie's boat. "You really carry the money about with you, then? Ah, there in the bilge, as casual as you please. Do you realize that boats sometimes sink? What would you say then to Sagmondo the Stern?"

Akadie's voice cracked under the strain of his displeasure. "The contingency is most remote."

"Undoubtedly true. But we're boring Duissane, who cares nothing for such matters. She refuses to visit me at Gensifer Manor—think of it! I've tempted her with luxury and elegance; she'll have none of it. Trevanyi through and through. Wild as a bird! You're sure you can't spare even a million ozols? What about half a million? A paltry hundred thousand?"

Akadie smiled with steely patience and shook his head. With a wave of his hand Lord Gensifer pulled back the throttle; the purple and silver boat lunged forward, swept around in a slashing arc and drove north toward the Prefecture Commons, the heel of which closed off the tip of Fleharish Broad.

Akadie and Glinnes proceeded more sedately. At Rabendary Island, Akadie chose to stop ashore for a cup of tea, but sat on the edge of his chair peering first up Ilfish Way, then across Ambal Broad, then through the row of pomanders which Screened Farwan Water. These, with their tall waving blades, created a sense of furtive motion which made Akadie more nervous than ever.

Glinnes brought forth a flask of old wine to soothe Akadie's apprehension, with such good effect that the afternoon waned into pale avness. At last Akadie felt obliged to go home. "If you like you can accompany me. Truth to tell, I'm a trifle on edge."

Glinnes agreed to follow Akadie in his own boat, but Akadie stood rubbing his chin as if reluctant to depart. "Perhaps you should telephone Marucha and let her know that we are on the way. Inquire also if she has noticed unusual circumstances of any sort whatever."

"Just as you like." Glinnes went to make the call. Marucha was indeed relieved to learn that Akadie was on his way home. Unusual circumstances? None of consequence. Perhaps a few more boats in the vicinity, or it might have been the same boat passing back and forth. She had barely noticed.

Glinnes found Akadie on the end of the dock, frowning up Farwan Water. He set off in his white runabout and Glinnes followed close behind, all the way to Clinkhammer Broad, clear, calm and empty in the mauve-gray light of evening. Glinnes saw Akadie safely to the dock, then swung about and returned to Rabendary.

Hardly had he arrived home before the telephone gong sounded. Akadie's face appeared on the screen with an expression of lugubrious triumph. "It went exactly as I had expected," said Akadie. "There they were, waiting for me behind the boat-house—four of them, and I'm sure Trevanyi, though they all wore masks."

"What happened?" Glinnes demanded, for Akadie seemed intent on arranging his tale to the best dramatic effect.

"Just what I expected; that's what happened," snapped Akadie. "They overpowered me and took the black case; then they fled in their boats."

"So. Thirty million ozols down the chute."

"Ha hah! Nothing of the sort. Only a locked black case packed with grass and dirt. There will be some sorry Drossets when they force the lock. I say Drossets advisedly, for I recognized the peculiar stance of the older son, and Vang Drosset's posture is also characteristic."

"You mentioned—*four?*"

Akadie managed a grim smile. "One of the thugs was somewhat frail. This person stood aside and kept a lookout."

"Indeed. Then where is the money?"

"This is why I called. I left it in the bait-box on your dock, and my forethought was amply justified. What I want you to do is this. Go out on your dock and make sure there are no

136

observers. Take the foil-wrapped packet from the box and carry it inside your house, and I will call for it tomorrow."

Glinnes scowled at Akadie's image. "So now I'm in charge of your confounded money. I don't want my throat cut any more than you. I fear I must charge you a professional fee."

Akadie instantly emerged from his preoccupation. "How absurd! You incur no risks. No one knows where the money is—"

"Someone might make a thirty-million-ozol guess. Don't forget who saw us together earlier today."

Akadie laughed somewhat shakily. "Your agitation is excessive. Still, if it gives you comfort, station yourself with your hand-gun where you can watch for trespassers. In fact, this is perhaps the judicious course. We'll both feel better for the vigilance."

Glinnes stuttered in indignation. Before he could speak, Akadie made a reassuring gesture and dimmed the screen.

Glinnes jumped to his feet and strode back and forth across the room. Then he brought forth his hand-gun, as Akadie had suggested, and went out on the dock. The waterways were empty. He made a circuit of his house, walking wide around the prickleberry bushes. So far as he could determine, there was no one on Rabendary Island but himself.

The bait-box exerted an intolerable fascination. He went back out on the dock and flipped up the lid. There indeed—a packet wrapped in metal foil. Glinnes took it forth and after a moment of indecision carried it into the house. What did thirty million ozols look like? No harm in soothing his curiosity. He unfolded the covering to find a wad of folded periodicals. Glinnes stared down aghast. He started for the telephone, then stopped short. If Akadie knew of the situation, his manner would be intolerably dry and jocular. If, on the other hand, Akadie were ignorant of the substitution, the news would shatter him, and might well be postponed until the morning.

Glinnes rewrapped the packet and replaced it in the bait-box. Then he brewed himself a cup of tea and took it out on the verandah, where he sat brooding across the water. Night now fully encompassed the fens; the sky was paved with stars. Glinnes decided that Akadie himself had transferred the money, leaving the foil-wrapped parcel as a decoy. A typically subtle joke . . .

Glinnes turned his head at the gurgle of water. A merling? No—a boat approaching slowly and softly from the direction

137

of Ilfish Water. He jumped down from the verandah and went to stand in the deep shade under the sombarilla tree.

The air was absolutely quiet. The water lay like polished moonstone. Glinnes squinted through the starlight and presently perceived a nondescript skiff with a single, rather frail person aboard. Akadie returning for his ozols? No. Glinnes' heart gave a queer quick throb. He started to step forward from the shade, then halted and drew back.

The boat drifted to the dock. The person aboard stepped ashore and dropped the mooring line over a bollard. Quietly through the starlight she came, and halted in front of the verandah. "Glinnes! Glinnes!" Her voice was hushed and secretive, like the call of a night bird.

Glinnes watched. Duissane stood indecisive, shoulders drooping. Then she went up on the verandah and looked into the dark house. "Glinnes!"

Glinnes came slowly forward. "I'm over here."

Duissane walked while he crossed the verandah. "Did you expect me?"

"No," said Glinnes. "Not really."

"Do you know why I came?"

Glinnes slowly shook his head. "But I am frightened."

Duissane laughed quietly. "Why should you be frightened?"

"Because once you gave me to the merlings."

"Are you afraid of death?" Duissane moved a step closer. "What is there to fear? I have no fear. A soft-winged black bird carries our ghosts to the Vale of Xian, and there we wander, at peace."

"The folk eaten by merlings leave no ghosts. And in this connection, where are your father and your brothers? Arriving by way of the forest?"

"No. They would grind their teeth if they knew I was here."

Glinnes said, "Walk around the house with me."

Without protest she came with him. To the best effort of Glinnes' senses, Rabendary Island was deserted except for themselves.

"Listen," said Duissane. "Hear the tree-croakers . . ."

Glinnes nodded shortly. "I heard them. There's no one in the forest."

"Then do you believe me?"

"You've told me only that your father and brothers aren't here. I believe that, because I can't see them."

138

"Let's go into the house."

Inside the house Glinnes turned up the light. Duissane dropped her cape. She wore only sandals and a thin frock. She carried no weapon.

"Today," she said, "I rode in a boat with Lord Gensifer, and I saw you. I decided that tonight I would come here."

"Why?" asked Glinnes, not altogether puzzled but not altogether certain.

Duissane put her hands on his shoulders. "Do you remember on the little island, how I jeered at you?"

"Very well indeed."

"You were too vulnerable. I longed for your harshness. I wanted you to laugh at my words, to take me and hold me close. I would have melted on that instant."

"You dissembled very well," said Glinnes. "As I remember, you called me 'despicable, untidy and gluttonous.' I was convinced that you hated me."

Duissane made a sad grimace. "I have never hated you—never. But you must know that I am solitary and wayward, and I am slow to love. Look at me now." She tilted up her face. "Do you think I am beautiful?"

"Oh indeed. I've never thought otherwise."

"Hold me close, then, and kiss me."

Glinnes turned his head and listened. From Rabendary Forest the susurration of the tree-croakers had never ceased. He looked back at the face close under his own. It swam with unusual emotions, which he could not define and which therefore troubled him; he had never seen such a look in any other eyes. He sighed; how difficult to love a person so intensely distrusted! How far more difficult not to do so! He bent his head and kissed Duissane. It was as if he had never kissed anyone before. She smelled of a fragrant herb, of lemon, and, vaguely, of wood-smoke. With his pulses racing, he knew he now could never turn back. If she had set out to enthrall him, she had succeeded; he felt he could never get enough of her. But what of Duissane? From around her neck she drew a heart-shaped tablet. Glinnes recognized it as a lovers' cauch. With nervous fingers Duissane broke the tablet and gave Glinnes half. "I have never touched cauch before," she said. "I have never wanted to love anyone before. Pour us a goblet of wine."

Glinnes brought a flask of green wine from the cupboard and poured full a goblet. He went to the verandah and looked up and down the water. It lay calm and dreaming, broken only by the ripple of a merling who somewhere had surfaced.

"What did you expect to see?" asked Duissane softly.

"Half a dozen Drossets," said Glinnes, "with eyes spurting fire and knives in their mouths."

"Glinnes," said Duissane earnestly, "I swear to you that no one knows I am here but you and me. Are you not aware of how my people regard virginity? They would spare me no more than you."

Glinnes brought the goblet of wine across the room. Duissane opened her mouth. "Do as a lover would."

Glinnes placed the cauch on the tip of her tongue; she washed it down with the wine. "Now you."

Glinnes opened his mouth. She put her half of the lovers' tablet upon his tongue. It might be cauch, thought Glinnes, or she might have substituted a soporific, or a poison drug. He held the tablet in front of his teeth, and taking the goblet, drank the wine, and then made shift to eject the tablet into the goblet. He took the goblet to the sideboard, then turned to face Duissane. She had slipped off her gown; she stood nude and graceful before him, and Glinnes never had seen so delightful a sight. And he was finally convinced that the male Drossets were not quietly approaching through the dark. He went to Duissane and kissed her; she loosened the fastenings of his shirt. He slipped from his clothes and, taking her to the couch, would have proceeded, but she rose to her knees and held his head to her breast. He could hear her heart thumping; he felt sure her emotion was genuine. She whispered, "I have been cruel, but this is all past. Henceforth, I live only to exalt you, to make you the happiest of men, and you shall never regret it."

"You intend to live here with me on Rabendary?" inquired Glinnes, both cautious and puzzled.

"My father would kill me first," sighed Duissane. "You cannot imagine his hate . . . We must fly to a far world and there live as aristocrats. Perhaps we shall buy a space-yacht and wander among the colored stars."

Glinnes laughed. "All very well, but all this requires money."

"No problem there; we will use the thirty million ozols."

Glinnes somberly shook his head. "I am sure Akadie would object to this."

"How can Akadie deny us? My father and my brothers robbed him tonight. His case contained trash. He had the money today in the boat and he has been nowhere but here. He left the money here, did he not?" And Duissane peered into Glinnes' face.

Glinnes smiled. "Akadie left a parcel in my bait-box, for a fact." And now he would wait no longer and drew her down to the couch.

They lay engaged, and Duissane, her face rapt, looked up at Glinnes. "You will take me from Trullion, and off and away? I so want to live in wealth."

Glinnes kissed her nose. "Sh!" he whispered. "Be happy with what we have now and here . . ."

But she said, "Tell me, tell me that you'll do as I ask."

"I can't," said Glinnes. "All I can give you is myself and Rabendary."

Duissane's voice became anxious. "But what of the parcel in the bait-box?"

"That's trash too. Akadie has fooled us all. Or someone else swindled him before he left Welgen."

Duissane stiffened. "You mean that there is no money here?"

"So far as I know, not an ozol."

Duissane moaned, and the sound rose in her throat to become a wail of grief for her lost virginity. She tore herself free from the embrace and ran across the dim room, out on the dock. She opened the bait-box, and pulling out the foil-wrapped package, tore it open. At the sight of the waste paper she cried out in agony. Glinnes watched from the doorway, rueful, grim and sad, but by no means bewildered. Duissane had loved him well enough, as well as she could. Heedless of her nakedness she ran blindly down the dock and jumped into her boat, but missed her footing and toppled screaming into the water. A splash, and her voice became a gurgle.

Glinnes raced down the dock and jumped into her boat. Her pale form floundered six feet beyond his reach. In the starlight he saw her terrified face—she could not swim. Ten feet behind her appeared the oily black dome of a merling head, with eye-disks glowing silver. Glinnes gave a hoarse call of desperation and reached for Duissane. The merling wallowed close and seized her ankle. Glinnes jumped at its head and managed to strike it between the eyes with his fist, which damaged his knuckles and perhaps surprised the merling. Duissane seized Glinnes in a frantic drowner's grip, and wrapped her legs around his neck. Glinnes swallowed water.

He wrenched the girl loose and, gaining the surface, thrust her toward the boat. A merling's palp seized his ankle, and this was the nightmare that haunted every mind of Trullion—to be dragged alive down to the merlings' dinner table. Glinnes kicked like a maniac; his heel ground into the merling's maw. He twisted and broke loose. Duissane clung whimpering to the dock piling. Glinnes floundered to the ladder; he clambered into the boat and pulled her over the gunwales and aboard. They lay limp and gasping like netted fish.

Something bumped the bottom of the boat—a disappointed merling. It might try to tip the boat in its hunger. Glinnes staggered onto the dock, pulled Duissane up after him, and took her back along the starlit path to the house.

She stood, withdrawn and miserable, in the middle of the room, while Glinnes poured two goblets of Olanche rum. Duissane drank apathetically thinking her own dreary thoughts. Glinnes rubbed her dry with a towel, and himself as well, then took her to the couch, where she began to cry. He stroked her and kissed her cheeks and forehead. Gradually she became warm and relaxed. Cauch worked in her blood; the thought of dark still water thrilled her mind; she became responsive and again they embraced.

Early in the morning Duissane rose from the couch and without words donned her gown and her sandals. Glinnes watched, dispassionate and lethargic, as if seeing her through a telescope. When she drew the cape around her shoulders, he sat up. "Where are you going?"

Duissane threw him the briefest of side-glances; her expression stilled the words in his mouth. He rose from the couch, wrapped a paray around his waist. Duissane was already out the door. Glinnes followed her down the path and out upon the dock, trying to think of something to say that would sound neither hollow nor petulant.

Duissane stepped into her boat. She turned him a flat glance and then departed. Glinnes stood looking after her, his mind whirling and confined. Why did she act so? She had come to him; he had solicited nothing, offered nothing . . . He discerned his error. It was necessary, he told himself, to see the situation from the Trevanyi point of view. He had seared her extravagant Trevanyi pride. He had accepted from her something of immeasurable value; he had returned nothing, let alone that which she had hoped to receive. He was callous, shallow, unfeeling; he had made a fool of her.

There were further, darker implications deriving from the

142

Trevanyi world view. He was not just Glinnes Hulden, not just a lecherous Trill; he represented dark Fate, the hostile Cosmic Soul against which the Trevanyi felt themselves in heroic opposition. For the Trills, life flowed with mindless ease—that which was not here today would arrive tomorrow; in the meantime it was negligible. Life itself was pleasure. For the Trevanyi, each event was a portent to be examined in all aspects and tested for consequences and aftermath. He shaped his universe piece by piece. Any advantage or stroke of luck was a personal victory to be celebrated and gloated over; any misfortune or setback, no matter how slight, was a defeat and an insult to his self-esteem. Duissane had therefore suffered psychological disaster, and by his instrumentality, even though from the Trill point of view, he had only accepted what had been freely offered.

Heavy at heart, Glinnes turned back to the house. His eye fell on the bait-box. A curious idea entered his mind. He raised the lid and looked within. There—the foil-wrapped parcel of wastepaper, which he took forth. He raked his fingers into the bottom layer of chaff and sawdust and encountered an object which proved to be a packet wrapped in transparent film. Glinnes saw pink and black Bank of Alastor certificates. Akadie had employed a sly trick to hide the money. Glinnes mused a moment, then took the foil-wrapped packet, discarded the wastepaper. He used the foil to wrap the money, which he replaced in the bait-box. Scarcely had he finished when he heard the sound of an approaching boat.

Down Farwan Water came Akadie's white boat, with two passengers: Akadie and Glay. The boat coasted up to the dock; Glinnes took the line and dropped the loop over the bollard.

Akadie and Glay jumped up on the dock. "Good morning," said Akadie in a voice of subdued cheer. He examined Glinnes with a clinical eye. "You are pale."

"I slept poorly," said Glinnes, "what with worrying over your money."

"It is safe, I hope?" asked Akadie brightly.

"Duissane Drosset looked at it," said Glinnes ingenuously. "For some reason she let it lie."

"Duissane! How did she know it was there?"

"She asked where it was; I told her that you had left a packet in the bait-box. She claims that it contains only wastepaper."

Akadie laughed. "My little joke. I concealed the money

143

rather cunningly, I do believe." Akadie went to the bait-box, removed the foil-wrapped package, which he dropped to the dock, and reached through the layer of chaff. His face froze. "The money is gone!' '

"Imagine that!" said Glinnes. "It is hard to believe Duissane Drosset a thief."

Akadie scarcely heard him. In a voice strained with fear he cried, "Tell me, where is the money? Bandolio will not be kind; he'll send men to tear me apart . . . Where, oh where? Did Duissane take the money?"

Glinnes could torment Akadie no further. He nudged the foil-wrapped packet with his toe. "What's this?"

Akadie swooped at the packet and tore it open. He looked up at Glinnes in gratitude and exasperation. "How wicked, to bait a man already on tenterhooks!"

Glinnes grinned. "What now will you do with the money?"

"As before, I wait for instructions."

Glinnes looked at Glay. "And what of you? Still a Fanscher, it seems."

"Naturally."

"What of your headquarters, or central institute—whatever you call it?"

"We have claimed a tract of open land not too far from here, at the head of the Karbashe Valley."

"At the head of the Karbashe? Is that not the Vale of Xian?"

"The Vale of Xian is close at hand."

"A strange choice of location," said Glinnes.

"How strange?" retorted Glay. "The land is free and unoccupied."

"Except for the Trevanyi death-bird and uncounted Trevanyi souls."

"We will not disturb their occupancy, and I doubt if they will trouble ours. The land will be used in joint tenancy, so to speak."

"What then of my twelve thousand ozols, if your land is coming so cheap?"

"Never mind the twelve thousand ozols. We have sufficiently discussed the matter."

Akadie had already stepped into his boat. "Come along then; let us return to Rorquin before thieves appear on the river."

# Chapter 17

★ ★ ★

Glinnes watched the white boat until it disappeared. He examined the sky. Heavy clouds hung over the mountains and loomed against the sun. The water of Ambal Broad seemed heavy and listless. Ambal Isle was a charcoal sketch on mauve-gray broad. Glinnes went up to the verandah and eased himself into one of the old string chairs. The events of last night, so rich and dramatic, now seemed stuff built of dream-vapor. Glinnes took no pleasure in the recollection. Duissane's motives, however ingenuous, had not been altogether false; he might have mocked her and sent her home in anger, but not in shame. How different everything seemed in the ashen light of day! . . . He jumped to his feet, annoyed at the uncomfortable trend of his thoughts. He would work. There was much to be done. He could pick musk-apples. He could go to the forest and gather pepperwort for drying. He could spade up the garden plot. He could repair the shed, which was about to collapse. The prospect of so much effort made him drowsy; he took himself inside to his couch and slept.

About midday he awoke to the sound of light rain on the roof. Glinnes drew a cloak over himself and lay pondering. Somewhere at the back of his mind hung a dark urgency, a matter requiring attention. Hussade practice? Lute Casagave? Akadie? Glay? Duissane? What about Duissane? She had come, she had gone, and would no longer wear a yellow flower in her hair. She might do so anyway, to hide the facts from Vang Drosset. On the other hand, she might risk his fury and tell him all. More likely, she might present an altered version of her nocturnal adventures. This possibility, already recognized by his subconscious, now caused Glinnes overt uneasiness. He rose to his feet and went to the door. A silver drizzle obscured much of Ambal Broad, but so far as Glinnes could detect, no boats were abroad. The Trevanyi, nomads by nature, considered rain an unlucky portent; not

145

even to wreak vengeance would a Trevanyi set forth in the rain.

Glinnes rummaged through the larder and found a dish of cold boiled mudworm, which he ate without appetite. Then the rain came to a sudden halt; sunlight spread across Ambal Broad. Glinnes went out on the verandah. All the world was fresh and wet, the colors clarified, the water glistening, the sky pure. Glinnes felt a lift of the spirits.

There was work to be done. He lowered himself into the string chair to consider the matter. A boat entered Ambal Broad from Ilfish Water. Glinnes jumped to his feet, tense and wary. But the boat was only one of Harrad's rental draft. The occupant, a young man in a semi-official uniform, had lost his way. He steered up to Rabendary dock and rose to stand on the seat. "Halloo there," he called to Glinnes. "I'm more than half lost. I want Clinkhammer Broad, near Sarpassante Island."

"You're far south. Who are you looking for?"

The young man consulted a paper. "A certain Janno Akadie."

"Up Farwan Water into the Saur, take the second channel to the left, and continue all the way into Clinkhammer Broad. Akadie's manse stands on a jut."

"Very good; the route is clear in my mind. Aren't you Glinnes Hulden, the Tanchinaro?"

"I'm Glinnes Hulden, true enough."

"I saw you play the Elements. It wasn't much of a contest, as I recall."

"They're a young team, and reckless, but I'd consider them basically sound."

"Yes, that's my opinion as well. So then—good luck to the Tanchinaros, and thank you for your help."

The boat moved up Farwan Water past the silver and russet pomanders and out of sight, and Glinnes was left thinking about the Tanchinaros. They had not practiced since the game with the Kanchedos; they had no money; they had no sheirl . . . Glinnes' thoughts veered to Duissane, who never again could be sheirl, and then to Vang Drosset, who might or might not be aware of the events of last night. Glinnes looked across Ambal Broad. No boats could be seen. He went to the telephone and called Akadie.

The screen glowed: Akadie's face was unwontedly peevish, and his voice was fretful. "Gong, gong, gong is all I hear.

The telephone is a dubious convenience. I'm expecting a distinguished visitor and I don't care to be annoyed."

"Indeed!" said Glinnes. "Is he a young man in a pale-blue uniform and a messenger's cap?"

"Naturally not!" declared Akadie. His voice caught abruptly. "Why do you ask?"

"A few minutes ago such a man inquired the way to your house."

"I'll watch for him. Is that all you wanted?"

"I thought I might come by later today and borrow twenty thousand ozols."

"Puh! Where would I find twenty thousand ozols?"

"I know one place."

Akadie gave a sour chuckle. "You must borrow from someone more intent on suicide than myself." The screen went dead.

Glinnes ruminated a moment but could contrive no further excuses for idleness. He took crates out into the orchard and picked apples, working with the irritable energy of a Trill caught up in an activity which he considers a barely necessary evil. Twice he heard the gong of his telephone, but he ignored it, and thus knew nothing of a fateful event which had occurred earlier that day. He picked a dozen crates of apples, loaded them on a barrow which he trundled to a shed, then returned to the orchard to pick more and finish the job.

Afternoon waned; the dismal light of avness altered to the gunmetal, old rose and eggplant of evening. Stubbornly Glinnes worked on. A cold wind blew down from the mountains and struck through his shirt. Was more rain on the way? No. The stars already were showing—no rain tonight. He loaded the last of his apples on the barrow and started for the storage shed.

Glinnes halted. The door to the shed was half ajar. Only half ajar. Odd, when he purposely had left it open. Glinnes set down the barrow and returned into the orchard to think. He was not wholly surprised; in fact, he had gone to the unusual precaution of carrying his gun in his pocket. From the corner of his eye he looked back toward the shed. There would be one within, one behind, and a third lurking at the corner of the house, or so he suspected. In the orchard he had been beyond the range of a thrown knife, and in any event they would hardly want to kill him outright. First there would be words, then cutting and twisting and burning, to ensure that he derived no advantage whatsoever from his offense. Glinnes licked his lips. His stomach felt hollow and odd . . . What to do? He could not stand much longer in the twilight pretending to admire his apple crop.

He walked without haste around the side of the house; then, picking up a stave, he ran back and waited at the corner. There were running footsteps, a mutter of rapid words. Around the corner bounded a dark shape. Glinnes swung the stick; the man threw up his arm and took the blow on his wrist; he uttered a yell of distress. Glinnes swung the stick again; the man caught the stick under his arm. Glinnes tugged; the two swung and reeled together. Then someone else was on him, a man heavy, smelling of sweat, roaring in rage—Vang Drosset. Glinnes jumped back and fired his gun. He missed Vang Drosset but struck Harving, the first man, who groaned and tottered away. A third dark shape loomed from nowhere and grappled Glinnes; the two struggled while Vang Drosset danced close, his throaty rageful roar never ceasing. Glinnes fired his gun, but he could not aim and burnt the ground at Vang Drosset's feet; Vang Drosset leapt clumsily into the air. Glinnes kicked and stamped and broke the grip of Ashmor, but not before Vang Drosset had dealt him a blow to knock his head askew and daze him. In return Glinnes managed to kick Ashmor in the groin, sending him staggering against the wall of the house. Harving, on the ground, made a convulsive motion; a metallic flicker stung Glinnes shoulder. Glinnes fired his gun; Harving slumped and was limp.

"Merling food," gasped Glinnes. "Who else? You, Vang Drosset? You? Don't move; don't even stir, or I'll burn a hole through your gut."

Vang Drosset froze; Ashmor leaned against the side wall. "Walk ahead of me," said Glinnes. "Out on the dock." When Vang Drosset hesitated, Glinnes picked up the stave and struck him over the head. "I'll teach you to come murdering me, my fine Trevanyi bullies. You'll regret this night, I assure you . . . Move! Out on the dock. Go ahead, run off if you dare. I might miss you in the dark." Glinnes plied the stave. "Move!"

The two Drossets lurched out on the dock, numbed by the failure of their mission. Glinnes beat them until they lay down, and beat them further until they seemed dazed; then he tied them with odd bits of cordage.

"So there you are, my fine lummoxes. Now then, which of

148

you killed my brother Shira? . . . Oh, you don't feel like talking? Well, I won't beat you further, though I well recall another time when you left me for the merlings. Now I must explain to you—Vang do you hear me? Speak, Vang Drosset, answer me."

"I hear you well enough."

"Listen then. Did you kill my brother Shira?"

"What if I did? It was my right. He gave cauch to my young girl; it was my right to kill him. And my right to kill you."

"So Shira gave cauch to your daughter."

"That he did, the varmous* Trill horn."

"So now, what happens to you?"

Vang Drosset was silent a moment, then he blurted, "You can kill me or cut me apart, but that's the good it'll do you."

"Here is my bargain," said Glinnes. "Write out a notification that you killed Shira—"

"I know no characters. I'll write you nothing."

"Then before witnesses you must declare that you killed Shira—"

"And then the prutanshyr? Aha!"

"Provide your own reasons; at this time I don't care. Assert that he struck you with a club or molested your daughter or called your wife a varmous old crow—no matter. Declare the affidavit and I'll let you go free, and you must swear by your father's soul to leave me in peace. Otherwise I'll roll both you and yonder murderous Ashmor into the mud and leave you for the merlings."

Vang Drosset moaned and strained at his bonds. His son raved: "Swear as you will; it won't include me! I'll kill him if it takes forever!"

"Hold your tongue," said Vang Drosset in a weary croak. "We are beaten; we must slink for our lives." To Glinnes: "Once more—what do you want?"

Glinnes restated his terms.

"And you won't prefer a legal charge? I tell you the great sweating horn thrust cauch at her and would have rolled her in the meadow yonder . . ."

"I'll prefer no legal charge."

The son sneered. "What about gelding or nose-cutting? Will you leave us our members?"

* varmous: dirty, infamous, scurrilous; an adjective often applied to the Trills.

"I have no need for your filthy members," said Glinnes. "Keep them for yourself."

Vang Drosset gave a sudden furious groan. "And what of my daughter whom you ravished, whom you fed cauch, whose value has now decreased? Will you pay the loss? Instead you kill my son and utter threats against me."

"Your daughter made her own way here. I asked nothing of her. She brought cauch. She seduced me."

Vang Drosset chattered in rage. His son cried out a set of obscene threats. Vang Drosset at last became tired and commanded his son to silence. To Glinnes he said, "I agree to the bargain."

Glinnes freed the son. "Take your corpse and be off with you."

"Go," droned Vang Drosset.

Glinnes pulled his own boat close beside the dock and rolled Vang Drosset into the bilges. Then he went into the house and called Akadie, but could make no connection; Akadie had turned off his telephone. Glinnes returned to his boat and drove up Farwan Water at full speed, pale foam veering to either side.

"Where are you taking me?" groaned Vang Drosset.

"To see Akadie the mentor."

Vang Drosset groaned again, but made no comment.

The boat nosed up to the dock under Akadie's eccentric house. Glinnes cut Vang Drosset's legs loose and hoisted him up to the dock. Tripping and stumbling, they proceeded up the path. Lights blazed from the towers, glaring into Glinnes' face. Akadie's voice came sharp, from a loudspeaker. "Who arrives? Announce yourself, if you please."

"Glinnes Hulden and Vang Drosset, on the path!" bawled Glinnes.

"An unlikely pair of chums," sneered the voice. "I believe I mentioned that I was occupied this evening?"

"I require your professional services!"

"Come forward then."

When they reached the house the door stood ajar, with light streaming forth. Glinnes shoved Vang Drosset forward and into the house.

Akadie appeared. "And what business is this?"

"Vang Drosset has decided to clarify the matter of Shira's death," said Glinnes.

"Very well," said Akadie. "I have a guest, and I hope that you will be brief."

"The affair is important," Glinnes declared gruffly. "It must be conducted correctly."

Akadie merely motioned toward the study. Glinnes cut Vang Drosset's arms free and thrust him forward.

The study was dim and peaceful. A pink-orange fire of driftwood blazed in the fireplace. A man arose from one of the fireside chairs and performed a polite inclination of the head. Glinnes, his attention fixed on Vang Drosset, spared him only a glance and received an impression of medium stature, neutral garments, a face without notable or distinctive characteristics.

Akadie, perhaps recalling the events of the previous day, recovered something of his graciousness. He addressed his guest. "May I present Glinnes Hulden, my good neighbor, and also"—Akadie made an urbane gesture—"Vang Drosset, a member of that peregrine race, the Trevanyi. Glinnes and Vang Drosset, I wish to present a man of wide intellectual scope and considerable erudition, who interests himself in our small corner of the cluster. He is Ryl Shermatz. From the evidence of his jade locket, I believe his home world to be Balmath. Am I correct in this?"

"As correct as needful," said Shermatz. "I am indeed familiar with Balmath. But otherwise you flatter me. I am a wandering journalist, no more. Please ignore me, and proceed with your business. If you require privacy I will remove myself."

"No reason why that should be necessary," said Glinnes. "Please resume your seat." He turned to Akadie. "Vang Drosset wishes to utter a sworn information before you, a legally accredited witness, which in effect will clarify the title of Rabendary and Ambal Isle." He nodded to Vang Drosset. "Proceed, if you will."

Vang Drosset licked his lips. "Shira Hulden, a dastardly horn, assaulted my daughter. He offered her cauch and attempted to force her. I came on the scene, and in the protection of my property accidentally killed him. He is dead and there you have it." The last was a growl toward Glinnes.

Glinnes inquired of Akadie, "Does this constitute a valid proof of Shira's death?"

Akadie spoke to Vang Drosset. "Do you swear by your father's soul that you have spoken the truth?"

"Yes," grumbled Vang Drosset. "Mind you, it was self-defense."

"Very good," said Akadie. "The confession was freely
151

made before a mentor and public counselor and other witnesses. The confession holds legal weight."

"Be good enough, in this case, to telephone Lute Casagave and order him off my property."

Akadie pulled at his chin. "Do you propose to refund his money?"

"Let him collect from the man to whom he paid it—Glay Hulden."

Akadie shrugged. "I naturally must regard this as professional work, and I must charge you a fee."

"I expected nothing less."

Akadie went off to his telephone. Vang Drosset said in a surly voice, "Are you done? At my camp there'll be great grief tonight, and all due to the Huldens."

"The grief is due to your own murderousness," said Glinnes. "Need I go into details? Never forget how you left me for dead in the mud."

Vang Drosset marched sullenly to the door, where he turned and blurted, "No matter what, it's fair exchange for the shame you put on us, you and all the other Trills, with your gluttony and lust. Horns all of you! Guts and groins, so much for the Trills. And you, Glinnes Hulden, stay out of my way; you won't have it so easy next time." He turned and stamped from the house.

Akadie, returning to the study, watched him go with nostrils fastidiously pinched. "You had best guard your boat," he told Glinnes. "Otherwise he'll drive away and leave you to swim."

Glinnes stood in the doorway and watched Vang Drosset's burly form recede along the road. "He carries grief too heavy for the boat, or any other mischief. He'll find his way home by Verleth Bridge. What of Lute Casagave?"

"He refuses to answer his telephone," said Akadie. "You must postpone your triumph."

"Then you must postpone your fee," said Glinnes. "Did the messenger find his way here?"

"Yes indeed," said Akadie. "I can justly say that he carried away a great load of my responsibilities. I am gratified to be done with the business."

"In that case, perhaps you have a cup of tea to offer me? Or is your business with Ryl Shermatz absolutely private?"

"You may have tea," said Akadie ungraciously. "The conversation is general. Ryl Shermatz is interested in the Fanscherade. He wonders how a world so generous and easy could breed so austere a sect."

"I suppose we must consider Junius Farfan as a catalyst," remarked Shermatz. "Or perhaps, for better comparison, let us think in terms of a super-saturated solution. It seems placid and stable, but in a single microscopic crystal produces disequilibrium."

"A striking image!" declared Akadie. "Allow me to pour out a drop of something more energetic than tea."

"Why not indeed?" Shermatz stretched out his legs to the fire. "You have a most comfortable home."

"Yes, it is pleasant!" Akadie went to fetch a bottle.

Glinnes asked Shermatz, "I hope that you find Trullion entertaining?"

"I do indeed. Each world of the cluster projects a mood of its own, and the sensitive traveler quickly learns to identify and savor this individuality. Trullion, for instance, is calm and gentle; its waters reflect the stars. The light is mild; the landscapes and waterscapes are entrancing."

"This gentle aspect is what strikes the eye," agreed Akadie, "but sometimes I wonder as to its reality. For instance, under these placid waters swim merlings, creatures as unpleasant as any, and these calm Trill faces conceal terrible forces."

"Come now," said Glinnes. "You exaggerate."

"By no means! Have you ever heard a hussade crowd cry out to spare the conquered sheirl? Never! She must be denuded to the music of—of what? The emotion has no name, but it is as rich as blood."

"Bah," said Glinnes. "Hussade is played everywhere."

Akadie ignored him. "Then there is the prutanshyr. Amazing to watch the rapt faces as some wretched criminal demonstrates how dreadful the process of dying can be."

"The prutanshyr may serve a useful purpose," said Shermatz. "The effects of such affairs are difficult to judge."

"Not from the standpoint of the miscreant," said Akadie. "Is this not a bitter way to die, to look out upon the fascinated throng, to know that your spasms are providing a repast of entertainment?"

"It is not a private or sedate occasion," said Shermatz with a sad smile. "Still, the folk of Trullion seem to consider the prutanshyr a necessary institution, and so it persists."

"It is a disgrace, to Trullion and to Alastor Cluster," said Akadie coldly. "The Connatic should ban all such barbarity."

Shermatz rubbed his chin. "There is something in what you

153

say. Still, the Connatic hesitates to interfere with local customs."

"A double-edged virtue! We rely upon him for wise decisions. Whether or not you love the Fanschers, at least they despise the prutanshyr and would obliterate the institution. If they ever come to power they will do so."

"No doubt they would expunge hussade as well," said Glinnes.

"By no means," said Akadie. "The Fanschers are indifferent to the game; it has no meaning for them, one way or the other."

"What a grim fastidious lot!" said Glinnes.

"They seem even more so by contrast with their varmous parents," said Akadie.

"No doubt true," said Ryl Shermatz. "Still, one must note that an extreme philosophy often provokes its antithesis."

"That is the case here on Trillion," said Akadie. "I warned you that the idyllic atmosphere is delusive."

A glare of light flooded the study, persisting only a moment. Akadie uttered an ejaculation and went to the window, followed by Glinnes. They saw a great white cruiser coming slowly across Clinkhammer Broad; the masthead searchlight playing along the shore, briefly touching Akadie's manse, had illuminated the study.

Akadie said in a wondering voice, "I believe it's the *Scopoeia*, Lord Rianle's yacht. Why should it be here in Clinkhammer Broad, of all places?"

A boat left the yacht and made for Akadie's dock; simultaneously the horn sounded three peremptory blasts. Akadie muttered under his breath and ran from the house. Ryl Shermatz wandered here and there about the room inspecting Akadie's clutter of mementos, bric-a-brac, curios. A cabinet diplayed Akadie's collection of small busts, each one or another of the personages who had shaped the history of Alastor—scholars, scientists, warriors, philosophers, poets, musicians, and on the bottom shelf, a formidable array of anti-heroes. "Interesting," said Ryl Shermatz. "Our history has been rich, and the histories before ours as well."

Glinnes pointed out a particular bust. "There you see Akadie himself, who fancies himself one with the immortals."

Shermatz chuckled. "Since Akadie has assembled the group, he must be allowed the right to include whom he pleases."

Glinnes went to the window in time to see the boat returning to the yacht. A moment later, Akadie entered the room, face ash-gray and hair hanging in lank strings.

"What's wrong with you?" demanded Glinnes. "You look like a ghost."

"That was Lord Rianle," croaked Akadie. "The father of Lord Erzan-Rianle, who was kidnaped. He wants his hundred thousand ozols back."

Glinnes stared in amazement. "Will he leave his son to rot?"

Akadie went to the alcove where he kept his telephone and switched the set back into operation. Turning back to Shermatz and Glinnes, he said, "The Whelm raided Bandolios' haven. They captured Bandolio, all his men and ships; they liberated the captives Bandolio took at Welgen, and many more besides."

"Excellent news!" said Glinnes. "So why walk around like a dead man?"

"This afternoon I sent away the money. The thirty million ozols are gone."

# Chapter 18

★ ★ ★

Glinnes led Akadie to a chair. "Sit down, drink this wine." He turned a glance toward Ryl Shermatz, who stood looking into the fire. "Tell me, how did you send the money off?"

"By the messenger you directed here. He carried the correct symbol; I gave him the parcel; he went away, and that is all there is to it."

"You don't know the messenger?"

"I have never seen him before." Akadie's wits seemed to snap back in place. He glared at Glinnes. "You seem very concerned!"

"Should I be uninterested in thirty million ozols?"

"How is that you did not hear the news? It's been current since noon! Everyone has been trying to telephone me."

"I was working in my orchard. I paid no heed to the telephone."

"The money belongs to the people who paid the ransoms," declared Akadie in a stern voice.

"Indisputably. But whoever retrieves it might legitimately claim a good fee."

"Bah," muttered Akadie. "Have you no shame?"

The gong sounded. Akadie gave a nervous start and stumbled to the telephone. After a moment he returned. "Lord Gygax also wants his hundred thousand ozols. He won't believe that I sent off the money. He became insistent, even somewhat insulting."

The gong sounded again. "You are in for a busy evening," said Glinnes, rising to his feet.

"Are you going?" asked Akadie in a pitiful voice.

"Yes. If I were you I'd turn the telephone off again." He bowed to Ryl Shermatz. "A pleasure to have met you."

Glinnes drove his boat at full speed west across Clinkhammer Broad, under the Verleth Bridge, down Mellish Water. Ahead shone a dozen dim lights: Saurkash. Glinnes drifted into the dock, moored his boat and jumped ashore. Saurkash was quiet except for a few muffled voices and a laugh or two from the nearby Magic Tench. Glinnes walked along the dock to Harrad's boat agency. An overhead light shone down on the rental boats. He went to the shop and looked in through the door. Young Harrad was nowhere to be seen, though a light glowed in the office. One of the men at the tavern rose to his feet and ambled down to the dock. It was Young Harrad. "Yes, sir, what might you be wanting? If it's boat repair, nothing till tomorrow . . . Ah, Squire Hulden, I didn't recognize you under the light."

"No matter," said Glinnes. "Today I saw a young man in one of your boats, a hussade player I'm anxious to locate. Do you recall his name?"

"Today? About mid-afternoon, or a trifle earlier?"

"That would be about the time."

"I've got it written down inside. A hussade player, you say. He didn't look the type. Still, you never know. What's next for the Tanchinaros?"

"We'll be back in action soon. Whenever we can collect ten thousand ozols for a treasury. The weak teams won't play us."

"For good reason! Well, let's look at the register . . . This might well be his name." Young Harrad turned the ledger first one way, then the other. "Schill Sodergang, or so I make it out. No address."

156

"No address? And you don't know where he can be found?"

"Perhaps I should be more careful," Young Harrad apologized. "I've never yet lost a boat, except when old Zax went blind on soursap."

"Did Sodergang have anything to say to you? Anything whatever?"

"Nothing much, except to ask the way to Akadie's house."

"And when he came back—what then?"

"He asked what time the Port Maheul boat came past. He had to wait an hour."

"He had a black case with him?"

"Why yes, he did."

"Did he talk to anyone?"

"He just sat dozing on the beach yonder."

"It's no great matter," said Glinnes. "I'll see him another time."

Glinnes drove pell-mell down the dark waterways, past the groves of silent trees, black stencils fringed with star-silver. At midnight he arrived in Welgen. He slept at a dockside inn and early in the morning boarded the east-bound ferry.

Port Maheul, named for its busy space-field rather than its site on the shores of the South Ocean, was the largest town of Jolany Prefecture and perhaps the oldest city of Trullion. The principal structures were built to archaic standards of solidity with glazed russet brick, timbers of ageless black salpoon, and steep roofs sheathed with blue glass shingles. The square was reckoned as picturesque as any in Merlank, with its perimeter of ancient buildings, black sulpicella trees, and herringbone pavement of russet-brown bricks and cobbles of mountain hornblende. At the center stood the prutanshyr, with its glass caldron, through the sides of which a criminal being boiled and the rapt crowd might inspect each other. Off the square sprawled an untidy market, then a clutter of ramshackle little houses, then the gaunt glass and iron space depot. The field extended east to the Genglin Marshes, where, so it was said, the merlings crept up through the mud and reeds to marvel at the spaceships coming and going.

Glinnes spent a toilsome three days in Port Maheul searching for Schill Sodergang. The steward of the ferry that plied between the Fens and Port Maheul vaguely remembered Sodergang as a passenger, but could recall nothing else, not even

Sodergang's point of debarkation. The town roster listed no Sodergangs, nor was the name known to the constabulary.

Glinnes visited the spaceport. A ship of the Andrujukha Line had departed Port Maheul on the day following Sodergang's visit to the Fens, but the name Sodergang failed to appear on the manifest.

On the afternoon of the third day Glinnes returned to Welgen, and then by his own boat to Saurkash. Here he encountered Young Harrad, whom he found bursting with sensational information, and Glinnes had to delay his own questions to listen to Young Harrad's gossip—which was absorbing enough in itself. It seemed that an act of boldest villainy had been effected almost under Young Harrad's nose, so to speak. Akadie, whom Young Harrad never had wholly trusted, was the cool culprit who had decided to seize opportunity by the forelock and sequester to himself thirty million ozols.

Glinnes gave incredulous laugh. "Sheer absurdity!"

"Absurdity?" Young Harrad looked to see if Glinnes was serious. "The lords all hold this opinion; can so many be wrong? They refuse to believe that Akadie closed off his telephone on the precise day that news of Bandolio's capture arrived."

Glinnes snorted in disparagement. "I did exactly the same thing. Am I a criminal on that account?"

Young Harrad shrugged. "Someone is thirty million ozols the richer. Who? The proof is not yet explicit, but Akadie has helped himself not at all by his actions."

"Come now! What else has he done?"

"He has joined Fanscherade! He's now a Fanscher. It's the common belief that they took him in because of the money."

Glinnes clutched his spinning head. "Akadie a Fanscher? I can't believe it. He's too clever to join a group of freaks!"

Young Harrad stuck to his guns. "Why did he depart in the dark of the night and travel up to the Vale of Green Ghosts? And remember, for ever so long he has worn Francher clothes and aped the Francher style.

"Akadie is merely somewhat silly. He enjoys a fad."

Young Harrad sniffed. "He can enjoy what he likes now, that's certain. In a way, I respect such audacity, but when thirty million ozols are at stake a switched-off telephone sounds pretty thin."

"What else could he say except the truth? I saw the switched-off telephone myself."

"Well, I'm sure the truth will be made clear. Did you ever find that hussade player, Jorcom, Jarcom, whatever his name?"

"Jorcom? Jarcom?" Glinnes stared in wonder. "Sodergang, you mean?"

Young Harrad grinned sheepishly. "That was somebody else, a fisherman down Isley Broad. I wrote the name in the wrong place."

Glinnes controlled his voice with an effort. "The man's name is Jorcom, then? Or Jarcom?"

"Let's take a look," said young Harrad. He brought out his register. "Here's Sodergang, and here is the other name; it looks like Jarcom to me. He wrote it himself."

"It looks like Jarcom," said Glinnes. "Or is it Jarcony?"

"Jarcony!" You're right! That's the name he used. What position does he play?"

"Position? Rover. I'll have to look him up sometime. Except that I don't know where he lives." He looked at Young Harrad's clock. If he drove at breakneck speed back to Welgen he could just barely connect with the Port Maheul ferry. He made a gesticulation of fury and frustration, then jumped in his boat and hurtled back east toward Welgen.

In Port Maheul, Glinnes found the name "Jarcony" as unknown as "Sodergang." Tired and bored beyond caring, he took himself to the arbor in front of the Stranger's Rest and ordered a flask of wine. Someone had discarded a journal; Glinnes picked it up and scanned the page. His eyes was caught by an article:

## AN ILL-FATED HOSTILITY AGAINST THE FANSCHERS

Yesterday news reached Port Maheul of an improper act commited by a Trevanyi gang against the Fanscher camp in the Vale of Green Ghosts, or, as the Trevanyi know it, the Vale of Xian. The Trevanyi motives are in doubt. It is known that they resent the Fanscher presence in their sacred vale. But also it will be remembered that the mentor Janno Akadie, for many years resident in the Saurkash region, has declared himself a Fanscher and now resides at the Fanscher camp. Speculation links Akadie with a sum of thirty million ozols, which Akadie claims to have paid to the starmenter Sagmondo Bandolio, but which Bandolio denies having received. It is possible that the leader of the Trevanyi gang, a certain Vang Drosset, apparently decided that Akadie had taken the money with him into the Vale of Green Ghosts, and so organized the raid. The facts are these: seven Trevanyi entered Akadie's tent during the night, but failed to stifle his outcries. A number of Fanschers responded to the call and in the ensuing fight two Trevanyi were killed and several others wounded. Those who escaped took refuge at a Trevanyi conclave nearby, where sacred rites are in progress. Needless to say, the Trevanyi failed to possess themselves of the thirty million ozols, which evidently has been hidden securely. The Fanschers are outraged by the attack, which they deem an act of persecution.

"We fought like karpouns," declared a Fanscher spokesman. "We attack no one, but will fiercely protect our rights. The future is for Fanscherade! We summon the youth of Merlank, and all those opposed to the varmous old life-ways: join Fanscherade! Lend us your strength and comradeship!"

Chief Constable Filidice declares himself perturbed by the circumstance and has launched an investigation. "No further disruptions of the public peace will be tolerated," he stated.

Glinnes threw the journal across the table. Slumping into his chair he poured half a goblet of wine down his throat. The world he knew and loved seemed in fragments. Fanschers and Fanscherade! Lute Casagave, Lord Ambal! Jorcom, Jarcom, Jarcony, Sodergang! He despised each of the names!

He finished the wine, then went down to the dock to wait for the boat back to Welgen.

# Chapter 19

★ ★ ★

Rabendary Island seemed unnaturally still and lonesome. An hour after Glinnes' return the gong sounded; he discovered his mother's face on the telephone screen.

"I thought you'd gone to join the Fanschers," said Glinnes in a voice of hollow jocularity.

"No, no, not I." Marucha's voice was fretful and worried. "Janno went to avoid the confusion. You can't conceive the browbeating, the bluster, the accusations which have come our way! We had no respite and poor Janno finally felt obliged to leave."

"So he isn't a Fanscher after all."

"Of course not! You've always been such a literal-minded child! Can't you understand how a person might be interested in an idea without becoming its staunchest advocate?"

Glinnes accepted the deficiencies imputed to him. "How long will Akadie stay in the Vale?"

"I feel that he should return at once. How can he live a normal life? It's quite literally dangerous! Did you hear how the Trevanyi set upon him?"

"I heard that they tried to rob him of his money."

Marucha's voice raised in pitch. "You shouldn't say such a thing, even as a joke! Poor Janno! What he hasn't gone through! And he's always been such a good friend to you."

"I've done nothing against him."

"Now you must do something for him. I want you to go to the Vale and bring him home."

"What? I see no point in such an expedition. If he wants to come home, he'll do so."

"That's not true! You can't imagine his mood; he is limp with passivity! I've never seen him so before!"

"Perhaps he's just resting—taking a vacation, so to speak."

"A vacation? With his life in danger? It's common knowledge that the Trevanyi plan a massacre."

"Hmmf. I hardly think that is the case."

"Very well. If you won't help me, then I must go myself."

"Go where? Do what?"

"Go to the Fanscher camp and insist that Janno return home."

"Confound it. Very well. Suppose he won't come?"

"You must do your best."

Glinnes rode the air-bus to the mountain town Circanie, then hired an ancient surface-car to convey him to the Vale of Xian. A garrulous old man with a blue scarf tied around his head was included in the rental price; he manipulated the antique device as if he were directing a recalcitrant animal. The car at times scraped the ground; at other times it bounded thirty feet into the air, providing Glinnes with startling perspectives over the countryside. Two energy-guns on the seat beside the driver attracted his attention and he inquired as to their purpose.

"Dangerous territory," said the driver. "Whoever thought we'd see such a day?"

Glinnes considered the landscape, which seemed as placid as Rabendary Island. Mountain pomanders stood here and there—clouds of pink mist clutched in silver fingers. Blue-green fials marched along the ridge. Whenever the car rose into the air the horizons widened; the land to the south fell away in receding striations of pallid colors.

Glinnes said, "I see no great cause for alarm."

"So long as you're not a Fanscher, your chances are tolerable," said the driver. "Not good, mind you, because the Trevanyi conclave is only a mile or two yonder, and they are as suspicious as wasps. They drink *racq*, which influences the nerves and makes them none the kindlier."

The valley grew narrow; the mountains rose steep on either side. A quiet river flowed along the flat floor; on each side stood groves of sombarilla, pomander, deodar.

Glinnes asked, "Is this the Vale of Green Ghosts?"

"Some call it so. The Trevanyi bury lesser dead among the trees. The true and sacred Vale lies ahead, behind the Fanschers. There—you can see the Fanscher camp. They are an industrious group, no question as to that . . . I wonder what they are trying to do? Do they know themselves?"

The car slid into the camp—a scene of confusion. Hundreds of tents had been erected along the river bank; on the meadow, buildings of concrete foam were under construction.

Glinnes found Akadie without difficulty. He sat at a desk in the shade of a glyptus tree performing clerical work. He greeted Glinnes with neither surprise nor affability.

"I am here to bring you to your senses," said Glinnes. "Marucha wants you back at Rorquin's Tooth."

"I will return when the mood strikes me," said Akadie in a measured voice. "Until you arrived life was peaceful . . . Though for a fact my wisdom has been in no great demand. I expected to be greeted as a noble sage; instead I sit here doing footling sums." He made a deprecatory gesture at his desk. "I was told that I must earn my keep and this is a job no one cares to undertake." He cast a sour glance toward a nearby cluster of tents. "Everyone wants to participate in the grandiose schemes. Directives and announcements flow like chaff."

"I should think" said Glinnes, "that with thirty million ozols you could easily pay your way."

Akadie gave him a glance of weary reproach. "Do you realize that this episode has blasted my life? My integrity has been questioned and I can never again serve as mentor."

"You have ample wealth even without the thirty million," said Glinnes. "What shall I tell my mother?"

"Say that I am bored and overworked, but at least the accusations have not followed me here. Do you plan to see Glay?"

"No. What are all these concrete structures?"

"I have made it my business to know nothing," said Akadie.

"Have you seen the ghosts?"

"No, but on the other hand I have not looked for them. You'll find Trevanyi graves across the river, but the sacred home of the death-bird is a mile up the valley, beyond that copse of deodars. I made a casual exploration and was exalted. An enchanting place, beyond all question—too good for the Trevanyi."

"How is the food?" asked Glinnes ingenuously.

Akadie made a sour grimace. "The Fanschers intend to learn the secrets of the universe, but now they cannot so much as toast bread properly. Each meal is the same: gruel and a salad of coarse greens. There is not a flask of wine for miles . . ." Akadie spoke on for several minutes. He remarked upon Fanscher dedication and Fanscher innocence, but mostly of Fanscher austerity, which he found inexcusable. He trembled with rage at the mention of the thirty million ozols, yet he showed a pathetic anxiety for reassurance. "You yourself saw the messenger; you directed him to my house. Does the fact carry no weight?"

"No one has required my evidence. What of your friend Ryl Shermatz? Where was he?"

"He saw nothing of the transaction. A strange man, that Shermatz! His soul is quicksilver."

Glinnes rose to his feet. "Come along then. You achieve nothing here. If you dislike notoriety, stay quietly at Rabendary for a week or so."

Akadie pulled at his chin. "Well, then, why not?" He gave the papers a contemptuous flick. "What do the Fanschers know of style, urbanity, discernment? They have me doing sums." He rose to his feet. "I will leave this place. Fanscherade grows tiresome; these folk will never conquer the universe after all."

"Come along then," said Glinnes. "Have you anything to bring? Thirty million ozols, for instance?"

"The joke has lost its savor," said Akadie. "I will go as I am, and to lend flair to my departure, I will perform an unfamiliar equation." He scrawled a few flamboyant flourishes on the paper, then slung his cloak over his shoulder. "I am ready."

The ground-car slid down the Vale of Green Ghosts and toward avness arrived at Circanie. Akadie and Glinnes put up for the night at a little country inn.

At midnight Glinnes awoke to hear excited voices, and a few minutes later detected the sound of running footsteps. He looked out the window, but the street lay quiet in the starlight. Drunken revelry, thought Glinnes, and returned to his couch.

In the morning they heard the news that explained the occasion. During the night the Trevanyi had waxed passionate at their conclave; they had walked through fires; they had performed their bounding mood-dances; their "Grotesques," as they called their seers, had breathed the smoke of baicha roots and had belched forth the destiny of the Trevanyi race. The warriors responded with mad screams and ululations; running and leaping over the starlit hills, they had attacked the Fanscher camp.

The Fanschers were by no means unprepared. They employed their energy-guns with dire effect; the bounding Trevanyi became startled statues limned in blue sparks. Action became confused. The first zestful onslaught became a mournful writhing of bodies up and down the Vale, and presently there was no more fighting; the Trevanyi were either dead or had fled in a horror as full and wild as their attack. The Fanschers watched them go in dismal silence. They had won but they had lost. Fanscherade would never be the same; its verve and vivacity was gone, and in the morning there would be dreary work to do.

Akadie and Glinnes returned to Rabendary without incident, but Glinnes' slipshod housekeeping made Akadie irritable, and before the day was out he decided to return to Rorquin's Tooth.

Glinnes telephoned Marucha, who had undergone a change

of mood; now she fretted at the prospect of Akadie's return. "There has been such turmoil and all unnecessary; my head is splitting. Lord Gensifer demands that Janno make instant contact with him. He is most persistent and not at all sympathetic."

Akadie's pent emotions burst forth in outrage. "Does he dare to hector me? I'll set him straight, and quickly too. Get him on the telephone!"

Glinnes made the connection. Lord Gensifer's face appeared on the screen. "I understand that you wish a word or two with Janno Akadie," said Glinnes.

"Quite true," stated Lord Gensifer. "Where is he?"

Akadie stepped forward. "I am here, and why not? I recall no pressing business with you; still, you have been incessantly telephoning my house."

"Come then," said Lord Gensifer, thrusting forth his lower lip. "There is still a matter of thirty million ozols to be discussed."

"Why should I discuss them with you, in any event?" demanded Akadie. "You have nothing at stake. You were not kidnaped; you paid no ransom."

"I am secretary to the Council of Lords, and I am empowered to look into the matter."

"I still do not take kindly to your tone of voice," said Akadie. "My position has been made clear. I will discuss the matter no further."

Lord Gensifer was silent a moment. "You may have no choice," he said at last.

"I really don't understand you," replied Akadie in an icy voice.

"The situation is quite simple. The Whelm is delivering Sagmondo Bandolio to Chief Constable Filidice in Welgen. Undoubtedly he will be forced to identify his accomplices."

"This means nothing to me. He can identify as he will."

Lord Gensifer cocked his head to the side. "Someone with intimate local knowledge furnished information to Bandolio. This person will share Bandolio's fate."

"Deservedly so."

"Let me say only that if you remember any helpful information, no matter how trifling, you may communicate with me at any hour of the day or night—excepting of course this day week"—Lord Gensifer chuckled benignly—"which is when I espouse to myself Lady Gensifer."

165

Akadie's professional interest was stirred. "Who is to be the new Lady Gensifer?"

Lord Gensifer half closed his eyes in beatific reflection. "She is gracious, beautiful, and virtuous beyond compare, far too fine for a person like myself. I refer to the former Tanchinaro sheirl Duissane Drosset. Her father was killed in the recent battle and she has turned to me for comfort."

Akadie added dryly, "The day has then brought us at least one delightful surprise."

The screen dimmed on Lord Gensifer's countenance.

In the Vale a strange quiet prevailed. Never had the fabled landscape seemed so beautiful. The weather was exceptionally clear; the air, a crystal lens, intensified, deepened the colors. Sounds were clarified but somehow muted, or perhaps the folk in the Vale spoke in somber voices and avoided sudden sounds. At night the lights were few and dim, and conversations were murmurs in the dark. The Trevanyi raid had corroborated what many had suspected—that Fanscherade, if it were to succeed, must defeat a broad array of negative forces. Now was a time for resolution and a hardening of the spirit! A few persons abruptly left the Vale and were seen no more.

At the Trevanyi conclave fury had broadened and deepened. If any voices urged moderation, they no longer could be heard for the strident music of drums, horns, and that coiled full-throated instrument known as the *narwoun*. At night the men leapt through fires and cut themselves with knives to yield blood for their rites. Clans from far Bassway and the Eastlands arrived, and many carried energy-guns. Kegs of an ardent distillation known as *racq* were broached and consumed, and the warriors sang great oaths to the skirling music of the *narwoun*, drums and oboes.

On the third morning after the night raid a squad of constable appeared at the conclave, including Chief Constable Filidice. He advised the Trevanyi to reasonable conduct and announced his resolve to maintain order.

Trevanyi, voices cried out in protest. The Fanschers encroached upon sacred soil, the Vale where ghosts walked!

Chief Constable Filidice raised his voice. "You have cause for concern. I intend to represent your case to the Fanschers. Nonetheless, whatever the outcome, you must abide by my decision. Do you agree?"

The Trevanyi remained silent.

Chief Constable Filidice repeated his demand for cooperation and again received no commitment. "If you refuse to accede to my judgment," he said, "obedience will be forced upon you. So be warned!"

The constables returned to their aircraft and flew over the hill into the Vale of Green Ghosts.

Junius Farfan conferred with Chief Constable Filidice. Farfan had lost weight; the garments hung loosely about his figure, and harsh lines marked his face. He listened to the Chief Constable in silence. His response was cold. "We have worked here for several months, without inconvenience to anyone. We respect the Trevanyi graves; there has been no irreverence; they are never denied freedom of passage into their Vale of Xian. The Trevanyi are irrational; we respectfully must refuse to leave our land."

Chief Constable Filidice, a bulky pallid man with ice-blue eyes, ponderous with the majesty of his office, had never taken kindly to recalcitrance. "Just so," he said. "I have enjoined restraint upon the Trevanyi; I now do the same to you."

Junius Farfan bowed his head. "We will never attack the Trevanyi. But we are ready to defend ourselves."

Chief Constable Filidice uttered a sarcastic snort. "The Trevanyi are warriors, every man of them. They would cut your throats with a flourish, should we allow them to do so. I strongly advise you to make other arrangements. Why need you build your headquarters in such a place?"

"The land was free and open. Will you provide us land elsewhere?"

"Naturally not. In fact, I see no reason why you need a great headquarters in the first place. Why not simply retire to your homes and avoid all this contention?"

Junius Farfan smiled. "I perceive your ideological bias."

"It is not bias to favor the tried and true ways of the past; it is ordinary common sense."

Junius Farfan shrugged and attempted no refutation of an irrefutable point of view. The constables established a patrol across the ridge.

The day passed. Avness brought a lightning storm. For an hour lavender strands of fire stroked the dark flanks of the hills. Fanschers came forth to marvel at the spectacle. Trevanyi shuddered at the portent; in their world-view, Urmank the Ghost-Killer stood on the clouds, spitting the souls of Trevanyi and Trill alike. Nonetheless they arrayed themselves, drank *racq*, exchanged embraces, and at midnight set forth upon their mission in order that they might attack dur-

167

ing the gray hour before dawn. They deployed under the deodars and along the ridges, avoiding the constables and their detection apparatus. In spite of their stealth they encountered a Fanscher ambush. Shouts and screams ruptured the predawn silence. Energy-guns flashed; struggling shapes created grotesque silhouettes against the sky. The Trevanyi fought with hissing curses, guttural cries of pain; the Fanschers strove in dire silence. The constabulary blew horns; waving the black and gray flag of government authority, they advanced upon the conflict. The Trevanyi, suddenly aware that they confronted an insensate foe, gave ground; the Fanschers pursued like Fates. The constables blew their horns and issued orders; they were handled roughly; the black and gray flag was torn from their grasp. The constables radioed Circanie; Chief Constable Filidice, aroused from his sleep and already out of sorts with Fanscherade, ordered out the militia.

Halfway into morning the militia arrived in the Vale—a company of Trill country-folk. They despised Trevanyi, but knew them and accepted their existence. The freakish Fanschers were outside their experience, and hence alien. The Trevanyi, recovered from their panic, followd the militia into the valley, with musicians loping along at the flank playing screes and warwhoops.

The Fanschers had retreated to the shelter of the deodar forest; only Junius Farfan and a few others awaited the militia. They no longer hoped for victory; the power of the state was now ranged against them. The captain of the militia came forward and issued orders: the Fanschers must leave the Vale.

"On what grounds?" asked Farfan.

"Your presence provokes a disturbance."

"Our presence is legal."

"Nevertheless, it creates a tension which previously did not exist. Legality must encompass practicality, and your continued occupation of the Vale of Green Ghosts is impractical. I must insist that you depart."

Junius Farfan consulted with his comrades. Then tears streaming down his cheeks for the destruction of his dream, he turned away to instruct those Fanschers who watched from the shade of the deodars. Addled by *racq*, the Trevanyi could not contain themselves. They sprang at the hated Farfan; a thrown knife struck squarely into the back of Farfan's neck. The Fanschers raised a weird moan. Eyes wide in hor-

168

ror, they fell upon militia and Trevanyi alike. The militia, uninterested in the quarrel, broke ranks and fled. Trevanyi and Fanschers tumbled about on the ground, each eager to destroy the other.

Eventually, through some mysterious process of mutual accord, the survivors crawled apart. The Trevanyi returned over the hills to the keening conclave. The Fanschers paused only a few moments in their camp, then wandered off down the valley. Fanscherade was finished. The great adventure was done.

Months later the Connatic, in conversation with one of his ministers, mentioned the battle in the Vale of Green Ghosts. "I was in the neighborhood and was kept apprised of events. It was a tragic set of circumstances."

"Could you not have halted the confrontation?"

The Connatic shrugged. "I might have brought down the Whelm. I tried this in a case not dissimilar—the affair of the Tamarchô on Rhamnotis—and there was no resolution. A troubled society is like a man with a stomach-ache. When he purges himself, he improves."

"Still—many folk must pay with their lives."

The Connatic made a wry gesture. "I enjoy the comradeship of the public house, the country inn, the dockside tavern. I travel the worlds of Alastor and everywhere I find people whom I find subtle and fascinating, people whom I love. Each individual of the five trillion is a cosmos in himself; each is irreplaceable, unique . . . Sometimes I find a man or a woman to hate. I look into their faces and I see malice, cruelty, corruption. Then I think, these folk are equally useful in the total scheme of things; they act as exemplars against which virtue can measure itself. Life without contrast is food without salt . . . As Connatic I must think in terms of policy; then I see only the aggregate man, whose face is a blur of five trillion faces. Toward this man I feel no emotion. So it was in the Vale of Green Ghosts, Fanscherade was doomed from its inception—was ever a man so fey as Junius Farfan? There are survivors, but there are no more Fanschers. Some will move on to other worlds. A few may become starmenters. A stubborn few may persist as Fanschers in their personal lives. And all who participated will remember the great dream and will feel as men apart from those who did not share the glory and the tragedy."

# Chapter 20

## ★ ★ ★

To Rabendary Island came Glay, his clothes stained and rent, his arm in a sling. "I have to live somewhere," he said glumly. "It might as well be here."

"It's as good as any," said Glinnes. "I suppose you didn't bother to bring along the money."

"Money? What money?"

"The twelve thousand ozols."

"No."

"A pity. Casagave now calls himself Lord Ambal."

Glay was uninterested. He had no emotions left; his world was gray and flat. "Suppose he were Lord Ambal; does that give him the isle?"

"He seems to think so."

The gong summoned Glinnes to the telephone. The screen displayed Akadie's face. "Ah, Glinnes! I'm happy to have found you at home. I need your assistance. Can you come at once to Rorquin's Tooth?"

"Certainly, if you'll pay my usual fee."

Akadie made a petulant gesture. "I have no time for facetiousness. Can you come at once?"

"Very well. What is your difficulty?"

"I'll explain when you arrive."

Akadie met Glinnes at the door and led him almost at a trot into the study. "I wish to introduce two officials of the prefecture misguided enough to suspect my poor tired person of wrong-doing. On the right is our esteemed Chief Constable Benko Filidice; on the left is Inspector Lucian Daul, investigator, jailer, and sergeant of the prutanshyr. This, gentlemen, is my friend and neighbor Glinnes Hulden, whom you know better perhaps as the redoubtable right strike for the Tanchinaros."

The three men exchanged salutes; both Filidice and Daul spoke politely of Glinnes' play on the hussade field. Filidice, a large heavy-chested man with pale melancholy features and cold blue eyes, wore a suit of buff garbardine trimmed with black braid. Dual was thin and spare, with long thin arms, long hands, long fingers. Under a clot of dead black ringlets, his face was as pale as that of his superior, with bony over-emphatic features. Daul's manner was polite and delicate in the extreme, as if he could not bear the thought of giving offense.

Akadie addressed Glinnes in his most pedantic voice. "These two gentlemen, both able and dispassionate public servants, tell me that I have connived with the starmenter Sagmondo Bandolio. They have explained that the ransom money paid to me remains in my custody. I find myself doubting my own innocence. Can you reassure me?"

"In my opinion," said Glinnes, "you'd do anything to gain an ozol except take a chance."

"That's not quite what I meant. Did you not direct a messenger to my house? Did you not arrive to find me in conference with a certain Ryl Shermatz and my telephone switched off?"

"Precisely true," said Glinnes.

Chief Constable Filidice spoke in a mild voice. "I assure you, Janno Akadie, that we come to you principally because there is nowhere else to go. The money reached you, then disappeared. It was not received by Bandolio. We have explored his mind, and he is not deceiving us; in fact, he has been most frank and cordial."

Glinnes asked. "What were the arrangements, according to Bandolio?"

"The situation is most curious. Bandolio worked with a person fanatically cautious, a person who—to quote you—'would do anything to earn an ozol except take a chance.' This person initiated the project. He sent Bandolio a message through channels known only to starmenters, which suggests that this person—let us call him X—was either a starmenter himself or had such an accomplice."

"It is well known that I am no starmenter," declared Akadie.

Filidice nodded ponderously. "Still—speaking hypothetically—you have many acquaintances among whom might be a starmenter or an ex-starmenter."

Akadie looked somewhat blank. "I suppose that this is possible."

Filidice went on. "Upon receipt of the message Bandolio

made arrangements to meet X. These arrangements were complicated; both men were wary. They met at a place near Welgen, in the dark. X wore a hussade mask. His plan was most simple. At a hussade game he would arrange that the wealthiest folk of the prefecture all sat in a single section; he would ensure this by sending out free tickets. X would receive two million ozols. Bandolio would take the rest . . .

"The scheme seemed sound; Bandolio agreed to the plan and events proceeded as we know. Bandolio sent a trusted lieutenant, a certain Lempel, here to receive the money from the collecting agency—which is to say, yourself."

Akadie frowned dubiously. "The messenger was Lempel?"

"No. Lempel arrived at the Port Maheul spaceport a week after the raid. He never departed; in fact he was poisoned, presumably by X. He died in his sleep at the Travelers Inn in Welgen the day before the news of Bandolio's capture arrived."

"That would be the day before I gave up the money."

Chief Constable Filidice merely smiled. "The ransom money was certainly not among his effects. So: I lay the facts before you. You had the money. Lempel did not have it. Where did it go?"

"He probably made arrangements with the messenger before he was poisoned. The messenger must have the money."

"But who is this mysterious messenger? Certain of the lords regard him as sheer fabrication."

Akadie said in a clear careful voice, "I now make this formal statement. I delivered the money to a messenger in accordance with instructions. A certain Ryl Shermatz was present at the time, and so much as witnessed the transfer."

Daul spoke for the first time. "He actually saw the money change hands?"

"He very probably saw me give the messenger a black case."

Daul fluttered one of his long-fingered hands. "A suspicious man might wonder if the case contained the money."

Akadie responded coldly. "A sensible man would realize that I would dare steal not so much as an ozol from Sagmondo Bandolio, let alone thirty million."

"But by this time Bandolio was captured."

"I knew nothing of this. You can verify the fact through Ryl Shermatz."

"Ah, the mysterious Ryl Shermatz. Who is he?"

"An itinerant journalist."

172

"Indeed! And where is he now?"

"I saw him two days ago. He said that he was soon to be leaving Trullion. Perhaps he is gone—where I don't know."

"But he is your single corroboratory witness."

"By no means. The messenger took a wrong turning and asked Glinnes Hulden for directions. True?"

"True," said Glinnes.

"Janno Akadie's description of this 'messenger' "—Daul gave the word a dry emphasis—"is unfortunately too general to assist us."

"What can I say?" demanded Akadie. "He was a young man of average size and ordinary appearance. He had no distinguishing features."

Filidice turned to Glinnes. "You agree to this?"

"Absolutely."

"And he provided no identification when he spoke to you?"

Glinnes cast his mind back across the weeks. "As I recall, he asked directions to Akadie's manse, no more." Glinnes broke off somewhat abruptly. Daul, instantly suspicious, thrust his face forward. "And nothing else?"

Glinnes shook his head and spoke decisively. "Nothing else."

Daul drew back. There was a moment of silence. Then Filidice said ponderously, "A pity that none of these persons you mention are available to confirm your remarks."

Akadie at last made a show of indignation. "I see no need for corroboration! I refuse to acknowledge that I need do more than enunciate the facts!"

"Under ordinary circumstances, yes," said Filidice. "With thirty million ozols missing, no."

"You now know as much as I," declared Akadie. "Hopefully you will pursue a fruitful investigation."

Chief Constable Filidice gave a disconsolate grunt. "We are grasping at straws. The money exists—somewhere."

"Not here, I assure you," said Akadie.

Glinnes could no longer restrain himself. He went to the door. "Fair weather for all. I must see to my affairs."

The constables gave him courteous farewell; Akadie spared only a peevish glance.

Glinnes almost ran to his boat. He drove east along Vernice Water, then instead of swinging south he turned north along Sarpent Channel, then out upon Junctuary Broad, where the Scurge River mingled its waters with the Saur. Glinnes turned up the Scurge. He proceeded back and forth up the meanders, every hundred yards cursing himself for his own stupidity. At the confluence of the Scurge with the Karbashe was Erch, a sleepy village almost hidden in the shade of enormous candlenut trees, where long ago the Tanchinaros had defeated the Elements.

Glinnes tied his boat to the dock and spoke to a man sitting outside the ramshackle wine-shop. "Where can I find a certain Jarcony? Or perhaps it's Jarcom?"

"Jarcony? Which one do you seek? Father? Son? Or the cavout dealer?"

"I want the young man who works in a blue uniform."

"That should be Remo. He's a steward on the Port Maheul ferry. You'll find him at home. Yonder, up the lane and under the thrackleberries."

Glinnes went up the path to where a great shrub almost engulfed a cabin of poles and fronds. He pulled a cord which swung the clapper of a little bell. A drowsy face peered from the window. "Who is it? And what for?"

"Resting after your labor, I see," said Glinnes. "Do you remember me?"

"Why, yes indeed. It's Glinnes Hulden. Well, well, think of that! Just a moment then."

Jarcony wrapped himself in his paray and swung back the creaking door. He pointed to a bower cut back into the thrackleberry thicket. "Sit down, if you will. Perhaps you'll take a cup of cool wine?"

"A good idea," said Glinnes.

Remo Jarcony brought forth a stoneware crock and a pair of mugs. "What conceivably brings you here to visit me?"

"A rather curious matter," said Glinnes. "As you recall, I met you while you were seeking the manse of Janno Akadie."

"Quite true. I'd contracted a small errand for a gentleman of Port Maheul. Surely there's been no difficulty?"

"I believe you were to deliver a parcel, or something similar?"

"Quite true. Will you take another cup of wine?"

"With great pleasure. And you delivered the parcel?"

"I did as I was instructed. The gentleman evidently was satisfied, as I haven't seen him since."

"May I ask the nature of those instructions?"

"Certainly. The gentleman required that I convey the parcel to the space depot at Port Maheul and place it in Locker 42, the key to which he gave me. I did as he required, thereby earning twenty ozols—money for nothing."

"Do you recall the gentleman who hired you?"

Jarcony squinted up into the foliage. "Not well. An off-worlder, or so I believe—a man short and stocky, with quick movements. He has a bald head as I recall, and a fine emerald in his ear, which I admired. Now, perhaps you'll enlighten me. Why do you ask such questions?"

"It's very simple," said Glinnes. "The gentleman is a publisher from Gethryn; Akadie wants to add an appendix to the treatise which he put into the gentleman's custody."

"Ah! I understand."

"There's nothing much to it. I'll notify Akadie that his work must already be in Gethryn." Glinnes rose to his feet. "Thank you for the wine, and I must now return to Saurkash . . . Out of sheer curiosity, what did you do with the key to the locker?"

"I did as I was instructed and left it at the accommodation desk."

Glinnes pushed westward at top speed, his wake bubbling the width of the narrow Jade Canal. He swept into Barabas River, hurling a white wave into the banked jerdine trees along the shore, and slid hissing westward, slowing only when he approached Port Maheul. He tied up at the main dock with a few deft twists of the mooring line, then half walked, half trotted the mile to the transport terminal, a tall structure of black iron and glass crusted pale green and violet with age. The field beyond was empty both of spaceships and local air transport.

Glinnes entered the depot and looked across the submarine gloom. Travelers sat on benches awaiting one or another of the scheduled air-buses. A bank of lockers stood along the wall beside the baggage office, where a clerk sat behind a low counter.

Glinnes crossed the room and inspected the lockers. Those available for use stood open, with magnetic keys in the lock holes. The door to Locker 42 was closed. Glinnes glanced toward the baggage clerk, then tested the door to find it immovable.

The locker was constructed of sound sheet-metal; the doors fit snugly. Glinnes seated himself on a nearby bench.

Various possibilities suggested themselves. Few of the lockers were in use. Among the fifty lockers, Glinnes counted only four closed doors. Was it too much to hope that Locker 42 still contained the black case? Not at all, thought Glinnes. It would seem that Lempel and the bald stocky off-worlder who had hired Jarcony were the same. Lempel had died before he had been able to claim the case in Locker 42 . . . So it would seem.

And now: how to get into Locker 42?

Glinnes examined the baggage clerk, a small man with wispy gray-russet hair, a long tremulous nose, and an expression of foolish obstinacy. Hopeless to seek either direct or indirect cooperation here; the man seemed a living definition of pettifoggery.

Glinnes cogitated for five minutes. Then he rose to his feet and walked to the bank of lockers. Into the coin slot on the face of Locker 30 he deposited a coin. Closing the door, he withdrew the key.

He approached the baggage desk and placed the key upon the counter. The clerk came forward. "Yes, sir."

"Be good enough to hold this key for me," said Glinnes. "I don't care to carry it around."

The clerk took the key with a twitch of mouth. "How long will you be gone, sir? Some folk leave their keys a remorseless time."

"I'll be no more than a day or so." Glinnes placed a coin upon the counter. "For your trouble."

"Thank you." The clerk opened a drawer and dropped the key into a compartment.

Glinnes walked away and seated himself on a bench where he could watch the clerk.

An hour passed. An airbus from Cape Flory dropped down upon the field, discharging passengers, engulfing others. At the baggage desk there was a flurry of activity; the clerk scrambled here and there among his racks and shelves. Glinnes watched him carefully. It would seem that after his exertions he might feel the need for a rest or a visit to the lavatory, but instead, when the last patron had departed the clerk poured himself a mug of cold tea, which he drank in a gulp, and then a second mug, over which he ruminated a few minutes. Then he returned to his duties, and Glinnes resigned himself to patience.

Glinnes began to feel torpid. He watched folk come and go and amused himself for a while speculating upon their occupations and secret lives, but presently he became bored. What did he care for these commercial travelers, these grandfathers and grandmothers fresh home from visits, these functionaries and underlings? What of the clerk? And his bladder? Even as Glinnes watched the clerk sipped more tea. In what organ of

176

his meager body was all this liquid stored? The idea provoked Glinnes himself to discomfort. He glanced across the depot to the lavatory. If he stepped within even for a moment the clerk might choose the same instant and his vigil would go for naught . . . Glinnes shifted his position. No doubt he could wait as long as the clerk. Fortitude had stood him in good stead on the hussade field; in a competition with the baggage clerk, fortitude once again would be the decisive factor.

People came and went—a man wearing a hat with a ridiculous yellow cockade, an old woman trailing an overpowering waft of musk, a pair of young men flaunting Fanscher costume and glancing from side to side to see who noticed their proud defiance . . . Glinnes crossed his legs, then uncrossed them. The baggage clerk went to a stool and began to make entries in a daybook. In order to slake his thirst he poured another mug of tea from the jug. Glinnes rose to his feet and walked back and forth. The baggage clerk now stood at the counter, looking out across the depot. He seemed to be gnawing his lower lip. He turned and reached—no! thought Glinnes, not for the jug of tea! The man could not be human! But the clerk merely tapped in the stopper to the jug. He rubbed his chin and seemed to consider, while Glinnes stood by the wall, swaying back and forth.

The clerk came to a decision. He stepped out from behind the counter and walked toward the men's lavatory.

Groaning in mingled relief and anxiety, Glinnes edged forward. No one seemed to heed him. He ducked behind the counter, opened the drawer and looked into the compartment. Two keys. He took them both, closed the drawer and returned to the waiting area. No one, so far as he could perceive, had noticed his conduct.

Glinnes went directly to Locker 42. The first key in his hand carried a brown tag stamped with the black numerals 30. The tag of the second key displayed the number 42. Glinnes opened the locker. He drew out the black case and closed the door once more. Was there time to replace the keys? Glinnes thought not. He walked from the depot into the smoky light of avness and headed back toward the dock. Along the way he stepped behind an old wall to relieve himself.

He found his boat as he had left it, and casting off the line, set forth to the east.

Steering with his knee, he attempted to open the case. The

177

lock resisted the grip of his fingers; he applied a metal bar and snapped back the latch. The cover slid aside. Glinnes touched the money within: neat bundles of Alastor certificates. Thirty million ozols.

# Chapter 21

★ ★ ★

Glinnes coasted into the Rabendary dock half an hour before midnight. The house was dark; Glay was not home. Glinnes put the case on the table and considered it a few minutes. He opened the lid and took forth certificates to a value of thirty thousand ozols, which he tucked into a jar and buried in the soil beside the verandah. Returning into the house, he telephoned Akadie, but elicited only expanding red circles, indicating that the telephone had been placed in a "non-receptive" condition. Glinnes sat on the couch, feeling fatigue but no lassitude. Once more he telephoned Akadie's manse without response; then he took the black case to his boat and set forth to the north.

From the water, Akadie's manse seemed dark. Yet it was not likely that Akadie, a man who enjoyed nocturnal activity, would be asleep . . .

On the dock Glinnes spied a man standing still and quiet. He sheered away and stood offshore. The dark figure made no move. Glinnes called out, "Who's that on the dock?"

After a pause a voice, throaty and muffled, came quietly across the water. "Constable of the Prefecture, on guard duty."

"Is Janno Akadie at home?"

Again the pause, and the low voice. "No."

"Where is he?"

The pause, the muffled disinterested voice. "He is in Welgen."

Glinnes jerked his boat around and sent it foaming back across Clinkhammer Broad, down the Saur, back down Farwan Water. When he arrived at Rabendary the house was still dark; Glay was elsewhere. Glinnes moored his boat and

178

carried the black case inside. He telephoned the Gilweg house; the screen brightened to show the face of Varella, one of the younger girls. Only children were home; everyone else had gone visiting, to watch stars or drink wine, or perhaps to Welgen for the executions—she was not quite sure.

Glinnes darkened the telephone. He tucked the black case out of sight in the thatch, then, flinging himself on his couch, almost instantly fell asleep.

The morning was gay and crystalline. A warm breeze blew flurries of cat's paws across Ambal Broad; the sky showed a lilac clarity not often observed.

Glinnes ate a few bites of breakfast, then tried to call Akadie. A few minutes later a boat pulled up to the dock and Glay jumped ashore. Glinnes came out to meet him. Glay stopped short and looked Glinnes carefully up and down. "You seem excited."

"I've got enough money to pay off Casagave. We'll do it before the hour is out."

Glay looked across the broad at Ambal Isle, which in the fresh light of morning had never looked lovelier. "Just as you say. But you had better telephone him first."

"Why?"

"To give him warning."

"I don't want to give him anything," said Glinnes. Nevertheless he went to the telephone. Lute Casagave's face appeared on the screen. He spoke in a metallic voice. "What is your business?"

"I have twelve thousand ozols for you," said Glinnes. "I now wish to void the contract of sale. I'll bring the money over at this moment, if it's convenient."

"Send the money over with the owner," said Casagave.

"I am the owner."

"Shira Hulden is the owner. I suppose he can void that contract if he chooses."

"Today I'll bring over an affadavit certifying the death of Shira."

"Indeed. And where will you get it?"

"From Janno Akadie, an official mentor of the prefecture, who witnessed the confession of his murderer."

"Indeed," said Casagave with a chuckle. The screen went blank. Glinnes spoke to Glay in a voice of puzzlement. "That isn't quite the reaction I anticipated. He showed no concern whatever."

Glay shrugged. "Why should he? Akadie is in jail. They'll put him on the prutanshyr if the lords have their way. Any certification of Akadie's is meaningless."

Glinnes rolled his eyes back and drew his arms high in the air. "Was anyone ever so dogged by frustration?" he cried.

Glay turned away without comment. Presently he went to his couch and fell asleep.

Glinnes strode back and forth along the verandah, deep in thought. Then, venting an inarticulate curse, he jumped into his boat and set forth to the west.

An hour later he arrived in Welgen, and only with difficulty found a mooring along the crowded dock. An unusual number of folk had chosen this day to visit Welgen. The square was the scene of intense activity. Folk of town and fen moved restlessly here and there, always with one eye turned upon the prutanshyr, where workmen adjusted the cogs of a ponderous mechanism, the functioning of which Glinnes found perplexing. He paused to make inquiry of an old man who stood leaning on a staff. "What goes on at the prutanshyr?"

"Another of Filidice's follies." The old man spat contemptuously upon the cobbles. "He insists on these novel devices, which can hardly be coaxed to perform their function. Sixty-two pirates to be killed, and yesterday the thing managed to grind asunder only a single man. Today it must be repaired! Have you ever heard the like? In my day we were content with simpler devices."

Glinnes went on to the Office of the Constabulary, only to learn that Chief Constable Filidice was not on hand. Glinnes then requested five minutes with Janno Akadie, but was denied the privilege; today the jail might not be visited.

Glinnes returned to the square and took a seat under the arbor of The Noble Saint Gambrinus, where so long ago (so it seemed) he had spoken with Junius Farfan. He ordered a half-gill of aquavit, which he drank at a gulp. How the fates conspired to thwart him! He had proved the fact of Shira's death and then had lost his money. He had gained new funds, but now he could no longer prove Shira's death. His witness Akadie was invalidated and his principal, Vang Drosset, was dead!

So now: what to do? The thirty million ozols? A joke. He would throw the money to the merlings before turning it over the Chief Constable Filidice. Glinnes signaled the waiter for another half-gill of aquavit, then turned a lambent glance toward the abominable prutanshyr. To save Akadie it might be necessary to surrender the money—though for a fact the case against Akadie seemed extraordinarily thin . . .

A shape darkened the entrance. Squinting up against the glare, Glinnes saw a person of middle height and unobtrusive demeanor, whom he thought to recognize. He looked more closely, then jumped to his feet with sudden energy. At his gesture the man approached. "If I am not mistaken," said Glinnes, "you are Ryl Shermatz. I am Glinnes Hulden, a friend of the mentor Janno Akadie."

"Of course! I remember you well," said Shermatz. "And how does our friend Akadie?"

The waiter brought aquavit, which Glinnes placed in front of Shermatz. "You will require this before long . . . I take it you have not heard the news?"

"I have only just returned from Morilla. Why do you ask?"

Stimulated by circumstances and by the aquavit, Glinnes spoke with a measure of hyperbole. "Akadie has been flung into a dungeon. He is accused of grand larceny, and if the lords have their way, Akadie may well be inserted into the cogs of yonder mincing machine."

"Sad news indeed!" said Shermatz. With a wry salute he raised the goblet to his mouth. "Akadie should never have aspired to chicanery; he lacks the cold decisiveness that distinguishes the successful criminal."

"You miss my point," said Glinnes somewhat testily. "The charge is absolutely absurd."

"I am surprised to hear you speak so definitely," said Shermatz.

"If necessary, Akadie's innocence could be demonstrated in a manner to convince anyone. But this is not the point. I wonder why Filidice, apparently from sheer suspicion, has imprisoned Akadie, while the guilty man goes free."

"An interesting speculation. Can you name the guilty man?"

Glinnes shook his head. "I wish I could—especially if a certain man is the guilty party."

"And why do you confide in me?"

"You observed Akadie transfer the money to the messenger. Your testimony will free him."

"I saw a black case change hands. It might have held almost anything."

Glinnes chose his words with care. "You probably wonder why I am so confident of Akadie's innocence. The reason is simple. I know for a fact that he disposed of the money as he claimed. Bandolio was captured; his aide Lempel was murdered. The money was never claimed. In my opinion, the importunate lords deserve the money no more than Bandolio. I am disinclined to assist either side."

Shermatz made a grave sign of comprehension. "A nod is as good as a wink. If Akadie is in fact innocent, who is Bandolio's real accomplice?"

"I am surprised that Bandolio has not provided definite information, but Chief Constable Filidice won't allow me a word wtih Akadie, much less Bandolio."

"I'm not so sure of that." Shermatz rose to his feet. "A few words with Chief Constable Filidice might be worthwhile."

"Return to your seat," said Glinnes. "He won't see us."

"I think he will. I am something more than a roving journalist, as I hold the commission of Over-inspector in the Whelm. Chief Constable Filidice will see us with pleasure. Let us go at once to make the inquiry. Where is he to be found?"

"Yonder is his headquarters," said Glinnes. "The structure is dilipidated, but here in Welgen it represents the majesty of Trill law."

Glinnes and Ryl Shermatz waited in a foyer only briefly before Chief Constable Filidice came forth, his face expressing concern. "What is this again? Who are you, sir?"

Shermatz placed a metal plate upon the counter. "Please assure yourself of my credentials."

Filidice glumly studied the plate. "I am of course at your service."

"I am here in connection with the starmenter Bandolio," said Shermatz. "You have questioned him?"

"To some extent. There was no reason to undertake any exhaustive inquiry."

"Have you discovered his local accomplice?"

Filidice gave a curt nod. "He was assisted by a certain Janno Akadie, whom we have taken into custody."

"You are assured, then, of Akadie's guilt?"

"The evidence very clearly suggests as much."

"Has he confessed?"

"No."

"Have you placed him under psychohallation?"

"We lack such equipment here at Welgen."

"I would like to examine both Bandolio and Akadie; Akadie first, if you please."

Filidice turned to an under-constable and gave the necessary orders. To Shermatz and Glinnes: "Will you be good enough to step into my office?"

Five minutes later Akadie was thrust complaining and expostulating into the office. At the sight of Glinnes and Shermatz he fell abruptly silent.

Shermatz said courteously, "Good morning, Janno Akadie; it is a pleasure to see you again."

"Not under these circumstances! Would you believe it? They have me pent in a cell, like a criminal! I thought they were taking me to the prutanshyr! Have you ever heard the like?"

"I hope that we will be able to clarify the matter." Shermatz turned to Filidice. "What precisely are the charges against Akadie?"

"That he conspired with Sagmondo Bandolio and that he has sequestered thirty million ozols which are not his property."

"Both charges are false!" cried Akadie. "Someone is plotting against me!"

"We will certainly arrive at the truth of the matter," said Shermatz. "Suppose we now hear what the starmenter Bandolio has to say?"

Filidice spoke to his underling and presently Sagmondo Bandolio entered the room—a tall black-bearded man, bald, with a black tonsure, lucent blue eyes, and a placid expression. Here was a man who had commanded five dire ships and four hundred men, who had dispensed tragedy ten thousand times for purposes he alone could define.

Shermatz signaled him forward. "Sagmondo Bandolio, out of sheer curiosity, do you regret the life you have lived?"

Bandolio smiled politely. "I regret the last two weeks, certainly. As to the period prior, the subject is complex, and in any event I would not know how to answer your question accurately; hindsight is the least useful of our intellectual capabilities."

"We are making an inquiry into the foray upon Welgen. Can you identify your local accomplice more definitely?"

Bandolio pulled at his beard. "I have not identified him at all, unless my recollection is at fault."

Chief Constable Filidice said, "He was subjected to mind-searching. He has retained no clandestine information."

"What information has he given to you?"

"The initiative came from Trullion. Bandolio received a proposal through secret starmenter channels; he sent down a subaltern by the name of Lempel to make a preliminary inspection. Lempel rendered an opitmistic report and Bandolio himself came down to Trullion. On a beach near Welgen, he met the Trill whom became his accomplice. The meeting occurred at midnight. The Trill wore a hussade mask and spoke in a cultivated voice Bandolio says he could not identify. They made their arrangements, and Bandolio never saw the man again. He assigned Lempel to the project; Lempel is now dead. Bandolio professes no other information and psychohallation corroborates his claim."

Shermatz turned to Bandolio. "Is this an accurate summation?"

"It is indeed, except for a suspicion that my local confederate persuaded Lempel to give information to the Whelm, so that the two might divide the whole of the ransom. After the Whelm was notified, Lempel's life came to an end."

"So then you have no reason to conceal the identity of your accomplice?"

"To the contrary. My dearest wish is to see him dance to music of the prutanshyr."

"Before you stands Janno Akadie. Is he known to you?"

"No."

"Is it possible that Akadie was your confederate?"

"No. The man was as tall as myself."

Shermatz looked at Filidice. "And there you have it: a grievous error which luckily was not consummated upon the prutanshyr."

Filidice's pale countenance showed a few of perspiration. "I assure you, I was exposed to intolerable pressure! The Order of Aristocrats insisted that I act; they authorized Lord Gensifer, the secretary, to demand definite activity. I could not locate the money, so then . . ." Filidice paused and licked his lips.

"To appease the Order of Aristocrats you imprisoned Janno Akadie."

"It seemed an obvious course of action."

Glinnes asked Bandolio, "You met your confederate by starlight?"

"So I did." Bandolio seemed almost jovial.

"What were his garments?"

"The Trill paray and the Trill cape, with wide padding, or

184

epaulettes, or wings; only a Trill would know their function. His silhouette, as he stood on the shore in his hussade mask, was that of a great black bird."

"So you came to stand close to him."

"A distance of six feet separated us."

"What mask did he wear?"

Bandolio laughed. "How should I know your local masks? Horns protruded at the temple; the mouth showed fangs and a tongue lolled loose. Indeed, I felt I faced a monster there on the beach."

"What of his voice?"

"A hoarse mutter; he wanted no recognition."

"His gestures, mannerisims, quirks of stance?"

"None. He made no movement."

"His boat?"

"An ordinary runabout."

"And what was the date of this occasion?"

"The fourth day of Lyssum."

Glinnes considered a moment. "You received all further signals from Lempel?"

"True."

"You had no other contact with the man in the hussade mask?"

"None."

"What was his precise function?"

"He undertook to seat the three hundred richest men of the prefecture in section D of the stadium, and so he did to perfection."

Filidice interposed a remark. "The seats were bought anonymously and sent out by messenger. They offer no clue."

Ryl Shermatz considered Filidice for a long thoughtful moment, upon which Filidice became uneasy. Shermatz said, "I am puzzled as to why you imprisoned Janno Akadie on evidence which even at first glance seems ambiguous."

Filidice spoke with dignity. "I received confidential information from an irreproachable source. Under the conditions of emergency and public agitation, I decided to act with decision."

"The information is confidential, you say?"

"Well, yes."

"And who is the irreproachable source?"

Filidice hesitated, then made a weary gesture. "The secretary of the Order of Lords convinced me that Akadie knew the whereabouts of the ransom money. He recommended that

185

Akadie be imprisoned and threatened with the prutanshyr until he agreed to relinquish the money."

"The Secretary of the Order of Lords . . . That would be Lord Gensifer."

"Precisely so," said Filidice.

"That ingrate!" hissed Akadie. "I will have a word with him."

"It might be interesting to learn the rationale behind his accusation," mused Shermatz. "I suggest that we undertake a visit to Lord Gensifer."

Filidice held up his hand. "Today would be most inopportune for Lord Gensifer. The gentry of the region are at Gensifer Manse to celebrate Lord Gensifer's wedding."

"I am concerned for Lord Gensifer's convenience," declared Akadie, "to the exact extent that he is concerned with mine. We will visit him at this moment."

"I quite agree with Janno Akadie," said Glinnes. "Especially as we will be able to identify the true criminal and take him into custody."

Ryl Shermatz spoke in a quizzical voice. "You speak with peculiar assurance."

"Conceivably I am mistaken," said Glinnes. "For this reason I feel that we should take Sagmondo Bandolio with us."

Filidice, with affairs slipping beyond his control, became correspondingly assertive. "This is not a sensible idea. In the first place, Bandolio is most supple and elusive; he must not cheat the prutanshyr. Secondly, he has declared himself unable to render any identification; the criminal's features were concealed by a mask. Thirdly, I find questionable, to say the least, the theory that we will find the guilty person at Lord Gensifer's wedding ceremony. I do not wish to create a tomfoolery and make myself a laughingstock."

Shermatz said, "A conscientious man is never diminished by doing his duty. I suggest that we pursue our investigation without regard for side issues."

Filidice gave a despondent acquiescence. "Very well, let us proceed to Gensifer Manse. Constable, confine the prisoner! Let the shackles be doubly locked and a trip-wire fastened around his neck."

The black and gray official boat drove across Fleharish Broad toward the Five Islands. Half a hundred boats clustered against the dock, and the walk was decorated with festoons of silk ribbon, scarlet, yellow and pink. Through the gardens strolled lords and ladies in the splendid archaic garments worn only at the most formal occasions, and which ordinary folk were never privileged to glimpse.

The official party walked up the path, aware of their own incongruity. Chief Constable Filidice in particular struggled between pent fury and embarrassment, Ryl Shermatz was placid enough, and Sagmondo Bandolio seemed actively to enjoy the situation; he held his head high and turned his gaze cheerfully this way and that. An old steward saw them and hastened forward in consternation. Filidice gave a muttered explanation; the steward's face drooped in displeasure. "Certainly you cannot intrude upon the ceremonies; the rites are shortly to take place. This is a most outrageous proceeding!"

Chief Constable Filidice's self-control quivered. He spoke in a vibrant voice. "Silence! This is official business! Be off with you—no, wait! We may have instructions for you." He looked sourly at Shermatz. "What are your wishes?"

Shermatz turned to Glinnes. "What is your suggestion?"

"One moment," said Glinnes. He looked across the garden, seeking among the two hundred folk present. Never had he seen such a gorgeous array of costumes—the velvet capes of the lords, with heraldric blazons on the back; the gowns of the ladies, belted and fringed with black coral beads, or crystallized merling scales, or rectangular tourmalines, with tiaras to match. Glinnes looked from face to face. Lute Casagave—Lord Ambal, as he chose to call himself—would necessarily be on hand. He saw Duissane, in a simple white gown and a wisp of a white turban. Feeling his gaze, she turned and saw him. Glinnes felt an emotion to which he could put no name—the sense of something precious departing, something leaving, to be lost forever. Lord Gensifer stood nearby. He became aware of the new arrivals and frowned in surprise and displeasure.

Someone nearby turned on his heel and began to walk away. The motion caught Glinnes' attention; he jumped forward, caught the man's arm, swung him around. "Lute Casagave."

Casagave's face was pale and austere. "I am Lord Ambal. How dare you touch me?"

"Be so good as to step this way," said Glinnes. "The matter is important."

"I choose to do nothing of the kind."

"Then stand here." Glinnes signaled the members of his group. Casagave once again sought to walk away; Glinnes pulled him back. Casagave's face was now white and dangerous. "What do you want of me?"

"Observe," said Glinnes. "This is Ryl Shermatz, Chief Inspector of the Whelm. This is Janno Akadie, a formerly accredited mentor of Jolany Prefecture. Both witnessed Vang Drosset's confession that he had murdered Shira Hulden. I am Squire of Rabendary and I now demand that you depart Ambal Isle at once."

Lute Casagave made no response. Filidice asked peevishly, "Is this why you brought us here, merely to confront Lord Ambal?"

Sagmondo Bandolio's merry laugh interrupted him. "Lord Ambal, now! Not so in the old days. Not so indeed!"

Casagave turned to depart, but Shermatz's easy voice checked him. "Just a moment if you please. This is an official inquiry, and the question of your identity becomes important."

"I am Lord Ambal; that is sufficient."

Ryl Shermatz swung his mild gaze to Bandolio. "You know him by another name?"

"By another name and by many another deed, some of which have caused me pain. He has done what I should have done ten years ago—retired with his loot. Here you see Alonzo Dirrig, sometimes known as the Ice Devil and Dirrig the Skull-maker, one-time master of four ships, as adept among the starmenters as any you might find."

"You are mistaken, whoever you may be." Casagave bowed and made as if to turn away.

"Not so fast!" said Filidice. "Perhaps we have made an important discovery. If this is the case, then Janno Akadie is vendicated. Lord Ambal, do you deny the charge of Sagmondo Bandolio?"

"There is nothing to deny. The man is mistaken."

Bandolio gave a mocking caw of laughter. "Look across the palm of his left hand; you'll see a scar I put there myself."

Filidice went on. "Do you deny that you are the person Alonzo Dirrig; that you conspired to kidnap three hundred lords of prefecture; that subsequently you killed a certain Lempel?"

Casagave's lips curled. "Of course I deny it. Prove it, if you can!"

Filidice turned to Glinnes. "Where is your proof?"

"One moment," said Shermatz in a voice of perplexity. He

spoke to Bandolio. "Is this the man with whom you conversed on the beach near Welgen?"

"Alonzo Dirrig calling on me to implement his schemes? Never, never, never—not Alonzo Dirrig."

Filidice looked dubiously at Glinnes. "So then, you are wrong, after all."

Glinnes said, "Not so fast! I never accused Casagave, or Dirrig—whatever his name—of anything. I merely brought him here to clear up an incidental bit of business."

Casagave turned and strode away. Ryl Shermatz made a gesture; Filidice instructed his two constables; "After him! Take him into custody." The constables ran off. Casagave looked over his shoulder, and observing pursuit, bounded out upon the dock and into his boat. With a surge and thrash of foam he sped away across Fleharish Broad.

Filidice roared to the constables, "Follow in the launch; keep him in sight! Radio for reinforcements; take him into custody!"

Lord Gensifer confronted them, face clenched in displeasure. "Why do you cause this disturbance? Can you not observe that we celebrate a solemn occasion?"

Chief Constable Filidice spoke with what dignity he could muster. "We are naturally distressed by our intrusion. We had reason to suspect that Lord Ambal was the accomplice of Sagmondo Bandolio. Apparently this is not the case."

Lord Gensifer's face became pink. He glanced at Akadie, then back to Filidice. "Of course this is not the case! Have we not discussed the matter at length? We know Bandolio's accomplice!"

"Indeed," said Akadie in a voice like a saw cutting a nail. "And who is this person?"

"It is the faithless mentor who so craftily collected and then secreted thirty million ozols!" declared Lord Gensifer. "His name is Janno Akadie!"

Ryl Shermatz said silkily, "Sagmondo Bandolio disputes this theory. He says Akadie is not the man."

Lord Gensifer threw his arms up in the air. "Very well then; Akadie is innocent! Who cares? I am sick of the whole matter! Please depart; you are intruding upon my property and upon a solemn ritual."

"Accept my apologies," said Chief Constable Filidice. "I assure you that this was not my scheme. Come then, gentlemen, we will—"

"Just a moment," said Glinnes. "We haven't yet touched

189

the nub of the matter. Sagmondo Bandolio cannot positively identify the man he faced on the beach, but he quite definitely can identify the mask. Lord Gensifer, will you bring forth one of the Fleharish Gorgon helmets?"

Lord Gensifer drew himself up. "I most certainly will not. What sort of farce is this? Once more I require that you depart!"

Glinnes ignored him and spoke to Filidice. "When Bandolio described horns and the lolling tongue of the mask I instantly thought of the Fleharish Gorgons. On the fourth day of Lyssum, when the meeting took place, the Gorgons had not yet been issued their uniforms. Only Lord Gensifer could have used a Gorgon helmet. Therefore, Lord Gensifer is the guilty man!"

"What are you saying?" gasped Filidice, eyes bulging in astonishment.

"Aha!" screamed Akadie and flung himself upon Lord Gensifer. Glinnes caught him and pulled him back.

"What insane libel are you setting forth?" roared Lord Gensifer, his face suddenly mottled. "Have you taken leave of your senses?"

"It is ridiculous," declared Filidice. "I will hear no more."

"Gently, gently," said Ryl Shermatz, smiling faintly. "Surely Glinnes Hulden's theory deserves consideration. In my opinion it appears to be definite, particular, exclusive, and sufficient."

Filidice spoke in a subdued voice. "Lord Gensifer is a most important man; he is secretary of the Order—"

"And as such, he forced you to imprison Akadie," said Glinnes.

Lord Gensifer furiously waved his finger at Glinnes, but could bring forth no words.

Chief Constable Filidice, in a plaintive grumble, asked Lord Gensifer, "Can you refute the accusation? Did someone perhaps steal a helmet?"

Lord Gensifer nodded vehemently. "It goes without saying! Someone—Akadie, no doubt—stole a Gorgon helmet from my storeroom."

"In that case," said Glinnes, "one will now be missing. Let us go to count the helmets."

Lord Gensifer aimed a wild blow at Glinnes, who ducked back out of the way. Shermatz signaled Filidice. "Arrest this gentleman; take him to the jail. We will put him through psychohallation, and the truth will be known."

"By no means," belched Lord Gensifer in a guttural voice. "I'll never stand to the prutanshyr." Like Casagave, he turned and ran along the dock, while his guests watched in fascinated wonder; never had they known such a wedding.

"After him," said Shermatz curtly. Chief Constable Filidice lurched off in pursuit and pounded down the dock to where Lord Gensifer had jumped into his runabout. Dismissing caution, Filidice leapt after him. Lord Gensifer tried to buffet him aside; Filidice, falling upon Lord Gensifer, drove him backward, over the gunwale and into the water.

Lord Gensifer swam under the dock. Filidice called after him, "It's no use, Lord Gensifer; justice must be served. Come forth, if you will!"

Only a swirl of water indicated Lord Gensifer's presence. Filidice called again. "Lord Gensifer! Why make needless difficulty for us all? Come forth—you cannot escape!"

From under the dock came a hoarse ejaculation, then a moment of frantic splashing, then silence. Filidice slowly straightened from his crouching position. He stood staring down at the water, his face ashen. He climbed to the dock and rejoined Ryl Shermatz, Glinnes and Akadie. "We may now declare the case closed," he said. "The thirty million ozols—they remain a mystery. Perhaps we will never learn the truth."

Ryl Shermatz looked toward Glinnes, who licked his lips and frowned. "Well, I suppose it makes little difference one way or the other," said Shermatz. "But where is our captive Bandolio? Is it possible that the rascal has taken advantage of the confusion?"

"So it would seem," said Filidice disconsolately. "He is gone! What an unhappy day we have had!"

"On the contrary," said Akadie. It has been the most rewarding of my life."

Glinnes said, "Casagave has been evicted; for this I am most grateful. It's an excellent day for me as well."

Filidice rubbed his forehead. "I am still bewildered. Lord Gensifer seemed the very apotheosis of rectitude!"

"Lord Gensifer acted at precisely the wrong time," said Glinnes. "He killed Lempel after Lempel had instructed the messenger but before the money had been delivered. He probably believed Akadie to be as unprincipled as himself."

"A sad case," said Akadie. "And the thirty million ozols—who knows where? Perhaps on some distant world the messenger is now enjoying his astonishing new affluence."

"That is probably the size of it," said Filidice. "Well, I suppose I must make some sort of statement to the guests."

"Excuse me," said Glinnes. "There is someone I must see." He crossed the garden to where he had seen Duissane. She was gone. He looked this way and that, but saw no Duissane. Might she have gone into the house? He thought not—the house no longer had meaning for Duissane . . .

A path led around the house to the beach, which fronted on the ocean. Glinnes ran down the path and saw Duissane standing on the sand looking across the water, toward that blank area where the horizon met the ocean.

Glinnes joined her. She stopped and looked at him, as if never had she seen him before. She turned away and went slowly eastward along the water. Glinnes moved after her, and in the hazy light of middle afternoon they walked together down the beach.